Sebastian's Way

The Torchbearers

BOOK III of A Tale From The Time of Charlemagne

George Steger

Table of Contents

Persons of the Story

Abul-Abbas	Indian elephant, a gift from the caliph of Baghdad to Charlemagne
Adela	Duke Gonduin's daughter, Sebastian's wife
Adelaide	Count Leudegar's daughter, courtesan
Alcuin	Philosopher and churchman, one of Charlemagne's wise men
Ajax	Adelaide's eunuch bodyguard
Arno	Charlemagne's Mayor of the Palace
Attalus Senior	Sebastian's birth father, horse master, constable and Charlemagne's guardian of the Saxon March
Attalus	Sebastian's third son, a captain in the Frankish army
Bardulf	Free peasant, a member of Sebastian's entourage; companion of Drogo
Baumgard	Former steward of Fernshanz
Bernard	Frankish veteran soldier; personal aide to Sebastian
Benedict of Aniane	Monk and personal advisor to Louis the Pious
Bjorn Torbjorn	Captain of Danish King Godofrid's personal guards (Bloodaxe)
Charlemagne	High King of the Franks, later emperor of all Francia (Karl der Grosse)
Charles the Younger	Charlemagne's oldest son, commander of his armies
Drogo	Fernshanz serf, companion of Bardulf in Sebastian's entourage
Father Pippin	Priest at Fernshanz, Adela's confidant
Godofrid	King of Denmark

Gonduin	Duke and general in the Frankish army; lord of Andernach, and father of Adela
Harun al-Rashid	Caliph of Baghdad and ruler of the Islamic Empire
Heimdal	Blind hermit; soothsayer, and advisor to Sebastian
Isaac	Famed Jewish traveler, merchant to kings
Joyeuse	Sebastian's string of famous warhorses
Karl	Sebastian's second son, later commander of the Frankish northern army opposing the Vikings
Konrad	Former count of Adalgray, later leader of Viking raiders, Adela's first husband
Liudolf	Soldier at Fernshanz; Sebastian's closest companion
Lothar	Eldest son of Emperor Louis the Pious, king of Italy and later Burgundy
Louis the Pious	Third and last son of Charlemagne, later king and emperor of Francia after Charlemagne
Magdala	Desert medicine woman, seer, and companion of Milo
Milo	Sebastian's one-armed son by Gisela, a Fernshanz peasant girl, later a well-known philosopher and teacher
Nadia and Nicoleta	Adela's courtesan companions
Pepin	King of Italy, Charlemagne's second son
Sebastian	Count of Fernshanz and Adalgray, Charlemagne's senior paladin, later count of Andernach on the Rhine, Adela's husband
Simon	World traveler and trader; a member of a network of Radhanite Jewish merchants ranging from Francia to the Baghdad Caliphate
Widukind	Saxon prince and war chief, eventually defeated by Charlemagne
Wolfram	Sebastian's peasant guide to the East Saxons

Prologue

The Road to Aachen

January 814

What happens when a great man dies? Does the world change all at once? Sebastian pondered the question as he leaned into the slanting snow and stood up in his stirrups to ease his aching back. Or does the world change like a great glacier, slowly, inexorably, but with such fearsome consequences?

The black January night shivered with such bitter cold that ice formed on Sebastian's beard and the muzzle of his plunging horse. Overhanging branches, burdened by heavy snow, slapped against horse and rider. Every creek and ford seemed to deny its shallows and threaten to suck them into icy depths. The grim night mimicked the catastrophe at Aachen.

But the great stallion knew the way so well there was no need for any guidance. He had been with Sebastian so long that he pounded through the silence and the gloom as if he were his master's spirit driven by an ominous wind, as if he knew his master's mind and shared his imperative.

The king was dying.

Charlemagne! The paragon of kings, the rugged monarch who ruled from the great western ocean to the steppes of the Rus. He was indeed an emperor, but he hated the trappings of the empire and preferred the title of king. For he was, first and always, King of the Franks. His people completely identified with him. He had ruled so long that hardly anyone could remember a time when his scepter did not command, regulate, and inspire everyone, noble and peasant alike. Throughout his reign, he had striven to surround himself with the wisest men he could find, yet most of those who served him believed there was no need for thinking. Charlemagne thought for everyone.

So what now?

That was the first monstrous question for Sebastian to ponder in the stygian gloom. But there was another, even more intimidating, one he had asked himself a thousand times: In the end, what was it all for? Without my clothes, the scars of my old wounds frighten even me. My bones, battered by the long marches over the years, protest at night. If I sleep, my dreams are filled with mayhem and slaughter. I am sickened by war. So many of my sword brothers are dead now or lie helpless in their beds, crippled by wounds or strokes.

Yet who could ever refuse him? Who could say him nay? I tried. From the beginning, I reasoned with him and risked everything to show him a better way than war. I cajoled, begged, and even left his service for a while. But always I came back when he summoned me. I don't know why. I still don't know what it was all for—this endless fighting, this struggle to subdue and rule over others, this hatred we created to make us crazed with lust for their blood—because their faith, their way of life, even their color and speech were not ours.

Sebastian was beyond fear of the road. Wrapped in an old army cloak, he did not even feel the cold. The question that filled his mind and burdened his heart was: What would come next?

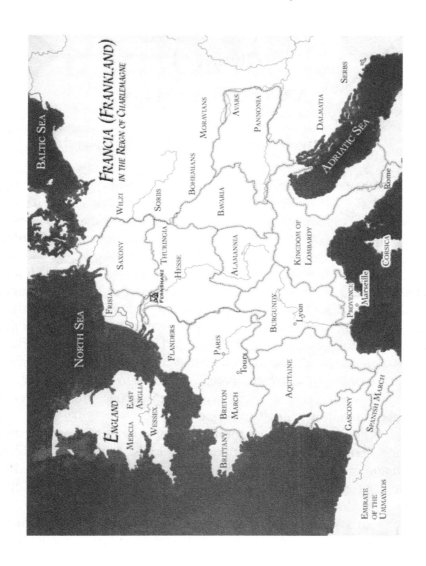

Chapter 1

A Woman Too Many

The Fortress Town of Fernshanz, Rhineland

When her boat pulled up to the landing at Fernshanz, Adelaide was sick and very fragile, not at all what she had been most of her life—especially in Constantinople, where she had been a ravishing beauty at the peak of her courtesan career in that fabled city.

An artful, many-faceted woman, she had appeared and danced at every important function, including every Hippodrome race. Behind her glamour and grace, however, was a sharp-witted, perceptive woman who could hold her own in the company of the highest personages of the realm. She could have had any one of them as her companion. But most of them had felt severely intimidated by her. She would just shrug and laugh and go on to the next suitor . . .

. . . until Sebastian had reappeared in her life, like some fateful djinn out of her discarded past.

When her small boat rounded the last bend of the river, and she saw Fernshanz, she almost burst into tears. At the height of her power and influence, Sebastian had changed her fortunes drastically. Because of Sebastian, she had found herself running for her life away from Constantinople.

I almost died a score of times on this Godforsaken journey, she murmured to herself as the boat slowly pulled up to the landing - just to get back to this godforsaken hamlet in the middle of nowhere! But it's the only place I know where I can be safe.

She owed her life on the perilous journey to three devoted companions, Ajax, her slave, and Nadia and Nicoleta, attractive young women from the lower levels of Constantinople society. She had seen them dance at a local festival and realized their talent. She had brought them up to perform with the palace company of courtesans, and they had become inseparable comrades. They had given up everything for her. Even now, she was wedged between their bodies for warmth. They had become her dearest friends in the world.

She turned to look at Ajax, standing at the prow of the boat. *And what would I have done without my precious Ajax? I owe him so much. I probably should have married him—except he's a eunuch!*

Ajax was a massive half-Greek, half-Arab eunuch whose tongue had been cut out for thievery. Adelaide had seen him one day while passing by the slave market. He was standing almost naked on the block, hands and feet bound. There were tears running down his broad, dark face. She had literally bought him on the spot. She'd cut his bonds with a borrowed knife in front of everybody, then turned on her heel and walked regally away. Ajax had followed her like a dog, glaring at one side of the crowd or the other as he moved menacingly along behind her with a fierce grin on his face. Since then, he had been one step behind her everywhere she went.

Adelaide shuddered at the memory of the night they had escaped across the straits and disappeared into the Arab community in the poorest part of Asian Constantinople. She recalled with abhorrence the several times she had needed to submit herself to various "protectors," powerful or wealthy men encountered here and there along the way. She'd stayed with them only long enough to gather resources and then break away safely, sometimes in the middle of the night, with money or jewelry obtained by feigning affection or pleasure. No matter how disgusted she might have felt, her strong will and innate survival instincts saved them.

She tried to raise herself up, searching for the man she had traveled a thousand miles to find. *He's the only thing that really kept me alive,* she admitted to herself.

In her mind, she clung to the image of Sebastian as he was in Constantinople when they had first shared such strong emotional and sexual attraction to each other.

God's blood! She thought ruefully. *Why didn't I go with him when he asked me? It was purely selfish. I couldn't believe he cared more for his cursed sense of duty than for me! I still didn't believe* he would actually leave me. But when everything went so damnably wrong, and he enraged the blasted empress of Constantinople, I couldn't let him die, could I? That's when I realized that I really loved him. And so I helped him. And then we both had to run.

***

As usual, a crowd gathered at the dock whenever a boat came up the river. Recently Sebastian had been in the middle of it, watching every boat that came into the landing dock, expecting and waiting anxiously for his wife, Adela. She had sent word that she was thinking of coming home by the end of the month. Since then, he had been unable to rest, sleeping little and even running along the river road at night to tire himself out, turning over and over in his mind the fateful decision before her. She had written that she was finally prepared to choose whether to stay with him permanently or return to the convent.

Sebastian was filled with hope and the joy of seeing her again after such a long separation. "Oh God," he said aloud to nobody, "Let her be on the boat! And let her want to stay with me this time." His expression instantly changed from joy to astonishment as he recognized the unexpected passengers.

It was a bizarre company: an obviously sick woman, with a thin but elegant face and a profusion of reddish hair, lying pale and inert in a worn gray blanket; two svelte young women in long, brightly colored dresses; and a veritable giant, half-naked, beturbaned and dark of color, menacing and powerful.

Sebastian's jaw fell open as he drew nearer, and his stomach reeled as if he'd been struck. To his surprise and dismay, the principal passenger was a beautiful but controversial woman who had once been his lover in a complicated past relationship. Great God! He thought as alarm bells rang out in his head. It's Adelaide!

Sebastian shook off his shock and ordered four nearby serfs to carefully pick up Adelaide's blanketed body and bring her to the manor house. But before they could move, the huge Arab had scooped her up as if she were a mere bag of flour and brought her toward Sebastian, to whom she was pointing frantically and calling out.

Sebastian could hardly move his legs and stood stock still with a stunned look on his face as the giant held her before him. She was eagerly reaching out her arms in profound relief. He finally offered a hesitant "Adelaide?" and bowed his head awkwardly before her. Hesitantly, he accepted her kisses on both his cheeks. Then he took her hand as Ajax bore her effortlessly up to the manor house.

*****

A few days were all Adelaide needed to start recovery under the expert care of Magdala, the resident healer and the close companion of Milo, Sebastian's oldest son. Sebastian visited her daily, but she hid her face from him and said little until she had recovered almost completely. But when she filled out and got her color back, Sebastian thought she was nearly as beautiful as she always had been.

While she was still sick, Sebastian had not had the heart—or the courage—to tell her that he might soon be reuniting with Adela, his wife of many years. But one perfect autumn day, when she had recovered and was relatively strong again, he invited her for a walk in the garden. They sat down in the shade on a bench surrounded by roses. There, in the ambiance of that peaceful, faultless day, he told her as gently as he could about Adela.

Adelaide's mouth dropped open as she took in what he said, and then she stood bolt upright and glared at him. Sebastian gritted his teeth against whatever was coming as Adelaide gathered herself like a raging thunderstorm and began to rain down hard on her hapless former lover.

She laid into him, arms akimbo, knees bent, teetering back and forth before a bewildered Sebastian as if she might attack him physically at any moment. Unable to control her anger, she shrieked at him. "She's what? Is Adela coming here? Why? Whatever for? She's not your wife anymore. She's a nun! She can't just pick up her skirts and come running up to see you whenever she feels like it. Didn't she take some bloody vows? Or doesn't that mean anything to the daughter of a duke?"

"She . . . she never took her final vows, Adelaide. Actually, we're still married," Sebastian stammered, feeling in his gut that he entirely deserved what was coming.

"Married? After all those years in the bloody convent? Well, by all that's holy, she cannot have you back! I won't allow it! You are mine, Sebastian! You owe me! It was I who saved your ungrateful arse from the clutches of the eparch of Constantinople, remember? Or did you never know that?"

"No! I didn't know that!" Sebastian blurted, grasping at any straw that might ameliorate his guilt.

"They knew I was sleeping with you. They were sure I would know your plans after you killed that fool, the senator's son. Oh, no! They weren't going to let you get away with that! But I delayed them, didn't I?"

"I did not know that, Adelaide. But, yes. Yes, I see now that you didn't betray us," Sebastian said, stumbling over his words. "But . . . but I didn't know it. I thought you would be forced to tell them where we were going if you wanted to stay in Constantinople."

"Well, you should have known it, you blighter. How could I let you die? How could I? You bloody well knew I loved you. You had to know that—after all, we said to each other! Why didn't you trust me, you ungrateful Judas?"

"I'm so sorry, Adelaide. I never knew what happened to you until now."

She paused a moment to catch her breath. "You could never imagine what we had to do. We had to slip away at once before they decided what to do with me. Ajax wound up killing three soldiers in the middle of the night when we escaped by the skin of our teeth—in a bloody rowboat with a sail! I had to leave a fortune behind and a brilliant career!"

With fire in her eyes, she stomped her feet in front of him and came close to slapping his face several times. "So now you owe me, Sebastian. I came here to marry you, and by God, that's what I'm going to do! In spite of your nun wife—ex-wife, whatever she is!" She paused for a few heartbeats, her chest heaving.

Sebastian stood as still as a stone, thunderstruck and speechless, completely unready to cope with the tirade. Adelaide tried but failed to suppress a mocking laugh.

"Oh, stop gawking like that, my darling. You look silly." She took a deep breath, softened her voice, and took a different tack.

"Listen, my heart, you still love me, don't you? You said you did, back there in Constantinople. You even said you would marry me and bring me back here to live with you. Didn't you?" Suddenly her bitter, angry face became almost pitiable and beseeching. She said in a small voice: "Well, I'm here now. I gave up everything for you."

He was silent for a long moment, unable to defend himself or avoid a growing sense of shame and guilt. Finally, he managed to mutter impulsively, "Oh, Adelaide, I'm so sorry."

Adelaide stiffened, and her ire welled up again. "Is that all you've got to say?"

When he didn't answer, she stifled with a fist what might have been a sob of frustration, turned on her heels, and stormed away to her quarters.

***

The following day was not much better. Sebastian sent word to Adelaide that he hoped very much to continue their conversation in the garden at her convenience. Desperate for some rational mediation, he brought with him to the meeting Adela's old confessor and dear friend, Father Pippin, whom he had sent for in anticipation of Adela's possible return. No one could ever be cross with the unassuming little priest, who had the soul of a saint and the gentle, reassuring manner of a trusted midwife.

They waited almost all morning until she came. Apparently, she had worked hard to erase all signs on her face of yesterday's angry tirade. Her hair was done up beautifully, and her gown was immaculate. But her eyes reflected hostility when she gave her hand to the little cleric—and bitterness when she met Sebastian's eyes.

If Sebastian hoped for a change, he was immediately disappointed. Adelaide exploded with a scornful remark whenever

Sebastian tried to speak. Finally, Father Pippin knelt before her and looked up into her eyes.

"Please, good lady. . . please sit, won't you? Please let me say a word. Perhaps if we are calm and well-intentioned, we might find a way to sort out this unfortunate strait in which we find ourselves."

Adelaide let out a sigh that sounded like "Humpff." Now who is this crazed little squirrel? She complained to herself. I'm insulted that Sebastian could think a comical mouse such as this could make me change my mind. Nevertheless, she sat down on a bench and prepared impatiently to listen. "Well, go on then, priest! But I don't care if you're the blooming Holy Ghost, you won't move me."

***

Father Pippin was ordinarily a very unassuming person. But those who truly knew him found in him a well of wisdom. He was often called upon to mediate between quarreling villagers and even in disputes among the nobility.

But the odd little cleric was never confident. He perceived himself to be inadequate. Each time before he faced a knotty controversy, he sustained himself with a single prayer: Oh God, it is you, not I, who will succeed here—if it is your will.

Now he sat down calmly on the other end of her bench and slightly bowed his head a moment before beginning. It is about her, Pippin, he said to himself. Concentrate on her, not Sebastian. Try to feel her pain.

He asked Sebastian to move away a bit so that he could speak to Adelaide in private. Then he began with a reverent, humble voice.

***

"My dear lady, it is plain to see how terribly you've been hurt. You must feel that your world has ended and all your hopes destroyed. The loss of love must be the cruelest pain in the world." He took her hand and was silent for a full minute.

12

"Well, that's a surprising gambit," Adelaide remarked crossly." "Well, what the devil can I do now, Father? If I lose the one I love most, I have lost everything."

"Dear lady," Pippin said in surprise, "you are one of the most beautiful women I have ever seen, and you have a quick-witted intelligence, from all I have heard. You are strong. You can start again and do whatever you please."

She relaxed her hand in his, and he was encouraged to continue.

"I do not make light of your pain, dear Adelaide. Grief never really ends, I'm afraid. And no one can escape sorrow. It's part of life. The trick is to overcome it."

Adelaide replied with mounting exasperation. "How, Father, how? He does not even know how much I really loved him."

"Listen, my dear. As I understand it, he did give you his love. Totally, there in Constantinople. It's just that time and circumstances got in the way by no fault of either of you.

"From the little, I know of you both, you can be thankful that you loved and loved well. In my experience, that is more than most people ever have. The memories may be bitter, but they can also be sweet." Adelaide breathed out a long sigh. At least he had quelled her fury.

"Dear Lady, you must also be thankful for what you have been spared. You might have died or been crippled for life. But now you can start again. You have every attribute. And Sebastian is not your enemy. On the contrary, I would wager you will find he will always be there for you when you need him, no matter what occurs."

***

Pippin could see that his words might have struck a nerve with Adelaide. He called Sebastian over to sit with them again.

Sebastian had been watching anxiously and wondering if there were anything he might say that would make a difference. He was glad to have another, calmer chance to speak to her.

He began with hesitation but then spoke from his heart. "I did love you, Adelaide. You see, I believed I had lost my wife, and in my regret and loneliness, I thought I could be happy with you. But you rejected me. You said you would have to give me up if I refused to live in Constantinople and renounce my duty to King Karl. That was a heavy blow to my pride and my trust in you. You had said you would love me forever. I believed you."

That last was hard for Sebastian to say. He knew it would make her feel her own guilt, and it seemed a cheap riposte. "My dear Adelaide, I must make you understand the bitter path by which I came to feel as I do now. He took a deep breath and began again.

"God forgives me, and it was all down to the dirty business of killing that senator's stinking son, Leo. He was the rat who betrayed us. I murdered him in a rage when they told me they had killed my men Archambald and Bernard. And then we got out of there just in time with nothing but our lives. I left, not knowing whether you would betray us or not. You knew all of our Jerusalem plans. And if you refused to betray us, I was mad with fear that they might torture you.

"On the voyage to Jerusalem, with nothing to do but think, I reached a point where I felt completely empty, worn out, mind and body. I had lost Adela and then you. I had killed a man in cold blood.

"I no longer cared about anything. I didn't even want to live. When we finally got to the Holy City, I was on the edge of taking my own life, and God help me. If it hadn't been for our healer, Magdala . . ." He paused for a minute, unsure how far he should go."

"I met her by accident through my son Milo. You might already realize what she was like. She had an aura of some kind, strange but compelling. I had a faint hope that she could teach me how to retrieve my sanity, but she did—she showed me a new way to look at life."

Adelaide sat impassively, watching him carefully. Sebastian was encouraged to continue.

"Magdala gave me a different kind of hope. I went through a very wretched period there for a while. But eventually, through some miracle or something, I felt I knew what to do with the rest of my life and what was most important to me.

"In these last few weeks since you came here, Magdala has healed you, too, hasn't she? You must know her power and insight."

His hopes rose when Adelaide nodded her head slightly. He clutched both her hands.

"You have to believe I'm telling you the truth. I did love you then. I still love you, as I love anyone who has been such a significant part of my life. And you will always be part of me.

"But dear Adelaide, I cannot marry you. Adela was in my heart first. She is the better part of me, the mother of my three sons. If she will have me this time, I must do whatever it takes to renew our marriage."

At that, Adelaide shook away his hands, stood up, and walked out again, this time without a word or gesture. Sebastian barely heard poor Father Pippin as he tried to give comfort and a bit of hope.

Chapter 2

The Spider

On a Rhine Boat

As Count Arno struggled to balance his heavy body on boarding the cumbersome riverboat at the port near Aachen, he was immediately stunned by the sight of the lovely passenger boarding ahead of him. He recognized her at once but could hardly believe his eyes. It was Countess Adela, the wife of the very man he was journeying to see and a woman in whom he had long had great interest.

For only a moment, Arno allowed himself to stare at her graceful figure just a few paces ahead, but then he averted his eyes lest she turned and saw his naked lust. Arno had a secret of his own: he was in love with Adela.

His heart pounded. This was the closest he had ever been to the woman he had dreamed of ever since she first appeared at the court of the king, a lovely maiden of sixteen accompanying her father to a great Maifeld gathering. There she was now, on the same small boat with him, a vision in white. It was the white of the convent, to be sure, yet she wore a blue shawl around her shoulders, and her thick auburn hair hung loose down her back, capturing the sun's rays as well as Arno's imagination.

He caught his breath as she turned and saw him.

"My lady," he said, bowing low, "what a delightful surprise to find you on the same boat!"

"Count Arno!" she exclaimed, a bit too cheerily.

He smiled broadly, gratified to know she recognized him. Since they had never really spoken to one another, he'd only been able to watch her from a distance. He suspected she might never have even looked at him. God, isn't she beautiful! I must find a way to make her understand that I am someone she must pay attention to. Somehow I must make myself important to her.

"May I say, Madame, you are truly a welcome sight. I thought never to see you again—that is, considering your vows and all." He bowed again.

"Well, Count, I've still never taken my permanent vows. I don't know yet if I ever shall. But I've taken advantage of my long service to the convent at Bischoffsheim to come home to Fernshanz for a while."

Sweating men gathered on the sides of the heavy riverboat, preparing to push it out into the Rhine's swift current. Arno was sweating, too, with the thought of the opportunity the voyage offered. Is she coming home for good? Will she be his wife again? He must know!

Wiping his face with a large kerchief, he called out to her. "Won't you please take a seat, Madame? I believe they are ready to launch."

With that, Arno plunked himself down on the bench beside her. He might have been handsome if he were not so fat. He had lively eyes, thick hair, and a slim black mustache on his shaven face. But that plump face turned almost beet red as he began to relish his good fortune. He had never imagined such fantastic luck—an extended river voyage with only the two of them as distinguished passengers, a golden opportunity to coax from his captive companion all he had always longed to know about her—and lo, perhaps even to win her approval of himself, perhaps even her sympathy, and—dare he think it—her affection?

"Whatever brings you to this rather primitive part of our realm, Count? After palace life for so many years and the luxury of the court, I would have thought our simple village in the wilderness would be little to your liking."

"The king, my lady—uh, that is, the emperor—is on a campaign at this very moment, dealing with the Saxons again. If your husband had not requested a leave of absence for family reasons—you, apparently—he would also be on that campaign. It seems there are some slight problems in Saxony and on the Danish border, but rather than send an impersonal message to his senior paladin, the kin—uh, the emperor—chose to emphasize the urgency of his present situation by sending me."

"Oh, please do call him the king. He much prefers it to the stuffy title of emperor. But what could be so important? The Saxons are always revolting—in both measures of the word!"

"Ah, I see that your wit is as fine as your beauty, Countess!" His compliment seemed unsuitable for the circumstances, and Adela looked away.

"But I'm afraid there's unusual business to be done with the Saxons. Something to do with a plan your husband suggested to the king about resettling many of our former Saxon enemies west of the Rhine so they will no longer be inclined to revolt. The king has decided to implement the plan and wants to consult Count Sebastian about how we should divide them."

"Well, I certainly hope the king will not need Sebastian until I have had a chance to greet him. We've not seen each other for months."

"Ah, yes. Well . . . uhm! We shall have to see," Arno said, averting his eyes.

"But now, Madame, if you please, tell me all about your return. Do you expect to see all of your sons, even the scholar Milo? And do you plan to remain at Fernshanz, perhaps for good now? I daresay the king would love to hear that. He admires you so."

Adela laughed merrily. "Ah, so it is true, Count, you never miss an opportunity to store more gossip in that clever head of yours. If I didn't know better, I'd accuse you of profiteering in rumor. Anyway, I'm sure what I do can't be very interesting to His Majesty."

"On the contrary, my lady. The king dotes upon you. If I don't have some colorful details of your homecoming, he might consign me to eat with the servants instead of at his table for a week or so."

She has got to know, he thought complacently, that I am the emperor's senior agent? No one is better than I at collecting information that might interest the high king—or myself.

In fact, that was his principal duty as Mayor of the Palace at Aachen—appropriately so, for he would never have made a warrior.

He was far to the other side of Portly. He moved slowly, cowlike, his rotund belly swaying from side to side, but the pointed face and beady eyes were those of a magpie. They never stopped moving, and they took in everything wherever he went.

Arno was excessively proud of the several budding plots against the emperor he had sniffed out. And he jealously guarded his power as Charlemagne's principal watchdog. Daily he perched spiderlike on a tiny stool at the palace entrance, offering an oily welcome to every invited guest and a scorching frown to every uninvited one. Later each evening, he debriefed the king thoroughly.

Eventually, he'd been promoted to Mayor of the Palace at Aachen, a position that made him a governor, only answerable to the king. He became Charlemagne's personal wizard of dark intrigue as well as entertaining gossip.

The information he sought at this moment, however, was more for himself than for the king. He resolved that by the time he got off the boat at the dock in Fernshanz, he would know every detail of the reasons and repercussions behind Adela's homecoming.

"As a matter of fact, dear lady, the king remembers you with great affection ever since you first accompanied your father, Count Gonduin, to that Maifeld war council at Worms a score of years ago or so. Remember?"

Actually, that was the occasion when Arno became obsessed with Adela. He had loved her as soon as he saw her youthful beauty, confidence, and natural grace. So unlike the other unripe and giddy maidens at the court, she had glided serenely into the pageantry as if she herself were its host.

"Indeed, I do, Count. Who could forget? It was not only my first look at the king and his magnificent court but also the occasion when I first met my future husband. How different he was at that grand assembly, so thoughtful and naive, so unlike the brutish warriors my father would have had me marry!"

Arno frowned and turned away, sniffing as if at a bad smell. He also remembered it well. He had felt then the despair of the unattractive male who knows he has no chance with the *belle dame* of the moment. Nevertheless, from then on, he had become obsessed with her and followed her life most avidly. He knew, of course, that she had chosen Sebastian to love and marry, and then he began to hate Sebastian.

He rejoiced when the king unexpectedly disrupted the lovers' plans and ruined their lives. He had announced that Adela would be commanded by reasons of state to marry Sebastian's cousin, Count Konrad, the most celebrated fighter in Charlemagne's army but also a notorious villain and brute. Arno had suffered for Adela, but he knew she could never love Konrad, and that was somehow a consolation.

"May I say, dear countess, that we all rejoiced with you when you were finally able to be joined to Count Sebastian after so many years of suffering? So much sorrow and confusion! I imagine your life has been devastated by the simple caprice of fate!"

Arno was intentionally treading on thin ice by mentioning the long-delayed marriage of Adela and Sebastian. He was curious to see if it would unsettle her to revisit that short, happy time and its disastrous end. He must find out for sure if Adela really meant to patch up their marriage. After all, he posited archly, she'd been in the convent for years while Sebastian gallivanted around the world, building his reputation as superhuman. Could they possibly have changed too much and grown apart?

Arno had been miserable when Sebastian and Adela had been reunited in marriage after the news that Konrad was dead. In his head, he had convinced himself, defying the odds, that somehow fate had meant her for him.

Those fears had turned again to delight when Konrad was found alive, and the Church declared her marriage to Sebastian invalid. Adela had then chosen to join the convent rather than defy Church law.

As fate wavered once more, Arno remembered the bitter pain he'd felt when Konrad was killed by one of Sebastian's own sons, and Adela was free to love as she pleased.

Still. . . Arno told himself Adela had remained inextricably for some time in the convent. Hmm! So there was still hope! Suddenly a grand idea flashed into his brain:

What if he could find a way not just to separate them but to put Sebastian in great danger? Perhaps he could convince the king to send him on a mission from which he might not return—something like Uriah the Hittite and David! He almost laughed aloud to think of it.

"Ah, my dear sir," said Adela, interrupting his scheming. "I wish you wouldn't touch upon such turbulent memories. I was never so happy as in those times. But they were also filled with some of my greatest disappointments—calamities, actually. I will tell you candidly that it was this turmoil that forced me to the convent—where I finally found a rueful peace. I'm sure you know all this, and I thank you for your care and sympathy, but it's no longer necessary, thank God, to think of such times."

"I humbly beg your pardon, Countess," Arno went on doggedly. "I never meant to open old wounds; I just think it must have been incredibly taxing to balance yourself between two such great men."

Adela sat upright on the edge of the bench and turned to Arno indignantly. "Taxing? Great men? Count, how can you say such things? Konrad was as evil a man as Sebastian is a good one. To belong to one was as maddening as being separated from the other. I'm sorry, but I must ask you to no longer bring up these old ghosts. I managed to banish them at the convent and forge a new life there. Now I think only of a happy reunion with my family." With that, she moved slightly farther down the bench and turned her gaze to the passing scenery.

"Of course, Countess. I only wish there had been something I could have done for you personally over those years. I would have gone to any length to help you."

"Thank you, Count. I'm sure you meant well."

Arno felt the sharp rebuff as she moved away from him entirely to a pallet arranged for her near the prow of the boat, but he hoped that he might at least have made a case for himself as a constant friend and admirer.

He would use this unexpected opportunity to insert himself further into her life and, more importantly, into her relationship with Sebastian. Ha! He reasoned to himself. I know it would be hard for her to love me, the fat clod that I am, but I might be content if she would only count me as a friend. I could speak to her alone once in a while, touch her hand!

And what if I could make her depend upon me? Who knows?

He shuddered with excitement at the thought and began immediately to spin a web for her.

Chapter 3

To Be, Rather Than to Seem

Sebastian was running—and without a thought for his dignity as lord of the manor. He could see her worried face, and he leaped ahead through the growing throng of peasants gathered at the landing. Is she really coming home to me? He thought desperately. And then his concern turned oddly to her safety as she disembarked. God, I hope that bloody dock holds up with all those people on it! Damn me for not building a stone dock!

He yelled ahead, "Make way, make way! Stop jostling the lady! Get back!"

Finally, she saw him, and the look of relief on her face blended into the dazzling smile he remembered so well. She dropped her bundles and almost leaped into his arms.

In that exhilarating moment, Sebastian was struck by the stunning notion that he might wake up beside her tomorrow. They would have breakfast together as if nothing unusual had ever happened. They could actually be married and not just suffer the illusion of it.

But he got no chance to linger on such a pleasant thought; the peasants crowded around as closely as they dared, and as they recognized her, a huge roar of approval rose up spontaneously, for the villagers knew her well and loved her. The couple might have savored it all for a while longer, except for Count Arno. The fat man elbowed his officious way to the couple and stuck his pudgy nose almost into their faces.

"Count Sebastian," he shouted over the crowd noise, "let me congratulate you on your long-delayed reunion with this beautiful lady! I say you must be overjoyed!"

What? Where in the blazing hell did he come from? Sebastian thought. Sweet God! It's what I feared. The king needs something! And he's sent this arrogant oaf to fetch me! He could feel his face growing red with disappointment and anger.

"I hate to spoil the moment," Arno bellowed as the crowd continued to mill around Adela. "But I must have your attention at once. I have important information from His Majesty that cannot wait. We need to speak in confidence. For God and the emperor, no?" He reached out to grasp Sebastian's forearm.

"What? Jesus, Mary, and Joseph, man!" Sebastian yelled back when he comprehended the ridiculous interruption. "Have you no decency? The emperor can wait one bloody moment."

He roughly shoved the blustering official aside and inserted himself between Arno and Adela. "I must speak with my lady first. And I have no doubt the emperor would thoroughly approve."

The astonished Arno nimbly jumped back and looked hastily around to see who had seen him being manhandled by Sebastian.

"Sorry, Adela," Sebastian whispered into Adela's ear, "I can't actually strike the fool. He'd probably die of indignation. But he's an important man. We've got to put up with him, at least for a while." He turned back to the crowd. Spotting Liudolf, his closest friend and long-time companion, he quickly motioned him over and shouted above the noise of the crowd, "Liudolf, do us all a great favor, will you, and escort this, uh, honorable count to our house. Put him in our best rooms. (Not mine, dammit," he whispered)— "Good rooms, right? Give him anything he wants—a bath, change of clothes, anything. Plenty of food."

Turning to Arno a bit more cordially, Sebastian offered a weak apology. "Sorry, my good man. No offense meant, but you took me by surprise. After such a long, hot journey, I'm sure you need some refreshments and a rest before we talk. I, for one, will have a clearer mind once I greet this wonderful lady properly. We'll take a short walk—alone—and I shall be up directly. In the meantime, the manor is yours. I beg you, please feel free and at home."

As Sebastian and Adela made their way hastily through the crowd, the red-faced Arno let out a long flatulation so egregiously that even the peasants moved away from him.

***

They almost ran along the river path up to the fortress, waving and smiling at those they met, then through the west gate, past the manor house, and out through the east gate to the path along the river again. It was blessedly empty of townsfolk at the moment.

They turned to each other, catching their breath, grasping their hands together, and laughing. "What a ridiculous show that was," Adela giggled demurely.

"Did you see his face, Adela? I thought he was going to burst in front of all the villagers! I don't know how we will face him tonight when we have to dine with him. God help me not to laugh as soon as I see him!"

"Don't, dear," Adela said, tugging his arm to begin walking again. "Count Arno has enough trouble maintaining his dignity as it is. We must treat him tonight as the distinguished guest he actually is. After all, isn't he as close to King Karl as you? In a different way, of course."

"That's right, my dear. He's certainly not a warrior. He has nothing to do with the army. But he's one of the most powerful men at the court. He's the king's news raven. He has informants everywhere and makes it his business to know everything about everyone, regardless of whether the information has any value or not. That's what he lives for. Nothing else. And, worse luck, the king trusts him."

Adela hugged Sebastian's arm tighter as an icy premonition intruded into her sense of delight at being home again. "I feel sorry for poor Arno," she said quietly. But I've seen enough of him already to know he could be dangerous. His eyes are cold and shifty, and several times on the boat, I caught him looking at me in an unsuitable way. And now this rude interruption of our homecoming?"

"Well, my dearest lady," Sebastian said gently, looking into her eyes, "this world is certainly not the convent. If you stay – and I fervently pray that you will - you have to choose between the safety of the convent and the daily challenge of being married to a man like me. You know that my life will never be without complications."

25

"Enough! I know that all too well. But we can deal with it later, can't we? For now . . . She stole a glance at Sebastian's strong face, his intense black eyes. They even seemed to shine in the dark, she remembered. She shook herself away from the thought.

"For God's sake, Sebastian, let's forget him for a moment. She took his hand and began to walk again. "My Lord!" she exclaimed, looking out across the river at the luxurious forest. "Oh, I have missed this place! Look at the deep green of those woods! And there is the dearest freshness here. It's like breathing a fragrant balm! This is all I need now—just to absorb this beautiful, tranquil place...and," she said, turning to look up at him, "to soak your presence into my body. My mind won't accept that you're actually here!"

He grasped her shoulders and held her at length. "How is it that you haven't changed? There's not even one white hair on your head! You're even more lovely than I remember." He squeezed her arms hard. "Hmm," he said with a grin, "just the shape of you drives me daft."

"Oh, stop, Sebastian. It's been too many years since we were together at Fernshanz. I might have been somewhat appealing then, but it's wicked of you to say such things now. Besides, in the strict sense of the word, I'm still a nun."

"Nonsense, my love, you still draw me like a bear to honey. But even if you didn't, you would always bring out the best in me."

"Oh, Sebastian. It's been so long. I barely know you."

"Well, let me introduce myself again." He pulled her closer. "May I kiss you, Adela?"

"Oh, yes, please," she whispered as he lifted her face to his. After a long moment, she broke away to catch her breath. "Wait. Wait, my love. Slowly. I'm not used to this. I haven't kissed anything but a pillow for years."

"But you're free now, my darling girl. We have each other again, and we can do anything. We can have the joy of being together completely."

"I know, love. At least I dare to think of you now without pain." She paused and reached up with both hands to touch his face . . .

She wanted him; she even ached to crush him against her breast. But then her ghosts interrupted.

"But Sebastian," she ventured anxiously, "it's not going to be as easy as you imagine. We've spoken about this before, but you never quite seem to understand. I have had to back away completely from married life. There was so much grief. I lost one son and was sick with fear that I would lose the others, too, if I stayed with you. I often thought I'd never see you again. I don't know if I can go through more crises like that."

"Of course, you can. You've proven how strong you are in a crisis. Besides, it's all right, my love, all right now. That's all in the past," he soothed. "We're together. It's all that matters."

She began to cry softly and wrapped herself tighter in his arms. For a long time, they stood silently in a communion of shared remembrances. Finally, she broke away, and they began to walk again. "Listen, love, try to understand why I was so hesitant to come back to you. Our lives were so torn apart that I thought we would never be man and wife again. During those years when you went off to the East for so long, I even thought you were dead. I had no purpose, no life left at all. I just wanted to die as well."

"I know, I know, dear. I felt exactly the same—for a long time."

"Well, while you went to war for the king, I had to immerse myself into a completely different life to keep my sanity. I turned to God. I decided to give myself up and be completely at God's mercy. I didn't know what else to do. Only the peace of the convent beckoned to me. And Mother Herlindis, my great friend at the convent, came to my rescue. She taught me how to retreat into my mind and find a different reason to be alive. Slowly I began to know I could be of use again somehow—I could think. I was trained in letters. She taught me how to use my talents. I began to write. And eventually, it was enough. I felt empowered. I thought less of my losses and of you. Finally, I offered you up to God. It gave me peace."

"I gave you up as well, Adela. I thought we would never have another chance. I even believed you had stopped loving me and would never leave the convent."

He stopped, looked down at his feet, and cleared his throat.

"Oddly, that brings me to something I have to tell you. Unfortunately, the sooner, the better."

When he hesitated, she took his hands and gently prompted him, "Go ahead love. We mustn't leave anything unsaid."

"When I thought I'd lost you forever, and when the king sent me out on one endless mission after another, I met another woman— a woman you might remember and one that I had once thought of marrying. Her name was Adelaide, and she was the daughter of one of the king's generals, Count Leudegar. Adelaide set her sights on me even before I met you. And after you married Konrad and I had lost hope, I took up with her for a brief time. But she was restless and capricious, and she couldn't think of spending her life in a wilderness village. So she finally ran off with a Jewish trader friend of mine."

"Uh-oh," Adela said cautiously, "there's another serious current here that I don't know anything about. I'm afraid to hear what's coming next." She pulled out a kerchief and twisted it around her hands to keep them from straying to her face.

"Incredibly," Sebastian went on gingerly, "we met again in Constantinople on the king's business. She was a famous courtesan by then, but she remembered me well—too well. We took up with each other again." He stopped for a moment to glance at her out of the corner of his eye.

Adela looked at him squarely and warned herself. It looks like a strong east wind is about to blow here. I need to stay in control of my feelings, no matter what he says. In spite of her resolve, she felt her stomach tighten in an alarming way, and she was reminded once again of the peace and surety of the white-walled convent.

"At that time," Sebastian labored on, "I thought I had lost you and desperately needed someone to love and share my life. Adelaide responded so eagerly I thought that perhaps I could start a new life with her. But when I suggested that, she insisted that any new life would have to be where she already was, in Constantinople, for that life was grand, and she couldn't imagine a better place. So my hopes for a new beginning were dashed, and I became sorely disillusioned with her.

28

"Ultimately, it all turned out badly for us in that Byzantine snake pit. Milo and I were almost killed. And, God damn their souls to hell, they did murder poor Archambald, the best friend of my youth, and Bernard, my mother's old guardian. The rest of us barely escaped with our lives.

"Lately, I discovered that Adelaide was not the one who betrayed us there after all. In fact, she had to flee for her own life when she refused to reveal where we'd gone. But I didn't know all that then, and I never knew what happened to her after that—until now."

"What do you mean? Why are you telling me all this?" Adela said uneasily.

"Well, Adela . . . uh, Adelaide is here—at Fernshanz. Please understand," he went on, speaking rapidly, "she showed up here only a few weeks ago. I couldn't believe it. But she was terribly sick, almost to death. Her escape from Constantinople was perilous, to say the least. She had to give up everything except a few attendants and friends. She had nowhere to go, so she returned to Francia. But her father is dead now, and her brother refuses to take her in. She came to me as a last resort.

"Our wondrous healer, Magdala, whom Milo coaxed here from Jerusalem, succeeded in saving her. She's on the mend now and is almost fully recovered."

Adela paused for a long moment, pressing her hands into her roiling stomach. "Oh, Sebastian, I had fears that you might not really want me anymore or that somehow the Church might not let us live together again. But this! This is really strange!"

Sebastian tried to hold her again, but she pushed him away. "I don't know what to say to you, Sebastian. Wait a minute. I must think." She walked a few paces away and turned her back to him.

Well, maybe all that Byzantine business is over, she conjectured hopefully. He can't still be in love with both of us, can he? Everything he's done so far shows he's still very much in love with me. I must believe in him and give him the benefit of the doubt. Besides, the poor woman is desperate. She turned back to him with a deliberate smile.

"Well, dear, I think I understand. Of course, you had to help her. It was the only thing to do."

"Wait, love, there's more."

"What more? What does she expect of you now?"

Sebastian looked across the river as if to find an answer in the trees beyond. He took a breath, looked back into Adela's eyes, and forced an answer.

"Adela, she expects to marry me."

Chapter 4

To the Sticking Point

When they finally turned back toward the fortress, every step Adela took was an effort. The wrenching decision she had taken so long to make began to look more and more like a colossal mistake. Behind the joyous welcome lurked a mockery.

Three specters waited for her on the threshold of the manor house: an irate royal count with soaring pretensions and bad manners, a husband she had not slept with for years, and a conniving jade who wanted to take that husband away from her.

The feeling grew as they passed through the west gate again and saw the manor house where she had once been so happy. Tension gripped her at the sight of the gathering crowd in front of the manor house, and a fleeting mental image of the quiet confines of the convent suddenly aroused in her a hint of loss.

Then she saw familiar faces: there was Liudolf, Sebastian's right arm, and closest friend, wearing his perpetual frown; Bardulf and Drogo, his devoted personal servants; Simon, the clever Radhanite trader; her own dearest friend, the ever humble Father Pippin; and a host of familiar house serfs and senior freemen from the village. The smiles and hurrahs made no doubt she was their lady and had come home. She yearned to embrace them all.

There was only one stranger in the crowd, a small, dusky raven-haired young woman, as plain of face as the simple dress and shawl she wore. Close beside her was a tall youth with a mass of bright yellow hair and a missing arm, her beloved son Milo. He stood so close to the foreign girl that the bond between them was unmistakable.

Adela went first to Milo and bent him down to her so as to plant kisses all over his face. He was really her adopted son, Sebastian's bastard child from a peasant mother before he had met Adela. But she had raised him and could not have loved him any less than the two sons from her own womb. Milo offered a mild protest

31

but was obviously moved by her affection. He broke off only to present the girl to her.

"Mother, this is my…uh, my companion Magdala. She's the healer we've all talked about so much—from Jerusalem, you know?"

"Of course, Milo, how could I not? You and your father have talked of little else since you returned from there." She turned to the girl, who stood quietly beside Milo, studying every word and gesture Adela made. Her serious face broke into a surprisingly lovely smile when Adela rushed to embrace her.

"My dear Magdala, what a richness you are! I know you already by reputation. Even in the cloister at Bischoffsheim, I heard about you, and the boatmen who brought us here said that you are already quite famous in the county . . . peasants coming every day to have you treat them for all kinds of afflictions. I can't wait to help you."

Clearly pleased, Magdala responded only with a smile and a shy thank-you, but she kept her hand in Adela's when they moved into the manor house.

Inside was what Adela had been dreading. At the end of the great hall, seated at the banquet table and sharing a flagon of wine, were Count Arno and Adelaide.

With Sebastian on one arm and Magdala on the other, she stopped momentarily at the door, myriad thoughts crowding her mind. Turning to Sebastian with a feigned smile, she leaned back to whisper in his ear, "Well, there sits my rival, darling. You didn't tell me she was such a raving beauty! My, she looks formidable! How am I supposed to compete with that?" Before he could answer, she turned back and began smiling and bowing her head to the welcoming guests on both sides of the aisle while fighting a sudden magnetic urge to flee at once to her peaceful convent. God, give me courage, she murmured softly between her teeth. I haven't faced this kind of challenge in years.

She lifted her chin, straightened her back, and walked confidently like a queen.

***

Sebastian had his own doubts as they approached the head table. Smiling, he whispered back to her, "Good Lord! What a homecoming! It's like having to fight enemies on both sides at once. Which to engage first?" He was saved the choice when Adela went immediately to Adelaide. Sebastian turned grudgingly to the count.

He approached Arno cautiously, sorry now that he had lost control of his temper earlier. He knew the king's Mayor of the Palace well enough, having suffered numerous delays and miscommunications in previous audiences with the king. Arno was a notorious gatekeeper, known to delay foreign delegations, papal legates, and even generals of the Frankish army for hours and days, depending on his own perspective of how important they were to the king or to his own designs. Sebastian knew him to be a very clever manipulator, with an alarming treasury of information he could draw from at will to disarm, confuse, and even doom rivals or visitors he did not like.

Keep your balance, Sebastian told himself. The scoundrel needs to be horsewhipped, but nothing's gained by openly dishonoring or making him look small. So patch this up somehow.

"Hello, Arno," he announced buoyantly, grasping the scowling count by the forearms. "Sorry for the confusion on the dock. But you were quite a surprise. And I hadn't seen my wife in ages, so I was a bit carried away. I'm sure a man of your perception understands. But come, let's go at once to my rooms, where you can tell me all about your fearful urgency. What's the king got himself into this time?"

He whisked Arno down the hall and into an adjoining room without a word to the others, praying that the ladies might find a way to tiptoe around the achingly awkward central issue between them. One dragon at a time, he told himself.

As they entered the room, Sebastian motioned to a house serf for ale and refreshments. When the servant had left, he slammed the door and pointed roughly at a table by the window. Once the annoyed count was settled, he sat down and drew his face four inches from Arno's, glaring coolly into the man's eyes.

"Now, you arrogant rogue, just what in blazes do you mean by coming into my home and frightening my wife and friends with your demands and posturing? Do you think that intimidates me? I'm a paladin of the king. I've been through more *scheisse* than you could ever imagine. Have a care, my too-hasty friend, I warn you. You are not King Karl, you're simply his messenger, and I'm no servant at your beck and call. I'm as close to the king as you are and have far more to show for my service to him. So if you try to threaten me or intimidate anyone in my household, especially my wife, you will see how fast your return to Aachen will be. And the king will hear about it. Is that clear?"

"Yes, yes, of course, Count Sebastian," Arno exclaimed with a nervous laugh. "I...ah-hum . . . I never meant to alarm anyone, I assure you. I only wanted to make you aware of the king's wishes."

"I understand," Sebastian said calmly, relaxing his tense posture. Careful now. This is how Arno always acts when he's out of his depth. Don't underestimate him!

In an attempt to regain his dignity, the flustered legate backed away from Sebastian's piercing eyes as far as the bench would allow, cleared his throat, and wiped his face with a silk kerchief. "Please understand me, my lord Sebastian. I am only the king's faithful servant. He charged me with letting you know his will. I hastened to do so. After all, the king comes first, no? And you, of all people, know how demanding he can be. Surely you realize that he would not have sent his Mayor of the Palace if it were not of the utmost importance."

"Fine, Arno. As long as we understand each other." What a treat to see the lordly spider squirm a bit, Sebastian reflected. He sat back and eyed his uneasy guest drolly. Finally, he said, "Look, Arno. I know you're no fool. I'm well aware of the good work you do every day for our good King Karl. And I don't want to regret your visit here. But just remember, I'm at least one person in this whole realm you can't bully!

"Now, let me show you the respect a legate of the king deserves." Sebastian clapped his hands. "From now on, while you are here, you will be treated with the utmost courtesy." The door opened, and a servant, at Sebastian's direction, splashed some ale into Arno's unsteady cup.

"So, tell me now, my good count, what is the king up to, and why does he need me so desperately? It must be of great moment for him to send the illustrious Mayor of the Palace to tell me. I'm very curious because his empire has never been so great. The threats he might face now are far fewer and less formidable."

"Yes, indeed, Count," Arno agreed, sliding back into his role as the sole custodian of secret information. "But there is once again a very serious situation with the East Saxons, those beyond the Elbe. They are close to yet another revolt against us. And, worse than that, there have been some alarming rumblings out of Denmark lately, where King Godofrid is said to be in league with those thrice-cursed Viking pirates. He has drawn their ships close to his army, which is now fully mobilized and sitting on our northern border as we speak."

Arno was now on more familiar ground. As Mayor of the Palace, he could speak with the king's voice. He used that power to build an edge over Sebastian, cleverly spinning a new web for his host.

"There is some good news, however! The king told me himself he was going to try 'Sebastian's way' with the Saxons. That's what he called it—Sebastian's Way! Despite his native inclinations, he told me he might be willing to parley with them, as you have always suggested. We have recently had some word that they might now agree to move west across the Rhine. But we need to go there and motivate them. The king thinks you're the only man who can do it."

"Oh, for God's sake! He thinks he can just draw me like a sword whenever he has a notion! There are other men, other paladins."

"Yes, Count, but he wants you. After all, as the king says, it's been your idea from the start."

Rats! Sebastian thought ruefully. No good idea goes unpunished. But what appalling timing! Just when I've got Adela home at last.

"Well, that's true," Sebastian admitted. "I've long advised him to meet with them. It worked with Prince Widukind, and he was a legendary Saxon hero. But until now, the king's not been willing."

"Well, he apparently is now. Based on some reports I received just a fortnight ago, there's a good chance the plan would succeed. For one thing, the East Saxons are being threatened by a new lot of pagan Slavs moving against them from the East. They're called Obodrites, and there's quite a slew of them, I'm told. The Obodrites hate King Godfrid in Denmark. They could help us, but the East Saxons are in the way. They're not just defying us, they're standing in the way of some potentially useful allies. The Saxons are too few and weak to win against the Obodrites, but it could be a long war. And we need those allies now to help us against the Danes.,

"God helps them, then," Sebastian said. "I know the bloody Saxons, and they're a stubborn lot. It'll take a miracle to budge them away from the graves of their ancestors, even if there is a serious danger to them."

"Too true," Arno agreed, "But in earlier years, King Karl would have just called up the army and marched out there pell-mell, burning everything and killing as many as he could. It's just simpler. But that would cost him a lot of men and treasure. And he still might have to face the Danes after that. So now he wants to try it your way. He wants you to come to him at Aachen without delay. He said now is the ripe moment, while the East Saxons are under attack by the Slavs."

Sebastian groaned inwardly. Right! "Now is always the ripe moment for the king."

Arno continued with a gleam in his eye. "Yes, of course. But the whole situation is tied to our new and pressing problems with Denmark. They seem to be building up along our border, and the king is considering moving against them again. But he wants you to scout the situation first—after you finish the business with the Saxons. I am to send a messenger as soon as I've found you. And now that I have, I plan to leave tomorrow."

"Impossible," Sebastian responded hotly, banging his fist on the table and sloshing Arno's ale. "I won't do it. Adela's only just returned. I've been waiting for years for her! I won't do it! Not until I've had at least a little time with her!"

"Shall I tell the king that?" Arno said with a thin-lipped smile, relishing Sebastian's dilemma. "He knew that you might object, Count Sebastian. That's why he sent me instead of an ordinary messenger—to give you to know just how important he considers your presence to be in these matters. You are his senior paladin. The opportunity with the Saxons may be slipping away, and the emperor is quite agitated by the thought of a Danish army on our border. He wants you to look into East Saxony and ensure the plan works there. And then to Denmark. Those are his orders. And he says you are to come to him at once."

"Bloody hell!" Sebastian muttered. He took a deep breath and looked away in silence for a long moment. I will not give this scheming parasite the pleasure of seeing me suffer, he said to himself. After a moment, he stood up and announced his decision without another thought. "All right then, I'll go as he wishes. But not until the day after tomorrow. I must have at least one full day with my wife. There are problems we must solve—as you might expect. You can leave tomorrow if you like, Count Arno. I'll come behind you. My horses are faster than your boat. I shall probably be at King Karl's side before you.

"Oh," he said as they went out of the room, "I won't be staying at the small banquet we're giving you this evening. I'm sure you can understand why. But there will be as many of my companions and family there as possible. They'll show you a courteous time. There will be music and singing. Please enjoy yourself. Liudolf, my lieutenant, will see you off tomorrow at the boat. I assure you, you have accomplished your mission. I will go to the king."

Chapter 5

The Choice

Smiling, Adela nodded gracefully to Count Arno and then turned to Adelaide, grasping both of her hands and greeting her warmly with no sign of fear or malice.

"My dear Adelaide, Sebastian has told me that you saved his life in that dreadful business in Constantinople. You are truly a courageous woman. I doubt if I've ever met one so brave. I'll be forever grateful to you."

Eyes narrowed and unsmiling, Adelaide drew back a bit and took her hands away. She was on the verge of throwing down the gauntlet. But Adela's conciliatory words and ungrudging flattery took her by surprise. For the moment, she said nothing.

"Come, dear," Adela tried again. "We've so much to say to each other. I know the others will excuse us." Taking Adelaide's arm with both hands, Adela led the way smoothly out of the room and into the garden behind the manor house. There she invited Adelaide to sit on a bench beside her.

Well, she's certainly pretty enough, Adelaide noted to herself. And she's marvelously calm and in control of herself. I thought she'd be as nervous as a cat and easily intimidated. After all, I did sleep with her husband. Wouldn't she like to know what a delicious revel that was!

Smiling grimly, she decided to bring it all out in the open, not bothering to fence around with niceties. "All right," she said. "Here it comes. I know you just brought me out here to avoid a scene. But let's see if you have any claws! I slept with your husband. Did you know that? Many times! He told me at one point he loved me. He said he would marry me. I saved his life in Constantinople. Now I want him to honor his words. I want him to marry me!"

"My dear Adelaide," Adela said with almost a cheerful laugh, "how strong and forthright you are! I've never met a Frankish woman like you. And how beautiful! No wonder Sebastian was so attracted to you. I'm so glad you've recovered so well from that terrible illness. Very glad, my dear. You've been through so much. I wish we could have known each other under different circumstances."

Adelaide sat bolt upright, frowning quizzically at Adela. "What's this? Why are you trying to avoid the main muddle between us? If I had known you earlier, I would have taken Sebastian away from you. It would have been easy since you stayed in the convent so long. Seems to me you didn't want him very much."

"That's a story I'll be glad to tell you when we know each other better," Adela continued softly, unperturbed by Adelaide's hostile gambit, "But now, you're right, unfortunately. We have this thing between us, this bizarre rivalry over Sebastian. Fate couldn't have served us a more uncomfortable dilemma. I know he asked you to marry him! But I also understand his reasons and also the reasons why nothing came of that proposal. From the outset, I want you to know that I hold nothing against you, although I know you wish to be Sebastian's wife. I understand that too. He's worth it."

Adelaide crossed and uncrossed her legs, desperate to start shouting and overpowering her rival with indignation and rage. But she checked her natural propensity for riot and listened to see how devious Adela might be in dealing with their prickly issue.

"Now you are here, as am I," Adela said softly, grasping Adelaide's hands again. "Obviously, we must solve this dilemma somehow. But before you say more, let me tell you—I have not yet taken permanent vows as a nun. I can return to the convent if I wish." She paused. "But I'm also free to return to Sebastian as his wife."

She hesitated and drew in a deep breath. "I've not made the decision to do either as yet. I confess this to you freely because I want to know you. You've been so very close to someone I love, and you gave up much for him. It's only fair that I know what it is you feel you must do and what is in your heart."

Adelaide was prepared for indignation, heated argument, or copious tears and wailing, but not for Adela's candor and sincerity. It was obvious what Sebastian saw in her. Anyone could see that Adela was genuine. She really was what she appeared to be, a loving and compassionate woman by nature, guileless and unselfish.

Adelaide thought to herself, if this woman is actually making a fight for Sebastian, she's doing it with completely different tactics. She's trying to disarm me with kindness!

Adelaide stood and turned away for a moment. She could feel her anger slipping away before Adela's solid wall of composure and goodwill. She tried a different approach designed to appeal to Adela's sympathy and sense of fairness.

"But why did you come out of the convent now, of all times?" Adelaide began. "You stayed there when you might have had him. You could have ignored the pronouncements of the Church. Even the king said he'd look the other way.

"I might never have met Sebastian again if you had just stayed with him when you could have. Ironically, if you had, he might never have come to Constantinople, and I would still be safely there, having the time of my life. Instead, I fell in love with him and tried to get him to stay with me. But he wouldn't. Oh no—duty, honor, et cetera. All that *sheise*! Bugger all!"

"I couldn't, Adelaide," Adela answered. "My conscience wouldn't let me. I felt I had to do it for all women whose husbands refuse to acknowledge the bonds of marriage. I did it to support the Church in making marriage a holy sacrament."

She hesitated a moment and continued in a low voice. "And all that time, I also felt a call from God. If I couldn't have Sebastian freely and rightfully, I would answer that call."

"Rubbish!" Adelaide waved a hand dismissively. "What has conscience ever done for a woman—or the bloody Church either, for that matter? And why, pray to tell, didn't you return to Sebastian as soon as you heard Konrad was dead? Seems to me that's no way to treat a husband and certainly doesn't say much about your love for him."

Adelaide could see that her words were having an effect. Adela's head was bent low, almost in her lap. But she rallied, took a deep breath, and sought Adelaide's eyes.

"I know. It was unfair. And unforgivable. But I wasn't sure." She paused a moment, searching for the words.

"I know my answer may be hard for you to understand, dear Adelaide. Your life has been so different from mine. But please sit. Let me try to explain the conflict in my heart."

Adelaide returned to the bench and reluctantly let Adela take her hands again.

"I was never free like you," Adela said. "My life was controlled by men: my father, though he meant well; my cruel first husband Konrad; even the king. When I first went to the convent, it was to escape all that. Then there was the miracle of Sebastian returning to me. But that dream, too, was crushed when we discovered Konrad was still alive!" She paused for a moment, remembering.

"I returned to the convent, and by the grace of God, I eventually discovered a new person in myself. I became immersed in that life, and I loved it too! I wasn't sure that God didn't want me to stay."

"Well, has God changed his mind? Are you sure now? Is that why you're back?"

"I don't know, Adelaide. I still don't know. I must see Sebastian for more than a few minutes, talk to him. We've had so little time. Perhaps I really could make a life here with him now. I've accomplished most of what I wanted to become and do in the convent. But first, I must see if I'm meant to return to married life. Perhaps I need some kind of sign or special insight if I'm to know for certain."

"What about Sebastian? What does he say?"

"He swears we can make it work. But he's always gone. He's always in danger. I never know when word will come that he's been killed. I live in fear of that each time he leaves. He and I need to see if we can overcome this nagging concern and rediscover the richness of our marriage. We were once very happy. I must know for sure."

Adelaide shook off Adela's hands and stood up again. "So I'm just supposed to sit around like some ornament in your great hall until you make up your mind, is that it?"

Adela also rose and clasped her hands before her as if ready to beg or pray. "Oh Adelaide, no! I don't want that. It isn't fair to you at all. He does owe you for what you did for him, and he has shared love with you before—quite intensely, apparently."

"You're bloody right, by God! The love I had for him was just as intense as yours. And I risked my life for it!"

"But, dear Adelaide," Adela continued firmly, "I just can't give him up to you because you feel you have a claim on him. I realize we must decide without delay. He's going to have to leave again soon, I know it. Either tomorrow or the next day. He has never been able to refuse the king. So, I promise you will have an answer before he leaves."

"Amen to that!" Adelaide said, nodding vigorously.

"But," Adela said, adding a conciliatory note, "whatever that answer may be, let me assure you from my heart that I will be your friend. If we decide that I should stay and be his wife again, we won't abandon you. We will help you do whatever you decide, and you can stay here for as long as you like. If the decision is that our reunion is not to be, I will return to the convent and leave you and Sebastian to decide for yourselves what you will do. Is that fair? Do you agree?"

Adelaide answered without hesitation. "It is fair. And I do agree, but you must give me at least an hour tomorrow with Sebastian. I must have a chance to make my own case to him."

"Agreed," Adela exclaimed eagerly. "It's a fearful decision. But at least it will be over soon. In the meantime, come, let me embrace you. We share the love of one man. That makes us sisters, no matter what happens tomorrow. Tonight, let us look forward to the banquet."

Chapter 6

The Banquet

By the time Adela and Adelaide returned from the garden, preparations for a festive banquet were well underway. Adela's return was reason enough for the feast, but the presence of Count Arno, a high-ranking lord of the realm, made it obligatory. Sebastian had instructed the manor's steward to spare no effort.

Thus a good deal of ale was already being consumed, and the delicious smells of roasting venison wafted through the hall. The tables were arranged in a *U* shape, facing the head table, which was slightly raised to show ascendancy. The lower tables were all filled with the village headmen and women and the leading warriors. Rising decibels of laughter and song filled the room.

Sebastian saw with pride that the host table groaned with savory dishes: pork pies, stewed chicken, fresh-caught fish in almond milk, mushroom pasties, baskets of fresh-baked bread, honey cakes and berries, apple pudding, and spinach tarts. The roasted venison would be the *pièce de résistance*.

There was even a small ensemble of local musicians. And a village minstrel who had just begun to play and sing.

As the great room filled, the celebration took on the feel of a comedic drama, and the whole crowd was in a jolly, expectant mood—that is, everyone except the three principal actors on the boards.

By virtue of unwritten law, Count Arno, as the highest ranking, sat at the center of the head table. On his right sat Sebastian, Adela, Milo, and Magdala; on his left Adelaide, Simon, and Liudolf.

An observer might have noticed that not all the smiles and cheerful words were genuine. But Adelaide used her time well at Count Arno's elbow, leaning in to whisper a saucy comment or flattering him shamelessly. Arno was so taken with the attention that he even went as far as to invite her to the king's court whenever she wanted to come.

Eventually, as the evening wore on and the wine and ale flowed freely, there were antics and spontaneous singing and dancing. There were calls for Adelaide. Everyone knew she had been a famous dancer, and even Adela joined in, urging her to perform for the celebration. After much modest protestation, she said something to ready the tambourine and lute players and stepped gracefully onto the floor and into the space in front of the banquet table.

Despite her recent sickness, Adelaide showed no signs of dysfunction. She started slowly, concentrating, her eyes half closed and unfocused as if she were bearing herself back into a far-off, fascinating place. The musicians followed her movements as she spun back and forth, arms upright and waving as a tree in a breeze, gradually increasing the tempo until her undulations merged into a reckless pace, rapidly rising and falling, spinning and weaving, whirling seductively, hands beckoning, from one end of the table to the other—finally ending in a heap upon the floor in front of Sebastian's place.

A long moment passed amidst the enthusiastic huzzahs and loud thumping of knives on tables. Everyone in the assembly below and at the head table was standing. Sebastian applauded just as enthusiastically. He had seen her dance many times before in Constantinople but never as alluringly. She seemed to be dancing in a dream, unaware of any onlookers.

But when she failed to rise after several long moments, the room fell silent except for murmuring undertones and alarmed whispers. Sebastian was the first on his feet, realizing with alarm that Adelaide had fallen too hard and might be gravely injured. He jumped down to her from the raised platform, but the giant Ajax was already there, bending down to pick her up as easily as a feather pillow. He exited the great hall at once, quickly followed by Sebastian, Adela, and Magdala.

Sebastian returned several minutes later, smiling and waving his arms to the crestfallen crowd. He explained calmly that Lady Adelaide had exerted herself too soon after recovering from a debilitating illness. But, he assured them, she was in no danger and only needed to rest and sleep. Everyone else should return to the celebration, as the lady would have wished.

Eventually, Adela also returned and reassured everyone that Adelaide was sleeping soundly with Magdala and the ever-vigilant Ajax watching over her.

"Great God!" Sebastian exclaimed in a low voice to Adela as she returned to her banquet seat. "I can't help but feel it's somehow all my fault. Poor Adelaide! She was trying to impress me—and everybody else as well. I will hate myself if she should not recover. More bad luck—her fall may have wrecked the only chance we're going to be alone together before I have to leave."

Chapter 7

Rendezvous

Sebastian had already arranged for their flight. Lightly packed horses waited in the nearby stable with an attending serf. He made sure with his steward and Liudolf that the banquet would go on for several more hours. Still, he and Adela stayed only long enough to see the room return to its former festive atmosphere, with most of the guests, including Count Arno, succumbing happily to the jugs of ale, the delicious food, and the mesmerizing strumming of the players. No one noticed when they quietly slipped separately out of the great room.

It took less than a minute for the pair to go off through the fortress gate and gallop down a path into the deep forest. Their destination was a hunting cabin several hours' ride away.

They sped recklessly through the autumnal woods, fully absorbed in the escape and sharing an exuberant joy they hadn't known in years. Sensing the energy and excitement of their riders, the two strapping stallions stretched out with a will, galloping buoyantly over a carpet of leaves, hardly making a sound. With a brisk wind in their faces, the liberated lovers leaned forward, laughing, and gave the charging beasts their heads.

At length, they slowed to a walk, and Sebastian had a chance to let his gaze absorb Adela's grace and beauty. She's the most precious thing in my life, he reflected. How could I have ever lost her?

She returned his intent look with an ardent gaze of her own. He reached across and caught her hand, and they tied themselves together for a while in tandem, feeling the energy and passion coursing through their joined hands.

Eventually, other, less friendly thoughts crowded into Sebastian's mind. He stopped the horses for a minute to see her better. "This is absurd," he said in exasperation. "You're still my wife, but I've only seen you a few times in a decade, and I haven't slept with you in so long I've almost forgotten what it was like. All I know is that I want you like that again—so close to me it feels like God himself fit us together perfectly. I feel like our bodies are the same, our desires the same, and even our thoughts run together.

"But to make that magic again, we have to run away from our home and find some fox's den deep in the woods—just to be alone! Damn, that wretched Count Arno! Damn duty and the bloody army! And, yes, damn the confounded king! Haven't I done enough for him? And damn the Church for making rules that blight the commandment to love one another."

She responded by leaning far over to kiss him briefly on the mouth. "Look at you," he said as she drew back. "You're like an angel. You've hardly changed in all these years!"

"Stuff and nonsense, Sebastian," she chided. But he could tell by her voice alone that she was pleased.

Still, he knew she was not an angel, not exactly. Thinking of the many times they couldn't agree, he called to mind her confounded stubbornness. She never cared about what passed for justice in the land. When one blasted thing, or another seemed right to her in the eyes of God, she became like a rock at the edge of the sea. She wouldn't budge, no matter how many waves pounded against her. He was torn between wanting her and trying to figure her out.

She never lied, he recalled, but she could be devilishly misleading. She'd retreat into silence and then do whatever she believed was right behind his back. Like that time after he was wounded in Denmark, she brought him back from the edge of death. Then, when he was almost healed, she slept with him - for just one glorious night. But then she'd left him at first light to return to the convent without saying a word about her decision.

Oh, I blamed her for that, he recalled, and for all those years when we could have been together—and weren't! How selfish, I thought then. Yet now, I finally realize that it wasn't selfishness—it was just her blessed unwavering sense of Right!

He wanted to stop and kiss her a hundred times and confess how little he had understood her. But he kept on, remembering his own faults in their long separations.

He delved into his accursed sense of duty as they rode steadily on. Whenever the king called, he had gone. Why? For one thing, Sebastian really loved him, even from the first time he saw him at twelve years old. Charlemagne was larger than life, greater than any other man, even including his own father, Attalus, whom he loved without reserve. He knew somehow that if anything were ever going to change things for the better, the High King Karl would do it.

He said I am talking to myself again, taking the blame. The ironic fact is that both our obsessions are alike! All our lives, we've sacrificed ourselves for these gilded fixations. It's our baneful sense of right and wrong, good and bad! Devil, take it!

***

The night turned darker as clouds covered the sky. They could no longer see each other clearly. But they kept bumping the horses together so they could reach out and feel for each other's presence.

Adela's thoughts remained riveted on the decision she had to make on the morrow. God or Sebastian? Sebastian or God! Her thoughts, too, led her to accept the burden of blame for their long separations. She had chosen God instead of him, though she felt her love for him so intensely, and it was so much stronger than her underdeveloped love of God. Yet she believed she instinctively knew what God wanted—at least for a while. And eventually, she did become fulfilled in the convent. She actually grew into a different person. Her life had meaning again. She was no longer a commodity, some asset to be handed back and forth by the will of men.

But there was Sebastian, always Sebastian. She looked up quickly to search for his form out in the darkness.

And then there came that fateful day when she felt her work at the convent was finished. She'd achieved enough and began to brood more often over Sebastian and their interrupted life. His voice was the pure note she heard in the silence of the convent. His presence, when he managed to visit—the way he looked at her, the smell of him—felt so familiar. She found to her surprise, that she dreamed more about him, dreams about just falling into his arms and being absorbed by him. It was all she could do not to go with him whenever he had to leave. But there was still that uncertainty lurking in the back of her mind. She still felt torn between her vows to God and the human love she used to have—the love that was so tangible, so sweet, so perfectly fulfilling.

She reached out a hand to him as if to pull him to her. But he couldn't see it. It occurred to her that the separating night between them and their floundering attempts to touch each other in the darkness was like the history of their separated lives.

Her life at the convent had become a self-imposed prison of work. She had to be busy every waking moment until he came again. It didn't matter what work she did—care of the sick, visiting the poor, scrubbing the floor, anything, as long as she could stop thinking about him and all they had missed not being together. She continued to write her psalms and letters, but they were less about heaven and increasingly more about natural things and the gifts of the earth. God, she would cry at the end of each day. Forgive me!

***

Finally, they stopped to rest the horses for a time and walked between them hand in hand.

"Sorry about all this maneuvering," Sebastian began. "I hated to take you by surprise, but we might never have gotten away from there tonight if we didn't take time by the forelock and jumped away quickly."

"Hush, love. It's all right. It was exciting and fun. But I was terrified at first that I'd forgotten how to ride!"

"Nonsense, you've always been a terrific rider. Better than most, man or woman."

"Ah, well, at least I stayed on the back of the beast. It was intoxicating! My heart was in my mouth the whole time. But . . . let's forget about all of *them* right now, can we? At this moment, no one else matters but you and I."

Sebastian couldn't have agreed more. It was all he could do to keep from sweeping her into his arms.

She stopped the horses suddenly and turned to him. "I must tell you something now because I know you feel I'm still uncertain about us. We have had so much pain and loss in our lives, so much sacrifice. One could say our lives have been one long sacrifice, spiced occasionally by blissful moments. But oh, those moments! They were unsurpassable! They managed to make up for all the misfortune. They lifted us to the peak of joy. I have come to realize that I want that again with you. I've never stopped loving you. Even when I chose the convent, the love I had for you was the gift I gave to God—because I had no greater gift to give."

Sebastian caught his breath. Now he had his answer. She still loved him and with all her heart! He felt weak with wonder and wished he could stop time so he could hear those words again.

"Finally," she went on, "Here's my decision: I feel that God may have set me free now to return that love to you. I realize now that it's right. Whatever time we have left, I want us to pledge once again to each other. And even when I can't be with you, that love and that joy in my mind will be lasting happiness as long as I live. I am a whole person because of you and only through you."

Sebastian felt paralyzed, almost afraid to move as she spoke. Her eloquence and sincerity shook him to the bone. When she had finished speaking, there was one profound moment of silence, and then he took her in his arms at once. "Amen!" he breathed and began to kiss her.

"Careful, my heart. We've been apart for so long." Even as she said it, Adela bent into his body and raised her mouth to his. He lifted her off the ground and hugged her so hard she gasped. He locked his hands in her thick hair, kissed her eyes and throat, and finally lowered her to the grass at the side of the path. She trembled as he kissed her and ran his hands over her body. "Slowly, love, slowly," she whispered, but she responded with increasing ardor, tears flowing down her face.

They stayed locked together for so long that the horses strayed, and they had to spend precious minutes collecting them. Later at the cabin, they lay together on a rough pallet on the floor, wrapped in blankets and fur against the brisk night air, with a single candle for light.

She wept, laughed softly, and made sounds in her throat as if she were savoring a good wine or a ripe pear. He watched her face as she went through the stages of yielding to the heat of her passion. He wanted to roar like a beast or laugh aloud with pleasure, but he held back lest he alarmed her. He could not tear his eyes from her as she slid her lips across his face and down his body, rediscovering the joy of intimacy.

For him, all the intensity and magic of lovemaking, wherever he had experienced it in his life, was perfected in her and this one night. For Adela, whatever was left in her from the convent died out in the rough bed of the little cabin as they clung to each other and even seemed to breathe as one.

They made love again and again, that night, resting only to listen to the sounds of the forest through the small window and watch the changing colors of the starlit night.

Chapter 8

A Peculiar Challenge

"This is how it should be, my incredibly beautiful wife," Sebastian announced happily as they continued to hold onto each other in the blissful comfort of their snug little bed. "It must continue to be like this forever."

"I was frightened to death," Adela responded with a small gasp. "I was afraid my body would let me down; it's been so long. But I'd forgotten how wonderful you make me feel. It's as if we never were apart."

"That's because it is as it was meant to be, my love. We were destined to be this way. Finally, fate has cast the die in our favor." He paused to gather her more closely to him and gaze into her eyes. "So I take it," he said with a grin, "you will stay now, won't you, precious girl?"

She hesitated only a moment and spoke with conviction. "I will stay. I am certain now. No matter what happens. You are my husband forever, whether we live to be a hundred or die tomorrow."

"What about your God? Does he say you can stay this time?"

"Hush, don't be irreverent. It's your God too, and I know you know that now."

"I do. And I'm eternally grateful that he has returned you to me."

***

They dressed slowly and reluctantly, pausing to touch each other multiple times in the process. Finally, Sebastian took one last long look at Adela standing in the middle of the rough little room before plunging through the narrow door. Adela lingered in silence as Sebastian went to see the horses, wishing fervently they could just stay immersed in the enchantment of this one brief night. Eventually, however, she made herself emerge into the day. As he came up with the horses, she turned and kissed the door and bowed her head a moment before the little cabin.

On the trail back, the conversation turned to more solemn subjects. "But what about the convent?" he asked. "What about your work there and the peace you prized so much? There won't be much of that peace around the manor, I'm afraid. Not with Adelaide still here and all the other things that happen at Fernshanz. Not to mention that exasperating monarch, our unfathomable king!"

"I can handle Adelaide," Adela said confidently. "I'll just tell her it's my duty to stay. The family reunion is what the king, the Church, and everybody else expects and will approve. And I, particularly, never want to be separated from you again."

"Nor I from you," Sebastian said emphatically. "But we can't just send her away. She has no place to go."

"Adelaide knows that well enough, I'm sure, poor thing. She has no allies and no ground to stand on. But I will make her my friend right away. I will learn to love her. I'll make her feel so welcome at Fernshanz that no matter how much she comes and goes, it will always be her home. We will all welcome her into our family. And you, my gentle friend, must not be upset about this arrangement. You must treat her as family. She has no one else now but us. I don't want her to be hurt ever again."

"Nor do I, Adela. But I warn you, she won't be content just to hang around and be like some pretty decoration in our manor house. She's too smart, too ambitious. In the end, God willing, she'll accept our decision and maybe even your offer to make Fernshanz her base. But she'll get into something, most likely something we won't approve of. Nevertheless, I'm all right with whatever you propose. It's just rotten to leave you with what's going to be the monstrous task of dealing with her. Nevertheless, I have to admit I'm relieved. I suppose that makes me a coward. But I'd rather face the Saxons or the Avars than Adelaide."

"You know, don't you, love, that you do have to face her before you go? I promised her at least an hour with you," Adela said as they rode back in the early morning twilight.

"Yes, I suppose I have to. She'd feel it was an unforgivable insult if I didn't. I just wish I could think of the right words to say."

"Nonsense. It's not that hard. Appreciate her. Tell her you're grateful for her love and what she's done for you. Tell her she'll always be a part of you. Because she will be, won't she? You won't be able to shake off her memory. It was too intense, from all I can gather. Just say that I'm the mother of your children, that the king and the Church and all of Fernshanz want to see us back together again. If you must, tell her, you'd be happy to marry her if you weren't already married. Well, wouldn't you?"

"No!" Sebastian protested with a start. "Not at all. After last night, I could see and feel how much you and I love each other. It was perfect. I could never spoil it by taking another woman."

"I know, I know. I feel the same," she said, reaching across to touch his arm and meet his eyes. "But be as gentle and caring as you can. Be careful. Don't say anything that would hurt her. She's been hurt enough already.

"And listen, my love. When you're done, as much as I hate to say it, I think you should go . . . get on the boat with Count Arno or go off by horse with your comrades. You don't want to add to her distress by being here another night. She and I need to start at once to love one another somehow. The longer you're here, the harder that will be."

"Aye, indeed! I've been brooding about that as well. But I desperately wanted at least one more day with you."

"God knows I feel the same, love. But there's nothing for it. We'll make it up when you return."

He hung his head low over the horse's neck and felt a sharp pang of frustration and hopelessness. "Why is it, Adela, that every time something really good happens for us, we have to pay for it with some crushing misfortune?

"I know, dear. But look on the good side. It's those bad times that make the good ones so incredibly sweet."

"You're right. I wouldn't trade them for anything. But let me tell you something, Adela," He said on a sudden inspiration, "I won't say that last night made up for all the times we've missed! But it was incredible, and I swear it will not be the last, by God! I will come back to you!"

When he raised his eyes again, there was Fernshanz in the tranquil early morning light. "Look, there's our polestar!" he observed to her softly. "Good Lord, what a treasured place! It's always been my beacon of promise and hope. It's where everything I've loved is. This place will lead me back to you! Last night may have been the best night of our lives. But we are owed, by all that's holy! And we will have more!"

Chapter 9

Gone Again

As a result of the general indulgence of the past night's feast, no one was stirring when they returned to the manor house. Sebastian went off immediately to roust his cohort for the unexpectedly early start of the journey. He would take only Liudolf, Bardulf, Drogo, and the old soldier Bernard, who, despite his age, was as tough as a hickory nut and seemingly indestructible. At Liudolf's urging, he consented to let a new man join their small troop, a young blacksmith called Wolfram, known for his good ideas and skills, who had been a captive of the Slavs for many years and could speak their language.

"And, my darling, you must take Father Pippin," Adela said, digging her fingernails into Sebastian's biceps and staring into his eyes.

"What?" Sebastian said, backing away in protest. "Pippin? On this mission? Are you joking?"

She held onto him tenaciously, backing him into a corner. "Listen to me, Sebastian. I'm deadly serious. I have a premonition about this. Father Pippin may be just the piece you will need to make this a successful mission."

Father Pippin had been Adela's personal confessor ever since she and Sebastian had first married. He advised her on every important decision. She had rescued him long ago from poverty and homelessness when he was an itinerant priest. He had given her comfort and good advice whenever she was grieving and spiritually adrift. She now trusted him implicitly and loved him as one of her closest friends.

At first, Sebastian had been a bit leery of Father Pippin. True, he was a nice enough little man, a humble priest with wispy hair, a long nose, skinny legs, and a bent-over torso that reminded Sebastian vaguely of a dark-colored stork. He was so unattractive that he was almost invisible wherever he went. People just didn't seem to see him. Sebastian suspected all he did for Adela was ask her the right questions.

Gradually, however, Sebastian saw what Adela had always known. Pippin truly feared no evil. He would step into any crisis, unselfishly willing to sacrifice his frail body to serve the needy or champion the wronged. He had an uncanny ability to sense what to do at the crossroads of crisis situations.

"I'm sorry, Adela, but I can't take him," Sebastian declared. "I'd love to, but he's not strong enough. He'd break in two on such a long ride. Come to think of it, I don't think I've ever seen him on a horse. Impossible!"

"That doesn't matter. I know him much better than you," Adela insisted passionately, still holding Sebastian in the corner. "I know what he's capable of. That's why he must go with you this time. If part of the agreement the East Saxons will have to make with King Karl is to forsake their pagan gods and embrace Christianity, I'm absolutely sure that only a man like Pippin might have a chance with them. He has a completely unselfish manner. He won't threaten or frighten them. He's the only person I know who could get the Saxons to accept something as repugnant as the ideas of Christianity would be for them."

She had thrown her arms around Sebastian's and captured his eyes with her own. "Listen, my love, I have a feeling in my bones about this. You'll be faced with the thorniest kind of task, one that could turn against you at any point. You're good at persuasion, my darling, but you're a warrior. You look like just the sort of agent the king would use just before he unleashes his heavy cavalry on some unsuspecting foe. You could be killed if they turn on you."

"But he can't keep up, Adela. He'd have to ride in a cart. And I can't wait for him. He could never find the way by himself. Even then, such an arduous trip would likely kill him."

"You're taking Bernard, aren't you? Let Bernard bring him. If anybody can get him there, that old scout can do it. Didn't he make his way by himself all the way back to Aachen from Constantinople?"

In the end, Sebastian surrendered, if only to have peace from Adela's insistence. "Well, he's worn out, Adela. Don't blame me if he dies on the trip. He's likely to die soon, anyway. I'll surely miss Bernard on the trek, but you're right. If anybody can keep that feeble little fellow alive over a hundred leagues of bumpy roads in a cart, it's Bernard. If he makes it, maybe that'll be a good omen. God help him! God help us all!"

One of the last things Sebastian did was beg Simon to put off going on his next trading journey and stay at least a few more weeks at Fernshanz. Adelaide would need somebody she knew well enough to vent to about himself and the betrayal she perceived he had done her.

He also spoke briefly with Milo and gave him complete rein in Fernshanz to continue with Magdala in building a network of hospices in the county and even in surrounding counties if possible. Once again, he blessed their plan to start a school for caregivers and those who would study healing, and he urged Milo to include his mother in their efforts and even Adelaide if she would. Finally, he spoke with the village headmen, urging them all to be of best use to Adela, who, as a countess, would have authority at Fernshanz in his stead.

***

Finally, he spoke to Adelaide. She was only a few minutes late at midmorning for their meeting in the garden behind the manor house. She had dressed meticulously, her dress and hair designed to emphasize every aspect of her beauty. Her perfection, however, could not completely cover the tension on her face as she approached this last meeting.

To enhance her confidence, she came with Ajax, who rarely left her side. She believed his presence augmented her power. He stood apart during the meeting, enormous arms folded, displaying his usual sphinxlike face.

Sebastian rose as she entered the garden and hurried to her, arms extended. But she warned him off with a short wave of her hands in front of her face. "No, Sebastian, no touching, no more of that!" she said as she seated herself.

I still love him, damn him, she warned herself. I want to kill him one minute, and I just want to hold him the next. But one thing is certain. We shall have no more touching—ever.

"In fact, I doubt if I shall ever see you again, Sebastian—if I ever manage to get out of this forsaken place!"

"Oh, Adelaide, don't leave it like that," he began.

"How else shall I leave it? I'm defeated. I know that. I thought to fight for you. But you didn't give me a chance. You snuck off when I fell sick last night. How do you think I felt? And then I had to wake up to all those bumpkins in your household. The only one I could stand to talk to was Milo. At least he's pretty, as you once were, and as good as gold. Maybe I should marry him. How would you like that, my old lover?"

"Hear me, Adelaide! Please. Adela's my wife. I've always loved her. I . . . ."

"Oh, stop! You needn't go through all that again. I understand. It's over. So be it! I'll survive. In fact, I'll be my old self again quite soon. You'll see! Probably well before you get back, I'll have found a new field to trust my luck to. I can do it. Just watch me. One day you may need me for some reason. For what, I don't know. And what I will do about that, I don't know either.

"But right now, I'm angry! I don't usually lose. Perhaps I'll just arrange for someone to kill you," she said flippantly. "I could have Ajax do it now, as a matter of fact. I need only snap my fingers."

She gave a short laugh at his consternation. "Oh, don't look so shocked. You know me better than that. Maybe I'll change my heart and pity you in whatever mess you're going to get yourself into. One thing is certain: we shall never have what we had in Constantinople again. Understand? That part is done, at least."

"I'm so sorry, Adelaide. I won't say I didn't love you then, in Constantinople. Or I don't still hold you in my heart because of that time. Fate played a role in our relationship. It could have gone quite another way. You know that. But I will always be glad of your memory and always be ready to help you however I can."

Adelaide felt her anger begin to ebb as he said these words. She lowered her head and closed her eyes. Dammit! Don't start bawling! Get a grip, she told herself... Am I lying to him—and to myself? But I still want him so much! This is not me! Things will change. I'm clever enough to find a way to get him back one day—if I still want him. Who knows?

But then her pride reasserted itself. She jerked her head upright, straightened her shoulders, and stood defiantly. "That's enough, Count! No more words. We'll see what fate has in store for us now. Go on! Go at once before I get angry again."

Without looking at him, she strode out of the room, tossing her long hair. She added softly as she disappeared through the door: "Be careful."

***

Sebastian and his men were gone within the hour. Everyone gathered in front of the manor house to bid farewell—everyone except Adelaide. Only Ajax appeared as if to mark her discontent. Always seeking to protect his beloved mistress from hurt, he stood silently at the back of the crowd, towering over everybody, arms folded and glowering like some dark angel ready to bring down fire bolts.

Adela stood by Sebastian as he mounted and rose on her toes to receive his parting kiss. Before he rode off, she kissed him again, this time on the knee, as she had done many times whenever they parted.

Chapter 10

A Royal Target

Whenever Adelaide was upset, she bade her two personal handmaidens sit beside her to comb her hair and rub ointments over her body. If she were particularly perturbed, she had Ajax massage her feet, back, and arms.

Such was the scene when Simon, the Radhanite trader, finally worked up the nerve to make a visit. He came into her quarters thinking of surprising her and was stopped squarely in his tracks by Ajax, who might have ripped off his head if Adelaide had not run, half-naked, to rescue him.

She knew Simon quite well. In fact, she knew him in the Biblical sense at one time.

"Simon, you devil," She scolded, pulling him out of Ajax's paw-like grip, "Have you come to revel in my misfortunes?" She allowed him to kiss her on both cheeks and then surprised him by giving him a generous hug. Then she dragged him to her dressing table and allowed him to comb her long hair. Once Ajax had relinquished his grip on Simon's neck, he settled cross-legged in a corner to watch the meeting with beady, suspicious eyes.

"You've turned out to be quite a famous fellow, I hear," she said as she looked Simon up and down. "Still quite handsome. Dashing as always."

Simon traded along the rivers of Francia in a boat manned by Danish sailors. Then he took his goods to Italy, as far away as Constantinople and Baghdad. After Sebastian, he was the most interesting man she had ever met.

As he combed and caressed her hair, Adelaide observed him appreciatively. "Hmm, you haven't changed much. Still the elegant, charming man I ran off with some years ago! We made quite a couple once upon a time."

Simon and Adelaide suited each other. Both had adventurous natures and were uninhibited by convention. Simon was darkly handsome, with a trim beard and mustache, shiny black hair, and a sleek body. He was a world traveler who was at least Adelaide's equal in intelligence and wit. He was also as sensual as she, and when they first met, they had wasted no time in becoming intimate.

"Right," she chided, "if it hadn't been for you, I might have actually married Sebastian long ago."

"What!" Simon protested, "I was just the means for your escape, not the cause. No one forced you to get into my boat that night. So don't blame me!"

"Well, it probably wouldn't have worked then either. I couldn't have stayed in this wretched place, Simon! I don't know if I could now. But it doesn't matter anyway. I have to find a new home and a new calling now. And soon!"

She'd met Simon just after Adela had been forced by the high king to marry Count Konrad, one of Charlemagne's generals. Denied his great love, Sebastian had been in a deep depression when Adelaide turned up at Fernshanz and implored him to give her sanctuary. Her father had condemned her for scandalous behavior and thrown her out of his manor.

Taking advantage of Sebastian's despair, she seduced him, and since everyone thought Adela would be gone forever, she even persuaded him that she could make him happy as his wife.

"You know, I suppose I did love Sebastian then," she mused as she allowed Simon to comb out her long hair. "But I didn't love him enough then to live the rest of my life on the far edge of everything. And in this shabby village surrounded by wilderness. And then you came, dear Simon, at the eleventh hour!" She smiled somewhat guiltily at the thought.

So she had stolen away on the trader's boat when he left for the East one early morning. Simon, tongue in cheek, had allowed it to happen, knowing that his friend Sebastian would be secretly glad to be free from an alliance made more out of loneliness and need than love.

But Adelaide had soon tired of long days at sea on a boat with twelve leering Danish sailors. And Simon was always too busy while in port. Adelaide had found little to do except buy clothes and trinkets, with no place to wear them. Eventually, she'd learned from other traders about the wonders of Byzantium and the opportunities there for beautiful women. She'd demanded money from Simon and made him arrange passage for her to Constantinople. Their parting had been amicable, even affectionate, but both had breathed a sigh of relief to see the back of the other.

Adelaide could tell that Simon was genuinely sorry for her and was concerned about what would become of her now. She shook her head and stopped him at once as he tried to cheer her up by gaily singing out an old sailing tune.

"You never spoke to me last night at that horrid banquet, you dog! You might at least have warned me about how deep the waters might be for me. But you never said a word."

"Alas, my dear girl, I wanted to, but you never gave me a chance. By the way, I adored your dance."

"Well, you're not likely to see it again. You don't expect me to stay here now that my false lover has chosen to have his nun wife instead of me? And now he has run off somewhere without giving me a chance to turn his head around. Bah!"

"I'm truly sorry, Adelaide. I hate to see you hurt like this. But I know you. Nothing brings you down for very long. Besides..." he paused a moment to leer at her once again..."your famous beauty is unfaded."

"Stop it, you liar! You'd just like to get me in bed again."

"Indeed not, madam. You know I'm a perfect gentleman. But you could run away with me again if I just had my boat here," he added playfully. "I'll have another boat before long. What about it? We weren't so bad together for a time, eh?"

"Bosh! I'm fond of you, Simon, you know that. But we're too much alike. Eventually, we would quarrel, as we did before. Besides, I couldn't stand any more weeks on that god-awful filthy boat!" She sat up on her couch and shook her finger at him emphatically.

"I must raise myself again, Simon! I must be somebody again, as I was in Constantinople. Am I not at least nearly as beautiful as before? And I'm bloody well sure I'm as clever as any man."

"You are indeed, my old love." They sat down together as the women brought some light ale and cheese. Simon stroked his beard and pondered a moment. "I have it, Adelaide—exactly what you might do! You must present yourself to our king! He would love you! He couldn't resist you." She laughed at how delighted with himself he was for having thought of this. He continued enthusiastically.

"You might have to sleep with him, old as he is," Simon cautioned, "but you could easily become a lady of his court. Since his wife died, he still keeps a few covert courtesans there. You would just need someone to get you in to meet the king. Once he sees you and realizes what a prize you are, he will demand that you stay and join the court at once.

"But," Simon said, curbing his newfound avidity, "who can we get to arrange an audience for you? It's not so easy to get in to see the king." Simon deliberated. "Matter of fact, I hardly know anybody at the king's court."

"Well, I do!" Adelaide responded triumphantly. "I'm well ahead of you, my old pet. And I have already got an invitation to the court."

"How? From whom?" Simon exclaimed in surprise.

"Well, what would you say to the fat spider? What about Count Arno?"

Chapter 11

Foes, Old and New

The King's Court, Aachen

Riding steadily with a small herd of remounts, they did indeed beat Count Arno's boat to the Rhine and found a barge ready to row them across to the road to Aachen. The king's men were waiting for them.

"Sebastian, you rascally dodger!" bellowed the king as his senior paladin bowed himself into the king's quarters. "I thought you'd never turn up. Come and embrace me, lad."

Sebastian braced himself for the customary bear-hug. "Oof," he said. "Strong as ever! You never change, m'lord." At least physically, he thought. If I could just get him to stop relying on the heavy cavalry as an answer to everything. Maybe this time.

"By the rood, I've missed you, my old champion! I've thought about you every blessed day. You're the only man I ever totally trusted—besides that fawning donkey Arno. I never trusted him, either. God knows what he's done behind my back. But he's useful."

"Came as soon as I could, my liege, even though it cost me sorely in terms of my love life," Sebastian inserted casually.

"What's this, say? Your love life?" the king exclaimed, holding Sebastian at arm's length. "Ooooh, right—I remember now. You hoped your wife would be coming home, innit? Well, she did, didn't she? That's it! I judge you're up and married again already! She agreed to stay with you this time, did she?"

"She did indeed, my king. Ah-hum…that is, we had exactly one night together," Sebastian said pointedly. "But at least she's staying. So, if I survive this new errand you have for me, I might at least enjoy the glorious pleasure of another evening or two with her."

"Tut tut! Don't get prickly with me, old son! Besides, you're my paladin, ain't you? And you took an oath to do whatever I bloody well tell you. Din't you?"

"I did sire. I know what my oath means."

"Well then..." The king suddenly stood up and began pacing back and forth in the room, pulling on his mustaches. Every now and then, he glanced at his favorite sideways, almost as if he felt a pang of guilt for sending Sebastian off once again just after Adela came home. Eventually, however, he cleared his throat and went on.

"Thing is, Sebastian. I'm the king, dammit, and it's my God-given duty, as well as my bloody misfortune, to do whatever this sprawling realm of ours needs. And it's you it needs right now.

"Thing is, the wretched Saxons have been rising against me again, as they're forever wanting to do. I can't seem to control 'em without pounding 'em. But that's a devil of a bother. These ones are way out there in the east, up against the Slavs. And it costs a fortune every time I have to bring our army out against 'em. So, I've decided to take your ruddy advice. After all, you always said, if we made a good enough offer, we could root 'em out of their stinking shitholes in the woods and plant 'em someplace safe across the bloody Rhine."

"It worked pretty well with Prince Widukind, my lord. We have some of his Westphalians in our army right now."

"I know, I know. But for God's sake, don't remind me of that nasty bugger. I hated him, and he hated me. I was sure you couldn't bring him over. But you did! So I had to swallow a lot of that scoundrel's insolent guff. But he did finally move—took himself and all his filthy Westphalians out of the fight. But I would still like to split him open and roast his guts. That devil killed a fearsome lot of my warriors before he was done. Good riddance! Wily old bastard!"

"Yes ... well, you showed a great lot of patience and wisdom, my king," Sebastian said, biting his tongue.

"Withal, dammit! I'm willing to try your way again, this time with the East Saxons. As you're so fond of saying, it's cheaper than having to beat 'em hollow every time. If you can do it, I won't have to weaken my army by fighting them."

"Right, sire," Sebastian replied, looking at the floor to suppress the temptation to make a gloating remark. Well, praise God almighty! He exclaimed to himself. We could have done this many times before with the Avars, the Bretons, the Slavs, and a batch of others.

The king carried on as if he were only asking a minor favor. "And I need you to chivvy right along, y'see. Don't spend too much time with that scrotty lot of bloody Saxons. Just tell 'em I said if they don't move at once, I'll bring the whole blinking army against them, and we'll rape their wives in front of 'em first before we kill 'em all. They'll wet themselves."

Sebastian sighed and dared to give the king a brief sour look. But he said only, "Um, not exactly the way to win their friendship, my liege."

"Pssh! No need to be nice to 'em, bloody pagans!

The dicier game, mind you, is this side of the Elbe, up by the sea and the flaming Danish border. The real reason I need to get the East Saxons the hell out of there is because I know they've been conniving against me with King Godofrid. I want to give their precious land to the Obodrites. You know who they are, don't you?"

"Aye, my king. But the Obodrites are Slavs, aren't they? And they're pagans, too, same as the Saxons."

"I don't give a flaming rat's arse what they believe in right now. The important thing is we need an ally against that pagan fornicator Godofrid. There's no love lost between Obodrites and Danes, and that's what I care about most. Better one ruddy bunch of pagans fighting another rather than me. But the price is that land the East Saxons are sitting on.

"So go up there and make 'em move quick time. And, oh, don't forget to bring a priest or two and get 'em baptized properly afore they move onto Christian ground."

"Oh, right, my liege. I'm sure they will just kneel right down and courteously respect your wishes."

"Don't get cheeky with me, you ruffian." The king began to pace and pull on his mustaches again.

"You know my rules, dammit. They have to surrender everything—totally, even their religion. Or else! No fudging on that, bet your arse. I'm a Christian king and the Sword of God! I'm his David, by thunder! I do whatever God tells me to do—and that's to cut down their cursed sacred trees and wipe out their evil pagan gods. When I'm done, there won't be any—anywhere in my realm!

"You tell 'em that, b'God! Tell 'em if they fight us, we'll grind their bloody bones into our stinking porridge! Nothing works better than being done over by my heavy cavalry! Then, once the Saxons are gone, I'll give all their land to the Obodrites, and that's who'll be our blooming ally against Godofrid!"

"Uh . . . right, my liege," Sebastian muttered a lukewarm assent, wishing that somehow he might finally find a way to mitigate the bloodthirsty side of Charlemagne's nature. "How soon would you want me to leave?"

"Well, bugger all, man! Right bloody now! 'Temples fludgit,' or whatever."

"That's *tempus fugit*, my king."

"Bedamned if it is! Well, get on with it then, will ye? And don't forget the missionaries."

"I have a plan for that, my king. It might take a bit of extra time. Priests don't move like cavalry. But we'll go ahead and meet with the Saxon chieftains. We may even go to the Obodrites too. We've found a young man, a blacksmith, who used to be a Slavic slave. He speaks both their tongues."

After a long moment of mustache-pulling, the king cleared his throat discreetly and said, "Uh, there is one more thing, though."

"One more thing, sire?"

Uh-oh, here comes the rest of it, Sebastian surmised, feeling new tension in his belly. As usual, he'll make whatever it is sound like a walkover, something I can do with my left hand.

"Arno's been telling me that brigand Godofrid has been marshaling nearly his whole army on our border again. And a flock of those rotten pirate Vikings has joined him with their ships."

"Is that so, my king? Well, I expect the good count should know."

"Bloody right! There's nobody like him for getting whatever I need to know. He has spies everywhere. I know whatever happens almost the day after it happens because of that tub o' lard."

Sebastian raised an eyebrow. "And good advice too, my king?"

"Well, I don't know about that always . . . Anyroad, about the Danes. Arno says he doesn't know whether they want war or not. He says we need to send somebody there post-haste because they're getting stronger by the day. He says we should send you!"

"Me? Why in God's name would he put the finger on me? I expect to be plenty busy enough with the bloody Saxons."

"He says you're the best we've got. He says you might be able to find a way to make Godofrid think twice about fighting me. And I agree with him. You have a direct way of talking to our enemies without riling 'em."

The king paused, pulling determinedly on his mustaches and putting on his best expression of innocence. "And so, all you've got to do is go up there and look around, see if that false king means business this time. See if you can judge his strength. Just talk with 'em a bit, if ye can."

Oh, is that all? Sebastian thought derisively. "Well, I'm sure that Count Arno has figured this all out. No real danger at all."

"Now, bide a wee bit, Sebastian. I'm not asking you to put your neck in a noose. Just go up there and take a look around. I'll be bringing the army up as soon as I can gather it. I'd just like to know what to expect when we get there. If you could convince that old rogue to back off from a fight, well enough. But . . . I'm . . . um...I certainly don't want you to take undue risk."

Sebastian lowered his head to stare at the floor, letting the preposterous statement hang in the air.

"It's a small thing, really." The king said edgily. Should be easy! Ah . . . right, then. You do know that beastly coward King Godofrid backed away from me the last time I faced him up in Schleswig."

"Indeed, my lord. It was quite a good show, I hear."

"Indeed it was, my fine soldier! I threatened him with my heavy cavalry, and he picked up and ran like a hounded deer. I thought that would be enough for a while. But the bugger seems to be returning and bringing his whole bloody army up behind that big wall. Arno's spies say he's building and stretching that whole wall across Denmark. What'd they call it?"

"The Dannevirke, my king."

"Bloody right! The scouts say he's sending hundreds of workers to the wall to lengthen and strengthen it. He must be spending a fortune. Doesn't he know an earth wall like that can be got over fairly easily, no matter how high they get it? And they can't guard every inch of it."

"No, my lord. It may be, uh, symbolic, more than anything else."

"That's it! I reckon it's a sign for sure that Godofrid considers us a serious threat. He must think I want to conquer all of Denmark! Ha! That's the last thing I want to do! Nothing but bogs and wind and shit piles for towns! Nothing I want up there. And I don't give a damn if they are pagans. They're not in my realm anyway."

"I'm glad to hear you say that, sire."

"To tell the truth, my good paladin, I'm tired of killing pagans. I want to settle a bit, do a little rogering here and there now that my last wife's gone—uhm—and go hunting in my forests, dammit, whenever I want to."

"Hmm, I can certainly understand that, my king!"

"Right." The king began to pace again, pounding his fists into his hands.

"Well, when you get done with the Saxons, you hie up there and scout out that wall the Danes are building. And while you're at it, you might just tell 'em I don't give a beggar's fart about owning Denmark. They can keep it and go to hell, as far as I'm concerned. Tell 'em the only thing that really makes me mad is if they keep raiding my towns and pirating my ships. I can get very bloody motivated if they keep that up. Tell 'em that!"

"Um, tell whom, my liege? Do you want me to seek out Godofrid himself?"

"Nooo, uh, not necessarily. Just go up to the wall with a white flag, find out who's in charge, and tell him. He'll be high enough. Godofrid'll get the message. Can you do that? Won't take you much longer, and then I promise I'll leave you alone. All right?"

Oh, God, where have I heard that before? Sebastian asked himself for the thousandth time as he studied his feet on the floor. The old answers cropped up once again: Because you made an oath to him; because he's making the land safe by keeping our enemies at bay; because he's an extraordinary man who can cause great change; and because you've loved him like a father all your life!

Sebastian took a deep breath, looked up at the king, and, closing his eyes, nodded his head once.

"Good!" The king paused, rubbing his nose and looking sideways at Sebastian. "But listen, old dog, don't you get y'self done in, ye hear? I wouldn't send you, except you're the only man I can think of who could survive a mission like this. I still can't believe you returned from that besotted business in Constantinople and Baghdad. If you didn't get pegged out then, you're not likely to die just searching out some jackleg Saxons and spying on the godforsaken Danes. You can tell 'em you're my personal herald."

"Yes, my king."

Sebastian had already made his decision. He would go because he believed both missions just might be achieved without shedding a drop of blood. And if he succeeded, it might actually change the way the king thought and acted.

"There's a good man! I knew you'd be keen for it in the end!"

In the end, Sebastian raised his eyes to the king's, bowed, and said the same simple thing he always said. "Aye, my king."

Chapter 12

The Forests of Wihmuodi

East of the Elbe

A flood of past-life remembrances accompanied Sebastian and his small band on the eight-day trip into Nordalbingia. It was in the eastern part of Old Saxony, a land of sunless, gloomy forests, giving way to windswept moors and frequent gritty gales from the northern sea, cold and wet even in summer. It also had the reputation of containing a collection of the unruliest tribes of all the Saxons.

Bardulf was the first to comment on the unwelcome feel of the land the farther they rode into the hostile quiet of this strange country beyond the Elbe.

"God's blood, this in't no joy! I thought we'd be havin' a bit of a lark now that we're shed o' the army. But all we been doing is wearing our backsides out. Ain't pretty, neither. Uncommon ugly country! No people, naught to look at but them empty ol' marshes stinkin' o' rotten fish."

"And what about the dark old woods we're-comin' through, full of haunts and demons?" piped up Drogo, who harbored the whole canon of peasant superstition in his head.

"Count your past blessings, boys," Liudolf countered laconically. "You may not want to think much about the kind of folks we're about to meet. From what I hear, they're most like this country—hard-bitten and mean as a badger."

Sebastian had said little over the whole distance except to inform everyone of what they would likely encounter and warn of the certain danger. Even though he knew they would refuse, he still offered each man the chance to skip this unpromising adventure.

"Why, it ain't much different from what we were doin' in Constantinople, wastin' time with them barmy Greeks," Bardulf snorted contemptuously. "I'd swear every one of 'em had a knife up his sleeve and would sell ye, soul and body, to them Arab pirates for half a piece of silver!"

"And we were worse off in the deserts over by Baghdad and that Afriky place," Drogo added. "There weren't a sip o' water most of the time. At least there was ol' Doggie to keep us company. 'E was fun! I wish we had, im still. We'd show them Saxons somethin'."

"Fun!" Liudolf exploded. "That blasted elephant nearly got us killed a hundred times. Have you forgotten all those swarming crocodiles when we had to move his fat arse across the Nile on that shaky ol' raft? And he wouldn't move at all if it was too hot or if we didn't give him a bath four times a day! So we spent most of our bloody time traveling in the dark and looking out for bandits. Nay! I'll take this little daytime holiday in my own kind of country anytime."

"Well, they were your remembrances. But I ain't sellin' that ol' elephant short," Bardulf observed. "I say he made us a bushel o' friends on the way. If it weren't for everybody overlooking us so they could take a look at 'im, we'd 'a-wound up murdered for sure."

Sebastian held up his hand and reined in quickly. "Get ready, gentlemen. That seems to be our hosts coming out of that little woods ahead. Pray they give us a chance to tell them why we're here before they set in to kill us.

"Get that white flag waving, Bardulf! And Liudolf, raise up the king's standard! The rest of you, keep your hands where they can see 'em and off your weapons."

Half a hundred riders of Saxon light cavalry came belting down the narrow road in a column. They made no war cries or threatening gestures, but their rapid approach was distinctly less than friendly.

Sebastian waved up Wolfram, the young blacksmith who had lived so long in this region east of the Elbe. "Son, the tribes in these parts don't speak much like the Saxons we're used to. You can speak their dialect, can't you?"

"I c-c-c-can, m'lord," the lad stuttered, wide-eyed with fear. "I was s-s-s-slave . . . to dem one year . . . den Slavs take me."

"Good. Just stand by me till I need you. And spit, boy. Spit! Clear your throat. I need you talking plainly."

"Aye, m'lord."

The dust the troop made as they pulled up abruptly shrouded the small cluster of Franks. When it cleared, they found themselves facing a bristling circle of ten-foot spears. A rather smallish, scar-faced captain with a heavy rust-colored beard and bright blue eyes glared balefully at Sebastian. His head was wrapped in a broad bandage from recent fighting, and his substantial chainmail vest bore signs of sword blows. He said nothing but only gave a slight nod to Sebastian.

Sebastian calmly told the boy, "Don't be afraid, now. They would have killed us already if they intended to. Just repeat after me everything I say."

"Aye, lord."

Sebastian dismounted and began by holding out two gold arm rings and bowing low to the gritty little captain.

***

They stayed two weeks in the nearest Saxon village, a run-down hodgepodge of hastily built huts on the bank of a small lake. Everyone in the village was on edge. The men constantly carried arms wherever they went. Clearly, the Slavic Obodrites had been pushing them hard of late and driving them farther and farther west.

There was a meeting around a small bonfire the first evening. Sebastian reasoned patiently with their chieftain, a small, round man with a wheezy voice and an air of fatalism. He was the gloomy epitome of a people in decline.

"High Chief," Sebastian began, "my king, the incomparable and all-powerful *Carolus Magnus*, greets you and urgently invites you and your people to come and live with him westward from here across the great river. You are in great danger; he feels you would be much better off west of the Rhine. There is plenty to eat. There is plenty of good land. And there is safety! A refuge from the Obodrites who wish to destroy you."

Judging from the looks that passed among the elders, Sebastian knew his argument was being taken seriously. These were poor people with little food to spare, ragged clothing, and a look of impermanence in their eyes. Nevertheless, the evening council around the fire floundered when the subject of conversion to Christianity came up.

The Saxons simply recoiled at the idea of giving up their gods and their sanguinary approach to life. The promise of Valhalla for a brave warrior who dies fighting was a strong image. Why, they questioned heatedly, would warriors anywhere want to worship a weak Outlander who claimed to be a king but let himself be crucified?

Sebastian brooded uneasily as each day went by with no results. What now? He worried. What if the Obodrites renewed their attacks and drew the Saxons away from these talks? What's happening on the Danish border? I'm running out of time.

Finally, a ray of hope trundled in on a cart. A cohort of Frankish cavalry rode ahead of it, followed by the old soldier Bernard, leading the cart. And in the cart was Father Pippin, buried beneath a nest of furs and blankets.

Despite his concerns, Sebastian could not suppress a smile as Pippin popped his head out of the furs and squinted at his new surroundings. There he was, prominent front teeth, a long, narrow nose, and weak eyes, precisely suggesting a mole emerging from a hole at first light. Sebastian made haste to extract the tiny priest and embrace him. He wound up having to carry the little man to the campfire,

The long journey had exhausted Pippin. He could not walk for several hours and seemed malnourished and dehydrated. Old Bernard explained curtly that "the little bugger won't eat. He doesn't like nothin'." Of course, Bernard's idea of a meal on the trail was little more than stringy smoked pork strips, small hard cakes of fried rye bread, and water to wash it down.

After a few hours of rest and a proper meal, Pippin revived and became cheerful and lighthearted. Sebastian discovered to his great surprise, that Pippin was devoted to beer. Most of the time, he shunned it like a temptation from the devil. But occasionally, he did take a cup or two.

Sebastian quickly found some stout Saxon beer, and it transformed him. Instead of the shy, modest churchman he normally was, the beer made him as merry as a jester. Sitting around the fire, he began to sing prettily in a high but quite melodious voice. It did not take much beer to put him soundly to sleep.

"By glory! What a surprising little bugger he is!" Sebastian remarked to Liudolf as they sat around the fire. "It's a "new" version of Pippin. He's already got the attention of our hosts, though they may think he's gone a bit balmy. Maybe, just maybe, he can reach them."

"Well, he's the best chance we've got," Liudolf added. "I've seen him do some strange things before, things that took a lot of courage. When there's a commotion of any sort, he's as unruffled and clear-headed as if he were in his chapel."

The next evening Sebastian brought Father Pippin to the elders' council. Crossing his fingers for luck, he introduced the skinny little priest as the emissary of the Christian God. He said he was a very holy man who could lift them all to a new understanding of the power of the One God and the inevitable triumph of Christianity.

There was an eruption of incredulous laughter, then dead silence. Sebastian stood up and pointed to the priest. "Listen to me, elders. This little priest has magical powers. You will see. Even the great King of the Franks holds him in high regard. Tomorrow he will speak to you about what may become the greatest change in your lives. Hear him! What he tells you will save you!"

The elders stared stoically at the comical sight of this slight, pale-as-a-ghost monk in a dirty brown robe. Sebastian bit his lip.

"We've really jumped into the *scheise* now!" Liudolf whispered as they left the meeting. "How on God's green earth are these tough warriors going to be able to accept anything this poor old mouse will say?"

"I'm afraid you're right," Sebastian said, shaking his head.

"And wait till he tells them that our savior God was nailed like a criminal to a tree but is still able to promise eternal life? I scarcely believe it myself!" Liudolf said. "We better pray that Lady Adela's unshakeable faith in him and his ability to perform miracles is justified!"

The next day, Sebastian rode off with most of his band to find the Obodrites and make a parley, leaving Pippin behind at the mercy of the Saxons. He also left Liudolf in case the good father had to be rescued.

But the little monk had strength nobody realized. He wasted no time. Over Liudolf's objections, he moved his few things at once right into the Saxon camp. There he sat or walked about as if he belonged there and had no cares in the world. Like a good Benedictine, he prayed seven or eight times a day, often praying aloud over his beads. He bowed low before every man he met, avoiding the eyes of the women, but he played with their children or sang to them. He showed at once that he was gentle, non-threatening, and generous. It was clear he wore his heart on his sleeve, for he bowed and smiled everywhere he went.

Soon the little priest could walk about freely, and everyone in the village seemed to like him. Simple, gracious, helpful, and often merry, Pippin won over the Saxons in a few short days.

One evening at the council fire, he happily took a cup of beer offered to him by a Saxon chieftain and then another. After the third one, he suddenly jumped up, hiked up his heavy brown robe, and began to dance around the fire, singing gaily, naked ankles notwithstanding. The Saxons were stunned. At length, Pippin sat down among the men with a thump, smiling brightly. Suddenly he let out a hearty, high-pitched laugh ending in a giggle. The burly Saxons roared with laughter, surprised and delighted at this completely unorthodox holy man.

That was the moment when Father Pippin began to win them over. The next day he began to preach.

Chapter 13

'Twas the Missionaries, Not the Heavy Cavalry

Sebastian found the Slavic Obodrites readily enough. The Saxon scouts simply took him to the wide meadow where the last bit of hard fighting had taken place and told him to march straightaway toward the tree line. Bardulf took out the white flag, Drogo unfurled the imperial pennant, and they moved gingerly across the field.

Almost at the end of the meadow, Sebastian halted the small band. At once, an Obodrite warrior stepped silently out of the tree line and then another and another until there were at least a hundred half-naked, blue-painted warriors with spears leveled or arrows nocked in their bows.

Magically, the tension evaporated when an Obodrite prince rode out of the woods on a dappled pony. He raised both hands high in a gesture of peace and pointed excitedly to the king's standard. It was clear that he knew, probably from one of Count Arno's agents, that the great King of the Franks might want to be his ally. Soon he was smiling and jabbering away to Sebastian as if it were already a done deed.

And so, indeed, it turned out to be. With the help of Wolfram, the former slave of the Obodrites, Sebastian learned his host was Prince Svetoslav, one of the highest nobles of the Obodrite tribe. A small supper and sharing some strong beer was all it took to seal a pact between Franks and Obodrites. The Franks promised to move the East Saxons to the west and turn over their lands to the Obodrites in exchange for their friendship and aid against their mutual enemy, the Danes, should it come to that. They swore an oath, spit on their hands, and rubbed them together, followed by some impromptu dancing and the draining of many cups. It was easy. All Sebastian really had to do was put forth a strong image of Charlemagne's invincible power and his magnanimous generosity.

After all, the Obodrites were getting a huge tract of land, and they already hated the Danes in any event.

There were just a couple of thorny little problems: the East Saxons still had to be convinced to vacate their lands and be converted to Christianity, all in a very short time. Sebastian assured the Obodrite prince that it would not take long, that the Saxons would be willing to go... soon. Again, he found his fingers crossing behind his back.

After much gift-giving and many reassurances, the small band of Franks withdrew the way they had come, and Sebastian felt, at the very least, that he had bought some time.

***

Holding a heavy wooden cross with both hands above his head was almost too much for the frail priest. Yet he thrust it to the sky and intoned his message to the assembled warriors:

"Credo in unum Deum,

Patrem omnipotentem,

Factorem caeli et terrae,

Visibilium omnium et invisibilium.

"There is only ONE GOD! He is the Father Almighty, maker of heaven and earth and all that is seen and unseen!

"And there is God's son, Jesus the Christ, one with the Father before all ages. He is the God-man who came down from heaven and was born of a virgin and the Spirit of God!

"He came as a sacrifice for all. He was killed—a sacrifice to pay for the sins of the world and the evil in men's hearts. And," Pippin pronounced in as stentorian a voice as he could manage, "he *rose again from the dead* and walked among the people!"

The Saxons drew back at these words, hardly able to imagine a dead man rising. Even Liudolf, taking the scene in from the back of the crowd, was moved by Pippin's words and his air of complete certitude. He marveled at how Pippin seemed to cast a spell over the Saxons, beguiling them from one new and astonishing idea to the next. They were particularly wide-eyed with awe when he spoke of the afterlife.

"He came to offer everlasting life to all who would believe in him and his Father, the One God."

"Afterlife? For everyone?" the Saxons murmured. "Even the poorest, the women, the non-fighters?"

Liudolf cringed a bit as Pippin made these bold announcements, knowing how hard it would be for the Saxons to embrace them. There were skeptical sideways glances and rumblings of doubt among the listeners. Even the women crowded behind the men to hear these strange prophesies.

As he spoke, Pippin constantly moved among the elders and senior warriors, looking them straight in the eyes as if he were speaking directly to each man. Small and weak as he was, his very energy and excitement seemed to lift him off the ground. He mesmerized them by his words and the images he conjured.

"Like any man, he lived and worked and was tempted by the devil. But he sinned not! When it was his time, he suffered shame and death for man's sake and was buried."

At this point, Pippin allowed the heavy cross to fall to the ground. He sank to his knees and then fell prone to the earth. For long moments he lay as if dead. The Saxons watched in awe. Suddenly the priest sprang to his feet, grasped the heavy cross, and thrust it once more toward the sky.

"But on the third day, he rose again from the dead!" Pippin exclaimed again in an exultant voice.

In the open-mouthed silence after this dramatic pronouncement, Pippin calmly donned a clean white cassock that he had carefully packed for the journey, and draping a crimson stole around his neck, he proceeded to say his first Mass for the pagan East Saxons, standing behind a large stump that served as his altar.

At length, Pippin raised the Host, a clump of coarse peasant bread, and proclaimed it to be the body of Christ. He took some cheap local red wine and declared it to be the blood that was shed for the forgiveness of sins. These he held out before him but did not offer them to the Saxons. Instead, he took the bread and wine and consumed them himself before them. Then he sank to his knees and prayed. After the last prayer of the Mass, he sang a melodic hymn in his high tenor voice. In the silence after the song, he folded the white cassock, put it in a small bag, and walked away without another word into the woods.

***

In the days that followed, Father Pippin sat for hours around the council fire with the Saxons and explained to them the One God and the Christian faith. For many years he had memorized the sermons and reflections of other monks and holy men. He recounted them and told stories from the Bible, as many as he could remember. He sang songs occasionally to emphasize the Scripture stories. He spoke frankly of both heaven and hell.

"There are only ten rules," he proclaimed. "They are called commandments. They all point to this one supreme rule: 'Ye shall love the Lord your God with all your heart, with all your soul, and with all your mind, and your neighbor as yourself!'"

This caused much consternation among the warriors. "Who is our neighbor?" they complained. "The Franks? The Obodrites? Those who have harmed us?"

With every outburst and every indignant remark, Pippin bowed his head, prayed for a moment, and then answered quietly as best he could. They shrank away in fear as he spoke of eternal damnation and the fires of hell. They shook their heads and sniggered as he described what the One God considered to be sin— a much different credo than the sanguinary Saxon outlook on life. They muttered to each other when Pippin declared that God meant his heaven for everyone, all believers—men, women, Saxon, Frank. All!

"Women? Non-warriors?" they objected vociferously.

"Yea, women too, my friends. 'My house shall be a house of prayer for ALL!'"

"Not so!" the Saxons groaned and shouted. "Should women have the same rights and benefits as men in this Jesus's heaven? Enemies too? No! Unheard of! Unacceptable!"

They were even more incredulous to hear that Jesus had willingly allowed himself to be captured, tried, whipped, and crucified, that he had been nailed to a tree like a common thief.

Pippin responded: "It was a sacrifice, don't you see? The ultimate sacrifice. Don't all of you make sacrifices? Do not your priests make them at special times of fear and danger when they offer the slaughter of bulls, sheep, goats, and sometimes, it is said, even your children?

"You even make sacrifices of your very selves in battle when you offer your lives to Odin and Thor and your king! Do you not? You do so to win glory, fame, and a place at Odin's table when you die in battle.

"But what of those who do not die in battle?" He opened his arms widely. "What happens to them, to the women, to the old ones who can no longer hold a sword when they die? Do they just disappear back into the dirt?

"The Lord Jesus made this heavy sacrifice, and then he rose from death after three days so that all would know that death here on earth is not the end. It is only the beginning of life. A new life where one can live forever!"

Shaking a skinny finger pointedly at the sky, Pippin proclaimed: "In my house, there are many mansions. I go to prepare a place for YOU." And he pointed the skinny finger back and forth at the crowd.

This last argument was the most compelling for the Saxons, along with the idea that there is only one God, all-powerful, all-knowing—a good God, not a vengeful one, who exists for all people, high and low, and for all time.

Such concepts were new and exhilarating. Liudolf noted that after each session with Pippin, small groups of men gathered together around a fire to discuss and argue late into the night. The women, too, had groups, which were usually much more lively and favored what Pippin had said.

It was clear to Liudolf that the Saxons were bone weary of fighting and sick of death and the fear of extinction as a tribe. The more Pippin preached in his humble, forthright manner, the more his own beliefs came through as genuine and inspired by his God, the more the Saxons admired and respected him, and the more they parleyed among themselves. Ironically, even Liudolf pondered his faith, though he had been a Christian all his life.

***

As soon as Sebastian returned to the camp, Liudolf reported that the elders were ready to move but that "taking the washing" was still a step too far. They were still doubtful about "the Risen Lord" and this invisible God who could be three persons simultaneously.

Sebastian quickly called a council that evening and spoke to them, surrounded by his men and their various flags. He kept the royal pennant of the king in his own hands as he spoke.

"I am very glad you have agreed to move your people to the safety of the West. However, I must speak to you now with the voice of the high king, Karl the Great. He has no time for those who would defy him. His protection is extended only to those who embrace the true God, the only God, the creator of all things. If you cannot do that, he will leave you to the tender mercies of the Obodrites."

The Saxons shifted uneasily in their places and turned to each other with worried glances. Sebastian continued.

"However, if you consent to 'take the waters,' as you say, here is what you can expect: safe passage for all of you to a land beyond the great river Rhine, where you will find sufficient land for all and a peaceful existence where you can expect your children to grow up and thrive. You will no longer be enemies of the king but his friends and allies.

"But you must abandon the false illusions of many gods and one chief god who lives in a tree and demands human sacrifices.

"As for the end of your life, as the holy priest explained to you, we Christians hold fast that each and every human being who believes can expect that a new life, a far better life, begins with the One God in a land of peace and plenty where there is no violence, no death, and our God loves every man, woman, and child.

"But you must decide tomorrow! After that, I can no longer hold back the Obodrites. I urge you, my friends, to choose the good!"

After that, Sebastian ceremoniously marched his troops out of the village and immediately began preparations for departure, praying with profound thanks that he had put his trust in the half-baked little priest. He was reminded once again of the words of his old advisor, the blind Hejmdal, who had assured him that more of Charlemagne's enemies were conquered by the bravery and conviction of Christian missionaries than by his heavy cavalry.

Bardulf had the last word as they departed the camp the next day after the big baptism. "Hallo, m'lads! We're ready, ain't we? I ain't pertickler if it was God or the Obodrites that made 'em move. What I care about is the state of our health and whether our own bloody king is pleased enough to allow us finally to go home!"

Chapter 14

Bloodaxe

The Dannevirke

"M'lord," Bardulf wheedled as they gazed from a distance at the great wall that divided Denmark from Charlemagne's empire, "if ye please, would ye be so good as to tell my bumfuzzled brain why ye're wantin' us four wee Christians to go up to that flamin' big wall with all the cursed Danish pagans in front of that bloomin' gate and have a parley with 'em?"

Only Liudolf, Bardulf, and Drogo had accompanied Sebastian to the Danes. Against Liudolf's furious objections, Sebastian had sent the king's guard back with Bernard and Father Pippin along a more direct route to the Rhine, painstakingly slowly.

"No soldiers? We're going up to that bloody wall without even one troop of soldiers?" Liudolf complained loudly.

"The soldiers are needed to protect Father Pippin. Besides, no one is going up to the wall but me."

"Well, I'm going, b'God! We agreed that I would always be with you when there's a risk."

"Not this time, old comrade—none of you," Sebastian said with a sideways smile. "It is I who must go up to the wall. All of you will stay back here and see what happens. If the Danes are not cordial and won't let me return to you, you must disappear like smoke and make all speed to the king. And you will be in charge of bringing the army back as quickly as may be. I know the king will already have the army mobilized and moving. I'm just not sure where he will be. You must find him."

Sebastian almost laughed at Liudolf's open-mouthed resentment. But when they arrived at the wall, the sight was worse than expected. Soldiers and workers crawled all over the parts of the wall they could see, and at least two warrior companies guarded the gate. Sebastian could feel his heart beginning to pound and his stomach clinching into a knot. But he knew from experience in many perilous times in the past that boldness often serves well, even against the odds.

"This is important, Liudolf! You heard those two Saxons yesterday who were just returning from trading at Hedeby. They were Count Arno's spies. They saw troops well beyond this gate—everywhere around that trading town. And they reported many Viking ships in the waters of both seas near Godofrid's host. The king must know post-haste that his old enemy King Godofrid is poised on our border with what may be his whole army!"

Sebastian knew that Liudolf would be torn between two compelling poles. Over a lifetime, he had rarely been separated from Sebastian. *I'll be sorry,* he thought, *not to feel the comfort of Liudolf's unfailing sword at my back!*

"Listen to me, dammit!" Sebastian cried urgently, grasping Liudolf's arm. "Do you think Bardulf or Drogo could find the king? I am under King Karl's orders to confront the Danes and speak to Godofrid if possible. I hope to convince that foolish king to back away again lest he is rash enough to cross over into Francia with troops. It would mean war!"

"All right, all right! I'll go," was Liudolf's terse reply. But his face was contorted with worry.

"Stay just long enough to see what they will do with me. If they won't let me go, then hie you to the king. Tell him that if there must be a fight, then he should have no trouble attacking over the wall. It's mostly earthworks, only a shallow ditch below and unfinished palisades," Sebastian shouted into the wind as Joyeuse trotted casually toward the huge gate.

***

"I am Sebastian, Count of Adalgray and Fernshanz, emissary of His Majesty Karl der Grosse, emperor of all Francian lands from the Great Sea to the lands of the Rus. I would speak with Godofrid, king of the Danes."

Sebastian's calm demeanor and authoritative voice hushed the soldiers clustering around him as he rode up to the gate bearing a white flag high on his lance. They stepped aside immediately when a very large young Dane bearing an officer's sash and distinctive helmet pushed his way through the men and stood before Sebastian, his head a foot above the horse's head.

"Will you get down, my lord, and state your business with my king?" the young man said politely, keeping an eye upon the distant group of riders from which Sebastian had come.

There followed a formal introduction from the young officer. "My lord Sebastian, I am Torbjorn, son of Bjorn. I am also known as Bloodaxe. My father and I are kinsmen of the great King Godofrid, and I am captain of his personal guard."

Sebastian returned the captain's formal bow, thinking all the while that there was something else besides formalities in the man's narrowed eyes and menacing face.

"If you come in peace, you are welcome to the hallowed land of the Danes," Bloodaxe said with cold formality. "May I ask what it is that brings you now to King Godofrid?"

Sebastian's face betrayed no fear or any telling expression at all. He merely nodded at the youth's introduction, hastily taking his measure. It was obvious that this Bloodaxe was both close to the king and a champion among warriors. His air of confidence and authority spoke no louder than the several deep scars on his arms and face. And, despite his words, he was definitely hostile.

As was his wont, Sebastian took a deep breath and paused for a long moment before replying. "I do indeed come in peace, Lord, uh . . . Bloodaxe. My liege, the incomparable King Karl, wonders why your king has brought such a large army to the gate of his empire and why you have so many people and such energy engaged in repairing and improving this old wall."

"My king," Bloodaxe replied coolly, "finds himself quite prosperous of late. He would use his wealth and power to improve his lands and secure his people—as any great king would do."

"I see," said Sebastian, "but it would seem that most of your king's efforts are projected in the neighborhood of my king's properties. Why this sudden interest in security? Surely your king knows that our emperor does not covet Denmark. At this time in his long life, he favors peace and goodwill. He has no kind of evil intent against his long-time neighbors, the Danes."

"Ah, I see, Count Sebastian. So . . . he is building an armada of new ships in Friesland simply to guard the trading routes against pirates. No?"

"That could be the reason, Captain Torbjorn."

"Our 'security work,' Count," Bloodaxe replied, stiffening and caressing the handle of his sword, "if I may be so bold, may coincidentally be partly due to yourself and what you did up in Dorestad in Friesland when you and your sons nearly destroyed a whole Viking fleet and slew its famous leader, Konrad."

Ah, thought Sebastian. So this is why the man has been so belligerent. He has another agenda!

"I must tell you, Count, King Godofrid was not behind that engagement, nor was he responsible for it, contrary to what you may have thought. He was, however, greatly saddened by the deaths of so many Danes, many of whom he knew personally."

Bloodaxe now brought his face closer to Sebastian's. "I, too, heard the news of that slaughter with great regret, for many of those warriors were, at one time, my sword brothers."

"What would you have had us do, Captain?" Sebastian asked without retreating an inch. "Just welcome Konrad in and let him rob and rape at his leisure, as he was so wont to do elsewhere?"

"Ha!" Bloodaxe laughed harshly. "Sir, I have never been certain that the merchants of Dorestad did not just invite Konrad's fleet in to trade, and your troops lay in wait for them, slaughtering them as they came peacefully ashore. You know that the Vikings are primarily traders. King Godofrid does not direct them, though he may profit indirectly from their trading activities."

He is not going to let me go, Sebastian realized. He has decided that I must be punished for the outcome of the Dorestad raid. It appears he wants to do it himself. Well. I will do some prodding of my own lest he thinks I fear him.

"That might have been true once, my good captain, in the days when the Vikings desperately needed to find a way to supplement their meager existence. But then they found taking what they wanted too easy and much faster than trading for it. Now they are nothing more than pirates, and they run if they get a whiff of the warriors of our emperor's heavy cavalry—which would have little difficulty climbing over your rather pathetic wall."

Bloodaxe's demeanor grew darker the more Sebastian cast aspersions on the Vikings and the old wall. His cheeks reddened, and he began to grind his teeth.

"Who knows what might have happened," Sebastian continued, "if Konrad had actually won that battle at Dorestad and your king was encouraged by it to the point of using it as an excuse to attack Francia? He came very close to doing so anyway, anticipating a victory. At the time it was fought, your king Godofrid had the entire Danish army poised here on the Danish border with Francia and many ships from the Viking fleet in the seas nearby. But as soon as he got news of Konrad's defeat and took a good look at King Karl's grand army forming in front of this very wall, he bolted back into the heartland of Denmark. I thought he might have learned then that King Karl would not suffer Danish piracy—or threatening Danish formations on the borders of Francia.

"But here you are again, Captain, with thousands of Danish soldiers massed on our border—and continuing to build this useless wall as well! What are we to think?"

"Think what you will Count," Bloodaxe said angrily. "It's clear that your King Karl looks upon us with disdain. It is he who threatens war here in the north. We build a wall to defend ourselves, lest your king decide that he will have Denmark as well as the rest of the world above the Middle Sea. I assure you that King Karl may take from others but not from us!"

"Very well, Captain," Sebastian said as he calmly moved toward his horse. "I will pass your message on to my king, the emperor of Francia. And we shall see what he has to say."

"Not so fast, Count Sebastian," Torbjorn warned, motioning to soldiers to seize the horse and Sebastian as well. Sebastian's sword was in his hand at once, and he crouched to defend himself.

"You would threaten an emissary of the high king and emperor under a flag of truce?" Sebastian shouted, glaring at the captain.

Torbjorn signaled his soldiers to stand back. But he narrowed his eyes and slipped his own hand onto his sword hilt. "I have no words to say to your 'emperor,' Count. That is for my king to do. And I would have let you go. But you have insulted all Danes and me personally because you killed so many of my friends, my brother among them!"

So this is it! Sebastian sighed. Of all the captains in the Danish army, I had to draw one who had a vendetta against me. Well, God rest his brother. I have no idea if it was me who killed him or not.

"I feel I cannot let this pass, Count! You will either throw down your sword now, or we will simply hang you. Or you must fight me. You have a great reputation as a swordsman. I imagine you are not intimidated by a lowly captain."

"No, I am not, Captain. But I am disappointed in you. I took you for an honorable man who would respect a white flag of truce and the emissary of a king." Good, Sebastian noted, that struck home. He's thinking of how he will explain to his king why he killed me. If, indeed, he can!

"I will fight you, Captain, if I must. But whatever the outcome, I doubt if my king will find the reception you gave to his personal herald a sign of your king's willingness to parley. On the contrary, he may very well see it as a reason for war. Have care, Captain Torbjorn."

"Nonsense, Count. This is personal. I feel insulted, and you must be made to pay for your remarks and my brother's killing. My king will understand and not let a little personal combat stand in the way of negotiations. Who knows, you might win your freedom. Come, Count, let us play!"

Chapter 15

The Duel

Bloodaxe began by bringing Sebastian's shield from his horse and inquiring politely if he needed anything else. He then signaled for his own shield to be brought—and a four-foot battle axe.

"I'm sure," Torbjorn began with a smile, "that you have faced every kind of weapon in your long and fabled experience as a Frankish warrior. The axe is all I ever use. I hope you do not find it inconvenient." He hefted the ugly weapon and swung it back and forth a few times as if to give Sebastian a preview of its fearful potency. "On horseback, I use a little longer one for crippling horses. I'm quite proud of them both."

Sebastian had indeed experienced fighting against axe-wielders. He did not think much of the weapon. It was often too heavy for sustained combat, and its cutting was straight down or awkwardly to the side. It was almost ineffective in striking to the left side if on horseback.

Torbjorn continued to admire his weapon for the benefit of Sebastian. "I have the best blacksmith in Denmark. The excellent steel of this axe was melted from the swords of two unfortunate Franks who strayed into Denmark. Observe the thin, knifelike blade, so sharp and with an edge precisely as long as a man's head. Are you not," Bloodaxe said with a grimly mocking laugh, "just a bit unnerved, my good count, by my formidable friend here?"

"I have found, Captain," Sebastian replied, limbering his sword arm with a few swings, "that a weapon is only as good as the man who uses it."

"Oh! Well then, let us see whose weapon will prevail here. Shall we begin?"

He began to circle, making short downward thrusts with the axe to draw Sebastian out. Suddenly he lunged and brought the axe down hard upon Sebastian's shield, cleaving through the leather and wood as easily as a knife was driven into the sand. A broken shield piece grazed Sebastian's leg, causing a long gash. It was clear at once that if Sebastian played Torbjorn's game, blow for blow, he would soon have no shield left at all, so he changed his tactics at once, slashing out with his sword at the big man's head, aiming for his eyes. He diverted the axe blows by leaping to the right and sweeping his shield sideways against the descending axe. The effect was to let the momentum of each blow carry the heavy axe head to his left and down toward the ground.

Sebastian was by far the lighter man, quicker on his feet and able to deliver two blows of his sword for every axe swing. He circled continuously since Torbjorn always struck from the right. Gradually the rapid forehand and backhand thrusts of his sword at Torbjorn's eyes caused him to raise his shield higher to a point just under his eyes. Sebastian waited until this occurred, then, quickly brushing aside an axe blow, he bent down below Torbjorn's shield and slashed sharply at his knees. They buckled at once, almost causing him to fall.

It was a lucky but decisive blow. Torbjorn no longer enjoyed total mobility. He limped slightly and was slow in turning. Sebastian moved more and more quickly, always striking at the eyes until the shield of his foe was jerked high enough to allow Sebastian to score more and more cuts on Torbjorn's legs. His blood began to flow copiously and pool on the floor. It seemed only a matter of minutes before the big Dane would fall.

Then, without warning, Sebastian slipped into the pool of blood and fell hard. Torbjorn jumped in to deliver a killing blow, but too eagerly. Sebastian thrust the edge of his shield into Torbjorn's face, and the weight of his descending axe also caused him to slip into the pool of blood. The axe blade buried itself into the dirt a few inches from Sebastian's head. Torbjorn followed the axe head and fell full length across Sebastian's body. The next thing he knew, he was feeling the point of Sebastian's dagger against his throat.

"Will you yield, sir?" Sebastian whispered into Torbjorn's ear, and he nicked the skin of the big man's throat for emphasis.

After a short moment, Torbjorn whispered bitterly, "Yes . . . yes, I will yield, damn you."

"Then roll off of me—slowly. Do not touch your axe. Don't try to get up, or I will finish you. Now roll off."

As Sebastian stood and recovered his shattered shield, he stood over Torbjorn and gave one last command. "Now, Bloodaxe, order your men to bring my horse." He stood, sword poised at Torbjorn's throat, until Joyeuse was brought up. Then he leaped at once into the saddle and tried to drive the powerful warhorse right through the ring of soldiers. But there were too many, and they were packed in tightly. Some leaped at Sebastian from behind as the horse reared and pulled him from the saddle. He landed heavily and was immediately secured by the soldiers.

Chapter 16

War No More!

Oddly, a sheaf of dried-out flowers sat in a pottery vase on the rickety table in Sebastian's cell, along with a small wooden plate. In the plate lay a dried-up beetle. Sebastian had been contemplating eating the beetle for two days. Finally, the craving in his belly got the best of him, and he popped the bug into his mouth. It had no taste and did little to assuage his hunger.

Contrary to his hopes, his victory over Bloodaxe did not result in his release. Instead, he was accused of foul play and immediately imprisoned. One of his guards eventually told him he was being held as a hostage.

He sat on an unstable stool by the table in the middle of the tiny room. There was a rude straw bed in one corner. In another sat a night pail emptied by two guards with drawn swords every other day. Once a day, a small mug of water and a meager plate of cold gruel came through a panel in the heavy wooden door.

Light and air entered through two tiny windows near the ceiling. Nothing else. The room was as bare and silent as a tomb. Its only good was that it reminded him of the room he had rested in when he served as a water boy and messenger in the Saxon siege of Adalgray so long ago.

"Enough! Enough!" he said to himself aloud after many days of this torture. "This is penance for my sins. I know it is! I made a vow to God and have broken it many times. My path has always led to violence. It is enough!"

He got up and began to pace back and forth between the narrow walls of the room, beating his fist against his heart. After what seemed like hours, he stopped, raised his arms to heaven, and shouted.

"I will not do it again! If I live, I shall not kill again. I shall do no harm to anyone, bad or good. I will cease to be a paladin of the king. I will refuse him even if it costs me my life!"

The next day Sebastian was bundled out of the small room after nearly three weeks of solitary confinement. The Danes returned his sword and lance, the ruined shield and helmet, and lifted him onto the back of Joyeuse. It took Sebastian several minutes before he could adjust to the glaring light, and he hid his eyes until they reached the gate. He opened them to the astonishing sight of Charlemagne's whole army arrayed at a short distance facing the Danish wall and gate, rank upon rank of horses and men. The king was recognizable at the head of his beloved heavy cavalry in the center.

There was no sign of Torbjorn Bloodaxe nor of the Danish King Godofrid, whose army was in the process of melting speedily back into Denmark. Later, spies disguised as Danish soldiers slipped through the confusion of the withdrawal to confirm that the armada of Viking ships had already sailed. Sebastian was simply allowed to ride off slowly into his waiting army. The king kept the army in front of the gate until the last Danish contingent disappeared into Denmark and the great door in the wall closed.

***

The road home was tortuously long, made more tiresome and uneasy by the king's stormy mood. In previous years, Charlemagne's spirits were always lifted by the prospect of battle. He expected to win and to feel once again the exhilaration of high risk versus great gain. This time, however, he was shocked when Godofrid blinked once again in the face of the Frankish host and backed away ignominiously. The Danish leader simply sent a herald with a white flag to announce his withdrawal from the wall.

Charlemagne was furious and highly disappointed. He felt insulted and was on the very verge of attacking anyway. The king sputtered and cursed in his anger, galloping his horse wildly back and forth in front of his troops, brandishing his sword at the retreating Danes. His warriors took up his mood, roaring their defiance and beating their spears and swords against their shields. For long minutes, it seemed that a charge was inevitable.

But Sebastian and a few others of the high command rode out to him quickly and worked urgently to calm him down, arguing that their purpose had already been achieved; the Danes were backing away from the border. Sebastian grabbed the reins of the king's horse and forced him to look into his eyes.

"Sire, let it go! Attacking them now would mean an invasion of Denmark! We don't have any ladders or siege equipment ready. Even if we crawled up and got over the walls quickly, we would be in for a long campaign, and high casualties would certainly weaken the army. You sent me to find a way to end the threat, remember? Well, whatever happened, we don't have to fight now. There's no need for an invasion."

"More's the pity!" the king exclaimed gruffly. Eventually, he relented, but he felt cheated. There would be no wetting of the spears now, no heavy adrenaline rush, no laurel wreath. When the last of the Danes withdrew from the gate of the great wall, he spat after them and muttered a curse.

***

Sebastian stalled for two long days on the long march home before approaching the king about taking a leave of absence. The king was still surly and brusque since the withdrawal from the wall. But he brightened a bit when Sebastian rode up beside him. "Well, ol' soldier, ye survived once more, d'in't you? And from the looks of ye, it wasn't much fun. You are all right, ain't ye, old lad?"

Sebastian hesitated for a long moment and then took a deep breath. "No, sire, I am not. I have been hurt this time. Not just my body. That will heal. It's in my head that I am hurt. I have been too long at war, away from my family and my long-suffering, precious wife. I no longer have the heart to fight and to kill, as I've been doing for you since I was a young lad. The thought of it sickens me now. I wish never to kill anyone again."

The king was taken aback by the confession. It had never occurred to him that Sebastian might not love fighting as he did or wished to give up the prestige of his role as a senior paladin. He shook his head as if to clear away a bad jest.

"Nonsense, my old champion! It's what you do. It's what we all do to make this realm a Christian land and drive back the forces of evil. No one does it better than you. Besides, you're my paladin, my army's best fighter and thinker. What would I do without you?"

"I thank you, my king, for your confidence in me, but truly, I am wounded in spirit. I'm drained. I'm sure I would be killed if you sent me out again. I ask you to remember my long service to you and what I have accomplished in your name. I ask you to release me from my vow to be your paladin. And I ask you humbly for a long leave of absence to recover in body and soul."

There was an uncertain silence as the king studied his long-time favorite as they rode. Sebastian felt compelled to speak again.

"It does not mean, sire, that I no longer wish to serve you. Far from it. I would never wish to be separated from you, and I stand ready to remain in your council and offer whatever wisdom my experience may have given me. But I would be no good to you anymore as your paladin or even as a commander in the army."

"God's blood! How has it come to this?" the king sputtered. "I thought you were invincible, that you could not even be killed." The king breathed a long sigh.

"Bloody hell! Everything's changing! The fact is, I'm old! My arse won't tolerate a horse's back all day long. My arms won't swing a sword for long in a fight. My whole body is telling me to quit as well. Ah, but the campaigns! I should miss them dreadfully! They were glorious! There was a time there, old lad when I'd far rather fight than fornicate. You used to feel that way too, I'll wager. Damn my eyes, a man can find a woman anywhere, innit? But nowadays, it's hard to find a bloody good fight!"

"Hmm," Sebastian responded, turning his head away with a smile.

"But," the king continued, pulling on his mustaches, "I suppose you are human after all. I can see it in your eyes. You've reached your limits. Besides, I love you like my own sons."

After a long pause, he finally said: "All right, I will release you from your vows as a paladin, and I will not call you up to fight again. But I will not release you from the bond you have with me. I would miss you too much. And I will always need your counsel."

"I assure you, my king, you will always have it. And it will always be a joy to see you."

"Go on, then, my old boy! You needn't come back to Aachen with me. Go on to that lovely wife of yours, you lucky scoundrel. By thunder, I reckon I'm getting pretty tired m'self of all this campaigning every bleeding year. Blessed Jesus, now's you bring it up, I should give the bloody main army over to my son Charles the Younger and let *him* ride his rear off to keep the wolves at bay from now on. Let's you and me retire together, by God, and go bloody hunting!" The king smacked his hands together and uttered a fierce "Ha!"

"I'm your man, sire! There's no one in the world I'd rather go a-hunting with than you.

Chapter 17

Trust the King!

Sebastian's sons, Karl and Attalus, had not seen their father since before he set off to resettle the East Saxons. On leave from the army, they returned to Fernshanz only a day after he had already departed with his small entourage to eastern Saxony. They were disappointed to have missed their father, whom they saw increasingly seldom. But their sudden arrival seemed to be a godsend for Adela. She had struggled even to have the shortest conversation with Adelaide, who stayed in her rooms almost exclusively.

But if the arrival of Karl and Attalus surprised and delighted Adela, it caused Adelaide to emerge immediately from her self-imposed exile—and in a grand way. She appeared at the table on the first night of their arrival, looking vibrantly alive and in her element again as if she were already at the king's court. "At last!" she had rejoiced privately to Nadia and Nicoleta. "Young men! Hallelujah! People I know how to talk to!" Suddenly she felt a twinge of guile. "I'm sorry for treating Adela so shabbily lately. But there's just been too much precious rubbish lying between her and me!"

She wore a low-cut gown of red silk and let her long, glossy hair spill over her partly exposed bosom. She betrayed no hint of controversy between herself and Adela. In fact, she behaved as if she had known Adela all her life and counted her as a best friend. At the small feast prepared to celebrate the homecoming, she managed effortlessly to place herself between the young men, chatting merrily with them, one after the other. She flirted shamelessly with them both.

***

Initially, Adela was delighted with the visit. It immediately lifted the gray pall that had hung over the manor since Sebastian left.

It made a dramatic, friendly change in Adelaide's attitude toward her. Above all that, Adela was beyond happy to see her beloved sons, strong and hearty, handsome and bronzed from weeks in the field.

As the evening wore on, Adela grew uncomfortable with the brazen teasing and suggestive innuendos Adelaide employed to toy with her young sons. Dying to hear their plans and how they had been faring, she barely had a chance to get a word into the lively exchange Adelaide was conducting. She began to feel a bit taken for granted.

But the boys loved their mother too much to neglect her for long. During a brief break in their animated conversation, she only had to say, "My darlings, I've missed you so much! Please tell me how you've been." They competed to tell her, which gave Adelaide a chance to assess her new prospects for a while.

She came to several conclusions early on. First of all, Attalus was a dear, she estimated, so innocent, starved for affection. Very handsome and smart but so tiresomely serious about everything and about as subtle as an anvil. Still, he mustn't be dismissed out of hand. If she led him along just a little, he might help her get to Count Arno and, who knows, perhaps to the king!

Adelaide did not have to try very hard. Attalus was swept away from the first day by her exotic looks and bold behavior. He was charmed by her salty conversation, so different from any woman he knew, and he was thrilled by the frequency of her touch. He was not accustomed to looking into the eyes of a beautiful woman for more than a few seconds. But Adelaide frequently held him in her gaze for a whole minute at a time. She smiled to herself to see how weak and powerless it made him feel, just like a deer facing a torchlight in the dark.

But Karl, Adelaide thought, appraising him with hunter's eyes, was quite a different game. He was more like the kind of man she was used to—big, strong, confident, and full of fun. She might be able to thrill him for a while. But he was the kind who would eventually say, 'That was nice, thanks, goodbye!' Besides, she doubted Sebastian and Adela would take kindly to a liaison between herself and either of the boys. She decided not to try. It would be too easy.

As she expected, Attalus fell in love with her almost immediately. He was far more sensitive and vulnerable to Adelaide's wiles. Karl, by stark contrast, was a warrior in every bone. There was no doubt that he saw himself as the successor to his father, perhaps even as a paladin to the king one day. He had no time for the courting of fine ladies. Any wench would do, as long as she was pretty and willing. He just joked and laughed and exchanged ribald suggestions with Adelaide.

Adelaide hesitated judiciously. Perhaps even Karl might prove useful someday. The main thing was just to get out of Fernshanz and lift herself again. Why not? She had done it in Constantinople. She could certainly do it in backward, Francia! They may be little more than barbarians, she judged, but these Franks are powerful, and right now, win or lose, she needed to be where the stakes were high! Fat Arno was the key!

***

Karl spent a few days hunting in the surrounding woods in the mornings and sparring with Adelaide at meals, but after a week at home, his restlessness got the better of him, and begging his mother's forgiveness, he left in haste to return to the army. Charlemagne had mobilized a good portion of the army, and he and his son Charles the Younger were marching to the Danish border for another confrontation with King Godofrid.

Attalus, by contrast, was not eager to return to the army. He sent word that "urgent problems" had arisen at home in his father's absence which he was obliged to settle. Of course, the "urgent problem" was his growing attraction to Adelaide and his determination to help her find a new life in Francia and perhaps, if lucky, join her.

Of course, Adelaide had no qualms about using Attalus to her advantage. They spent every day together in some form or another—long walks, long rides, and even hunting with the dogs. On one of these long rides into the surrounding deep forest, Adelaide let Attalus kiss her passionately but stopped short of seducing him. It was just not necessary, she concluded confidently.

***

Adelaide's extended stay at Fernshanz had not brought her closer to Adela. The two were courteous and attentive to each other, but it was more like a fragile truce than a budding friendship. Adela lost sleep, worrying about what would happen once Sebastian returned. She'd received little information about him until a courier from the army brought the frightening news that Sebastian had been captured and was being held in a Danish prison. The message also mentioned that the count might have been wounded.

Ironically, the bad news served to unite the two women. Adelaide dropped her airs of high dudgeon and became genuinely close to Adela. They began to spend more time together, sewing or walking together in the garden. Adela avoided mentioning Attalus's obvious infatuation with Adelaide, attributing it to the adulation a naive young man might have for an attractive older woman.

But as soon as the news came that Sebastian had survived and was on his way home, Adela began seriously to develop her plan to do something about Adelaide's continued presence at Fernshanz. Little did she know that Adelaide's plan was exactly like her own.

Late one evening, she brought Attalus to her chambers, dreading what she had to say to him and praying she could find the right words.

"Darling boy!" she began as they sat facing each other by the fireside in the great room. "Your father is safe now and on his way home, thank God! We know he's been wounded again, but we don't know how seriously. So it may still be a while before we see him. Meanwhile, the king, we're told, has already returned to Aix la Chapelle."

She hesitated momentarily, looking down at the handkerchief wound tightly around both hands. She took a deep breath and raised her head to meet Attalus's eyes.

"You may not be aware that while I was in the convent for so long, your father, under dire circumstances in Constantinople, developed a rather intimate relationship with our guest Adelaide. Uh . . ." she hesitated a moment as Attalus tried hard to comprehend and then went on quickly.

"He had known her since his youth. Their liaison, of course, was not a betrayal of his marriage to me. We desperately loved one another, but before we could wed, I was forced to marry another man, a very bad man. You know him. It was Konrad. I finally had to enter the convent to escape him. As far as your father knew, I would never return from the convent." At this point, she reached across quickly to grasp Attalus's hand with both of her own. "What he did with Adelaide, my precious boy, was out of sheer loneliness and deep disappointment. In any case, eventually, circumstances drove them apart.

"After much soul searching, I finally decided to leave the convent, and we renewed our love for each other. I'm confident that he has always wanted nothing more than for us to be together for the rest of our lives. And that is all I want as well."

Struggling to control her emotions, Adela wiped her eyes and continued. "Dear Attalus, I'm desperate for you to understand all this. Your father is not to blame. I love him with all my heart. And both of us have nothing but sorrow and goodwill toward poor Adelaide. She loved him too—and now she realizes she has lost him.

"All told, she's become a serious problem—for all of us. She came here, dear boy, expecting to marry your father!"

Stunned, Attalus almost rose to his feet, but she motioned for him to sit. "Please listen, dear! Adelaide feels she has a right to him since they were close in Constantinople, and she saved his life in harrowing circumstances there. That is a story you must one day hear from your father. However, Adelaide has no place to go and no future of any consequence to anticipate."

Adela bit her lip and continued hesitantly. "I couldn't help but notice, my son, that she clings to you, hoping perhaps to find a way out of her dilemma."

"Mother," Attalus interrupted anxiously, "before you go on, you must know that I've indeed become increasingly fond of Adelaide. In fact, I've never met a woman like her, and it's very hard now not to want to be with her. But considering what you've told me—I...God help me. I don't know what to do. I've fallen in love with her!"

Attalus became red-faced and increasingly agitated. He went down on one knee. "Mother, believe me, I had no idea about this. I'm appalled! But Adelaide . . ."

Adela hesitated and let her son's words hang between them. Finally, she asked gently, "Even if Adelaide would have you, do you think you could face your father? And what about me, my son? Such a liaison would hurt me deeply. I'm afraid it would mean I could never see you again. I love you so much, my dearest. I wish only for your happiness, but this . . . this would tear us apart."

Attalus held his head in his hands for a long minute before speaking. At last, he groaned and raised his eyes to Adela's. "I know it, Mother. I can see how wrong I've been. It's just that she is . . . this is the first time I've ever cared for anyone. But . . . but I will give her up! I know I must...it just cannot be!" After a minute, he added, "But what can we do now? How can we help her? She has nothing."

As tears began to well again in her eyes, Adela breathed a sigh of relief, clutching his hands before answering. "Thank you! Oh, thank you, my blessed boy. I'm so sorry for you. Believe me, I know full well how hard it is to love someone you can't have. But you are right. It cannot be, even if Adelaide herself would have it. Still, there is a way we can help her. We can get her to the king!"

"What? How? What does the king have to do with anything?"

"Son, Adelaide is not a nobody. Her father was a count, very loyal, and close to the king. He fought in all the king's wars until he died. She even has distant ties to the king's own family. And, as you have seen for yourself, Adelaide can handle herself in any company."

Adela stood up and began to pace about the room, eyes bright with excitement.

"Let us bring her to the king! We will present her as a potential lady in waiting at the court. There are many ladies there, mostly wives of men in the army . . . I think. They would gladly have her company. And if I know the king, he would be positively captivated by her wit and beauty. You just need to bring her to the court and report to the king that this is a lady to whom your father, Count Sebastian, owes his life. You will do it, won't you? And before your father returns?"

"I will, Mother, and as soon as may be. What's more, I know Adelaide will see this as the solution to all her problems. If the king accepts her, she need not worry for the rest of her days. The king's court is where she belongs! We will leave on the morrow if possible," she exclaimed eagerly.

***

When it was clear the king had returned to Aachen, Attalus waited a day or two and then packed Adelaide and her small retinue into carts for the journey to Aachen. It was late autumn, on the cusp of winter, but they traveled during a week of almost perfect weather, cool yet beautiful everywhere, as the trees morphed from deep green into bright patches of gold and scarlet. They arrived at the palace just one day before the first winter storm.

Adelaide perceived Adela was anxious to get her out of the manor before Sebastian returned. She was just a bit puzzled that Attalus also seemed to waste no time. No matter, she thought with satisfaction. She didn't want to see that vow breaker again anytime soon. She would show him! Wouldn't Sebastian be surprised if the next time she saw him, she was the king's favorite instead of him!

***

At the palace gate, the reception of Attalus's small party was briefly unnerving. Guards with drawn swords were quick to surround Ajax and the two Greek women before they could even get through the entrance to the great hall. Just beyond the entrance, ensconced like a predatory arachnid in a throne-like chair on an elevated dais, sat a powerful enemy of the house of Sebastian—the scowling, black-robed Mayor of the Palace, Count Arno, fatter and more pompous than ever. As he did every day, Arno held court like a judge before every prospective visitor to the palace. Half a troop of soldiers spread around the hall insured his security.

Ah, there's the mark. Adelaide smirked behind her veil. Good lord, she thought, what a pudgy old potentate he does make of himself! She wondered offhandedly if he would remember her. And then she bet herself twenty gold florins that he would.

After a considerable wait, Attalus was allowed to approach the forbidding official. As he approached the dais, without raising his eyes, Arno said, "State your name and business!"

"I am Attalus, son of Count Sebastian, paladin for the king, and this is . . ."

"The Lady Adelaide!" exclaimed the oily count, suddenly spotting her as she removed her veil at the door. He popped right up on his skinny legs and stepped sideways down the three steps of the dais. Ignoring Attalus, he held out his chubby hands and grasped Adelaide's in a grip a bit too eager and familiar for acquaintances only.

Adelaide smiled graciously but carefully kept a regal distance from his paw-like groping. Um-hmm, she thought to herself. She would have won those gold florins easily. My God, she marveled. What an eager puppy the haughty count is! King or not, there was no longer any doubt in her mind that she could find a home in those exalted chambers!

"What a pleasure, my lady! I hardly expected to see you again so soon. Is something wrong? Please come and sit with me a while and let me greet you properly." He held her arm tightly as he led her into a small room off the main hall and then to a nest of covered benches where a small fire was already burning in the hearth. Maintaining his possessive grip on Adelaide's hands, he motioned imperiously to the guards to allow Adelaide's servants to follow and called to a house serf to bring refreshments at once.

"Dear lady," he gushed enthusiastically, "what brings you to us? Let me say at once, whatever it is, and you may count on me to help you facilitate it."

It was widely said by her friends and enemies alike that Adelaide never missed an opportunity and that she achieved where others failed by the simple artifice of making everyone she met believe that he or she was the most important person in her life. Her charms were already at work. As she accepted the corpulent count's eager welcome, she already sensed the first signs of triumph.

From their first meeting at Fernshanz, Adelaide had gone out of her way to make Arno believe she was the only one in the entire place who really liked him. In fact, she pressed herself against him while laughing at every lame witticism he uttered. She held onto his arm excitedly while he related the simplest news. And she complimented him so often that even he felt she might have exaggerated.

After all, she told herself, he is the Mayor of the Palace, the mortal doorway to the king. As they fell into the same rapport as before and chatted away like old friends, it occurred to her, happily, that she might already have caught the spider in her web.

It became perfectly obvious to the dumbfounded Attalus that they would have no trouble at all getting an audience with the king.

***

Let no one say that Charlemagne would ever be uninterested in a charming, beautiful woman. Over the course of his long reign, he almost always had several such "ladies of the court" in his entourage. They commonly stayed among his daughters, and he was just as protective of them as he was of the daughters, whom he never even allowed to marry.

However, his appetite for new amorous adventures had cooled considerably as he reached his sixties. He kept fewer "extra ladies," even though his last wife had died several years before. Still, his court was enlivened by two or three such attractive courtesans. They mixed easily with his daughters and grandchildren and even birthed a few of his illegitimate children.

"Well, Arno," the king shouted gruffly, "what in the devil's name are you bothering me with now? Get out of the way, man. Let me see who you think is important enough to interrupt my nap!" Arno stepped aside with a bow. And there was Adelaide at her bright and shiny best.

Attalus stepped back as well, the better to behold the scene as it opened. He already knew about the king's appetite for charming ladies from bits and pieces Sebastian occasionally dropped after a visit to the court. But he was not quite prepared to observe how completely the king was captured in the first five minutes of his introduction to Adelaide.

First, she thanked Count Arno and, without waiting, introduced herself. She made a low curtsy, bending just low enough for the king to look at her bountiful breasts. Then, all smiles and graces, she pronounced herself to be "Lady Adelaide, of the house of Kostheim, daughter of the late Count Leudegar and sister to the present count of Kostheim—and also," she added, dropping her eyes, "a distant cousin of yourself, my king."

Mouth agape in surprise and wonder, the king finally exclaimed, "And so you are, my fine lady! I have heard much about you, most of it lately. It seems you are a close friend of my paladin Count Sebastian. Count Arno recently gave me a report of your presence at Fernshanz. Fascinating! I am delighted to meet you. Come and sit with me. Oh, and who's this?" he said, waving a hand toward Attalus.

"I am Attalus, High King, son of Count Sebastian, and a captain in your army."

"Marvelous, young fellow! Come and sit with us. Any son of Sebastian is like a son of me own." Attalus sat down anxiously, hoping for the best. He needn't have worried. For the next while, he might as well have been a fly on the wall for all the attention he got. He was astonished at what happened.

Suddenly and incredibly, without effort, the domestic problems of the house of Sebastian began to melt away. The king was delighted with Adelaide's wit and experience. None of his wives or "extra ladies" could have boasted of anything like the life Adelaide had led. My God, Attalus thought to himself, she treated the king as if he were just any other man! Even for his unpracticed eye, she seemed endlessly interesting and possessed of a wit that would be the envy of most men! If she could bewitch the king himself, what chance would he have ever had with her? But still, he would have died trying to have her if not for their extraordinary circumstances.

It only took one visit. She made the king roar with laughter as he listened spellbound to her tales. They talked for over an hour, and in the end, he had already promised the main goal she sought— an invitation to join the court's official ladies in waiting.

Attalus was welcomed warmly too, and he answered a few questions about Sebastian and Adela. But the king could hardly keep his eyes off Adelaide. Attalus actually felt jealous and rued the fact that he must leave Adelaide. But the good news was that she was safe and in good hands, even if those hands would likely be the king's. He left in pain at the loss of her but also in wonder and admiration for her prowess. In one visit, he thought, as they rode away waving goodbye, she had succeeded, smoothly and painlessly, in charming the trousers off the two highest officials of the land, the king and his right hand, Count Arno. Was there anything she couldn't conquer?

Chapter 18

The Grand Design

Sometimes, very rarely, something happens in life that is so intoxicatingly surprising that the only response is to break out laughing.

When Sebastian and his troop finally returned home, Adela ran down the steps of the manse and threw herself against the side of Sebastian's horse, trying to reach up to him. "Oh, thank God! And you're still in one piece! God be praised! Get down, and let me hug you, for God's sake. And I have some fantastic news to tell you! Adelaide is gone!"

For a moment, he could say nothing, and then he began to laugh, hardly able to catch his breath. "Really? How ... where ... ?" he sputtered as he dismounted awkwardly, favoring his wounded leg.

Adela immediately hugged him close to her lest he fall. "Oh, my love, I'm so sorry. I forgot about your wound. But you look so good! Are you all right? I'm so glad to have you home!"

"I'm fine, Adela. It's just a little stiff. Now tell me at once. What's happened? Where's Adelaide?"

"She's at the king's court, and he has accepted her as a lady in waiting!" Adela giggled. Another burst of explosive laughter from Sebastian was so infectious that Adela began to laugh impulsively. But she caught herself quickly, hugged him closer, and whispered rather guiltily, "Shush, Sebastian, we're being naughty. Actually, I'm very happy for her. She deserves some good luck after all she's been through."

"I agree wholeheartedly," Sebastian said, giving the horse to a groom and taking her arm to limp into the manor house. "It's just that it's about time we had some luck. Adelaide has been one knotty problem after another. We've all been so tense! I worried about it all the way home from Denmark.

"True, she'll probably always be an important figure in our lives. But no one was happy with the situation while she was here, especially her! The wounds were just too raw. The king is the answer to everyone's prayers."

"Amen to that," she said, suppressing another giggle. "But God help the poor king!"

"Right, she will take him by storm. Whew!" Sebastian whistled. "Jolly good luck to him!"

"And to her!" they both said together.

"So now," Sebastian said, as he sat down on a bench and took Adela onto his lap, "for God's sake, tell me, what in the world just happened?"

"Careful, you brute! Stop squeezing the breath out of me, and I'll tell you."

Adela related the whole bizarre episode as nearly as she knew it—Attalus's infatuation with the entrancing older woman, Adelaide's blitzing seduction of the king, and her rather peremptory rejection of their poor son. Attalus had returned home quickly, hurt and disappointed but nevertheless glad for Adelaide and relieved that the family had been spared further turbulence. He had set off immediately the next day to return to the army.

Suddenly, they were alone together in the manor house for the first time in years. They rejoiced in each other and the unexpected gift of their freedom. Yet, even as they held each other tightly in the room's silence, it was hard to dispel the old feeling, after so many years of uncertainty and separation, that it would only be temporary.

***

The king did require Sebastian to come to court often to hunt with him and sit late into the night by the hearth fire, drinking ale and recounting old adventures. Charlemagne loved to relive old campaigns, and he could not get enough of prying out the details of Sebastian's many exploits as a paladin. He would laugh and hoot and slap his leg no matter how many times Sebastian related an escapade. It was the king's way of being there himself.

Such visits, however, caused Sebastian considerable concern. He dreaded the possibility of encountering Adelaide somewhere around the palace. But no matter how many times he visited the king, she never appeared.

He spent a great deal of time with the king, regaling him with many a nightly rendition of past travels and travails. One strong memory they always shared was of Abul-Abbas, the Indian elephant Sebastian and Isaac, the famous Jewish trader, had brought back from Baghdad.

"Ye gods, he was the most stupendous animal in the world," the king declared effusively. "I loved him more than all my horses and most of my men. I rode 'im all over my kingdom for ten years, b'God! When I was up on his back, I felt like I was king of the world! And the people loved it! I cried for a week when he died." The king sniffed.

"Well, he was a bloody lot of trouble, if you ask me," Sebastian replied laconically. "He nearly got us killed a score of times. It took us nearly three years to bring him home to you.

"And," Sebastian continued somewhat testily, "we would have never made it without Isaac, who knew every monarch and headman we met from one end of the Middle Sea to the next."

"Well, it was worth it to me, you rogue! And it did us a great deal of good, says I. That ol' Harun bugger of a caliph gave us the right to protect all the Christians in Jerusalem and the rest of the Holy Land. How bloody good is that? And he agreed to a peace treaty with me against that snake pit of Byzantines and that rotten lot of rebel Musselmen in Spain. I'd say all that was worth your bloody sweat and tears any day!"

"I suppose so, my king. I'm just saying it took a long time to bring that hulking beast back."

For the king, Abul-Abbas had become, for a few years, the symbol of his power and greatness. He junketed with it all around the realm, riding regally on its back as they entered a town or village. For Sebastian, the beast symbolized the incredibly high price of serving the king at the highest level.

"Feathers! You should be proud. Nobody but you could have done it. Never mind old Isaac. He could never have made it without you and your intrepid little band. What's more, you have your king's profound gratitude, b'God!"

"Thank you, sire." Sebastian stifled any other reply. The elephant had cost him almost three years of his life. Consequently, his admiration for the beast was heavily tempered by his resentment of him. The king truly loved to hear about all the derring-do of his favorite paladin's adventures. For Sebastian, they mostly recalled pain and loss, incredible effort and risk.

Regarding the Constantinople chapter of his tales, Sebastian clung carefully to a sketchy outline of the facts, resisting every attempt of the king to draw some information about Adelaide from the episode. He would say only that she had given him unselfish, life-saving help in escaping from the city after he had been condemned to die. The king was no fool, and Sebastian could tell he sensed much more.

***

The most important aspect of Sebastian's new visits to the king was Charlemagne's growing interest in leaving a legacy. As he grew older and less physically active, he began to think more and more of a great plan by which he could leave something of value behind beside the bloody wars he fought to conquer paganism in the realm. Sebastian was astonished and delighted by the king's new interest. He rode to Aachen more often and plotted with the king about finding and achieving such a lofty goal.

"Y'see, my old lad," the king said, leaning toward Sebastian as they sat across from each other in the king's private chambers, "I want to leave something to the people—to the Frankish folk, whom I've always loved so much! I know the realm ain't perfect. I see the poverty, don't think I don't! I hate the constant crop failures and famines. And the sickness and plagues that come year after year." Charlemagne paused to spit into the fire and take another swallow of ale as he looked wild-eyed around the room, searching for hidden answers.

"And now that we've pushed the bloody pagans back away from the realm and Christianity is strong and growing, we can finally be doing something for the little people of this land. By God, they certainly deserve something! They've served me almighty well. They're hardy and loyal. They've always done anything I've ever asked of 'em. And look at the mighty empire we've created together! No race like the Franks!"

The king's enthusiasm spellbound Sebastian. Up to this moment, he'd had no idea what was hatching so dramatically in the king's fertile brain.

"Well, what do you think? Does it make any sense? What comes to mind, Sebastian? Can we do something? What? How?"

"Whoa, my king. That's a pretty big dragon you're asking me to slay. I completely agree with the idea. It's tremendous! But it's so big and many-faceted. It touches everything and everybody."

"Well, that's it! That's what I want—everybody! I want the Church, the army, the whole nobility, the whole country involved. No one is to be exempt. Everybody must take this plan most seriously, whatever it turns out to be! And I want you, Sebastian, my old champion, to dive into it and come up with a plan!"

***

Several weeks later, on one long ride to confer with the king again, Sebastian had a sudden inspiration. He turned to Liudolf, riding beside him. "Listen, brother, how many times do you suppose we've made this ride to see the king?"

"Huh! I'd not care to try to tote 'em all up," Liudolf replied lazily. But he thought momentarily and then said, "What about all those bloody times when we wore our pants off as part of the *missi dominici*?"

"That's it, my old comrade!" Sebastian shouted into the wind. "That's how we can do it!"

They discussed and pondered that seminal notion the rest of the way to Aachen, and that evening, as he and the king sat staring into the fireplace seeking ideas, he brought it up. "You know, sire, we've had considerable success with our old *missi dominici* system. The king's agents we send out still cover the entire empire to convey your justice and proclaim your will to all. Why could we not devise

115

a similar system to spread your intentions to improve the lives of the people?"

For a moment, the king was stunned. "Why in blazes didn't I think of that?"

He wasted no time. The result was a final edict declaring, "The realm must undertake to improve and enrich the lives of the Frankish people and to make of Francia a new civilization."

Of course, the teeth of the decree was a massive amount of gold and silver the king astonishingly released from the royal treasury to be used for this purpose. Sebastian was named a key agent, along with certain high churchmen and leading men of the aristocracy and army, to invent the program, administer its funding, and see its speedy promulgation. No one could doubt that Charlemagne intended that Aachen should become "the New Rome."

***

On one of his journeys to plan with the king, Sebastian met Louis, Charlemagne's youngest son and a potential successor. He had traveled all the way from Aquitaine just to hear his father's command to endorse the "plan for the people wholly."

Sebastian had never even seen Louis. Nevertheless, he felt his stomach tighten when the short king of Aquitaine marched purposefully into the king's quarters. He was not alone. Several black-robed monks followed close behind him. Sebastian noted the truth of the presumption that Louis never went anywhere without the Church.

Louis, the so-called Pious, was not the man his father was. The people identified with Charlemagne, a strong, decisive, lusty war leader. His successful wars, the treasures he won, and his capitularies establishing law and order over the land were a glory shared by every Frank. The people loved him.

Not so with Louis. It was commonly felt that the king did not see much potential in his third son and did not expect him ever to succeed him. As Sebastian bowed before Louis, he was not surprised to find in him an unremarkable middle-aged man, physically

116

unimposing, with delicate hands and a dry, unvaried face. He acknowledged Sebastian with no more than a slight nod. Sebastian immediately felt edgy around him and noted that he looked like one of those Aquitanian monks he brought with him. He also felt that Louis and his companions had resentment written all over them.

It was common knowledge that the high king preferred his first son as heir to the throne. Charles the Younger was a strong-willed, independent thinker and a good general. Apparently, Louis also knew of or felt the king's preference and realized he had only a meager chance to succeed to the throne. He also was aware that most people in the Rhineland part of the empire did not even know about him. This awareness only made him angry. He hated being ignored by both his father and his brothers. After all, he was King of the Aquitaine, a huge part of the empire. Their relative indifference only made him more ambitious.

The meeting was anything but warm. Everyone, including the king, was stiff and uneasy. Only one of the churchmen dared to say anything at all. Sebastian immediately knew him as the Goth, Benedict of Aniane, who influenced most of Louis's decisions. He was a tall, thin, unsmiling monk with a serious, no-nonsense approach to everything.

The king met with Sebastian later that night, asking for his opinion of Louis. "Well, my king, he certainly matches his reputation. I'm not sure he's his own man. Arno told me Louis generally follows Benedict's advice. And most of the time, the monk's advice is good. But he's no friend of yours, my liege. No matter how much you may do for the Church, Benedict disapproves of you, your lifestyle, and even the sometimes rough way you talk. Most of all, he might object to your firm conviction that the Frankish king, not the pope in Rome, must be the head of the Christian Church! There's the real rub."

"Well, damn his eyes then!" exploded the king. "What's wrong with the way I talk? It certainly ain't 'church talk.' Never mind. I'll talk and do whatever I bloody well please as long as I'm alive. And Louis would do well to learn how to think for himself if ever he takes my place, God forbid!"

Later in the visit, Lothar, Louis's firstborn son, also arrived to hear Charlemagne's imperative decree. As soon as Sebastian met him, he knew the youth would one day be a huge problem. Just meeting the boy left a nasty taste in his mouth. When the king later asked for Sebastian's assessment, he readily replied. "To be frank, my king, Lothar, seems to me to be wildly rash and combustible. He says whatever comes into his head, and he's astonishingly ignorant about the empire and how it functions. He doesn't even know the geography! He lays claim to land he wants to be added to his portion of the empire without ever having been in such land or even knowing precisely where it lies. Worst of all, he's jealous of his father, bragging openly about what he would do after his father dies. Lord, save us!"

"My impression exactly, the saucy pup," the king snorted. "God help the realm if he ever does become emperor."

"Amen, Your Majesty!" Sebastian echoed wryly.

***

The meeting with Louis was short, lasting only a few days. Still, in the end, Benedict surprised everyone by supporting "the people plan" and convincing Louis that it was indeed important and that he and the entire Church should approve it without reservation. Reluctantly Louis vowed his full support.

Lothar, to the contrary, memorably said, "It's just a bloody pile of horseshit! Too much work, a waste of the king's treasure. We'd be better off spending all that on building a stronger army!"

***

Sebastian let out a whoop only a few miles out on the ride home with Liudolf. "Hurrah! We're free!"

"What?" Liudolf responded in alarm. "You just resigned your exalted rank as the high king's paladin, and then he gave you an impossible job. And you're cheering?"

"Hurrah to all of that, old companion! The king says I'm free! I don't have to kill anybody anymore. Oh, he's still got his

118

clutches on me with our so-called 'plan for the people.' He wants me to devise and see to the implementation of the thing. It's an enormous task! But it's something I'd far rather do, actually. The king wants it quite urgently now that he's getting older. So we, my skeptical friend, will no longer have to go traipsing into the maw of the king's enemies or fighting his battles with him. Don't you see? This is a whole new life! It's going to take all our time. And best of all, I get to spend it with Adela!"

Thinking of that, he let out another wild whoop, raised both hands high above his head, and kicked Joyeuse into a gallop.

Chapter 19

Reconstructing Rome

"Good Lord, Father! How came you by all this ruddy *gold*?" Milo exclaimed as Sebastian, with a theatrical gesture, lifted the lid of a large box full of shiny gold coins. "Have you dug up another trove of Irminsul loot or robbed some new Avar stronghold?"

"No, my son, I did not. But I would be willing to wager that most of this glittering hoard was once among the booty of one or another pagan nation we've beaten into submission."

Sebastian felt more than a twinge of guilt as he presided over the treasure, remembering clearly how he had been a part of the seizure of much of it after victorious battles against the Avars and Saxons. To the victor belongs the spoils, he said to himself. It's an ancient, universally accepted conviction. But he knew full well that such tolerance was almost always accompanied by the pale horses of destruction, hunger, and death for the defeated. At least now, in the king's extraordinary largesse, Sebastian could discern the vague image of redemption.

The gold and grand venture to make Francia a benevolent realm and a powerful one was already the talk of noble houses up and down the Rhine. Most great lords lustily approved of the venture since it stood to be financed largely from Charlemagne's treasury. The Church, of course, was also among the major planners. But Sebastian was not content. So far, the plan was vague and just barely underway.

He chose Andernach, Duke Gonduin's sprawling estate along the Rhine and Adela's ancestral home, as the headquarters for his "Council of the New Civilization," the name given to the informal group he hoped would be the spearhead of the movement.

Sebastian thought that the council sitting around the central fireplace of the manor's great room was certainly bizarre. No great lords or high churchmen or bloody Mayor of the Palace to veto our decisions. There was only himself and Adela, Milo, Magdala,

Simon, Liudolf, Father Pippin, and the venerable Heimdal, who had
to be carried everywhere now but whose brain was still very much
intact.

Sebastian felt exhilarated as he looked at the earnest faces of
close friends and family. He was willing to bet that this manor house
and this small group of talented, hard-working, and imaginative
people would get more done than any ten of the king's councils! And
if the king approved what this tiny, seemingly insignificant group
did, the great lords and all the notable clergy would have to go along,
no matter what they think of us!

***

They met at Andernach for its generally reachable location
along the Rhine and its imposing reputation among Franks as a
symbol of the Frankish heartland and power. From Andernach,
serious things could be accomplished throughout the realm.

Duke Gonduin was long dead, and Charlemagne had handed
over Andernach to the duke's only child, Adela, and her husband,
Sebastian. From Andernach, the council intended to reach out to all
the great lords of church and state and enlist them in the endeavor.
The gold – and the king's whip hand - would drive their cooperation.

"What, then, are the priorities, my friends?" Heimdal began,
assuming his usual role as the voice of order and reason.

Milo was quick to respond. "Healing!" he exclaimed
enthusiastically. "We've already got a good start!"

"Safety! Protection on the roads and rivers," Simon added
quickly. "We cannot improve trade or see our towns grow and ideas
multiply unless the people are safe to travel."

"Books!" Father Pippin declared, skinny finger in the air.
"Preservation. Copying the wisdom of the ancients, religious as well
as classic. Too many manuscripts have already been lost forever."

"Father Pippin is right," Sebastian added. "But it's more than
copying books. It's Learning. It's teaching people to read those
books—or any written thing. As it is now, reading is still almost
solely the monopoly of the Church. King Karl has dreamed all his
life of teaching the people to read. And he has finally caused a

miraculous new script to be created, with spaces between words. Which trashes the old Merovingian script and makes any writing wonderfully easier to read. It's now possible, my friends, to teach anyone, and everyone, to read! That means we need a great many more schools—schools open to anyone with the ability to learn!"

A long pause followed Sebastian's disclosure as everyone contemplated its overarching promise. He was pleased to see that his words had struck home. In a quiet voice, he added with certitude, "I believe with all my heart that any progress at all depends on teaching and learning."

"Ah," intoned Heimdal. "So then, we have many paths toward our holy dream of a new Rome. But only so much gold! Such ambitious endeavors will take a very long time and much more gold than we have here, as great a treasure as it is. One more time, I ask: Where shall we begin, and how?"

Though he was the youngest at the council, Milo jumped in again. "I agree with Father on the importance of schools, but Magdala and I feel we must name medicine and healing to be our priority. There is so much suffering among our common folk! And there is constant danger of plague and other diseases."

Magdala added quickly, "We already have a good start here at Andernach. We have at least fifteen native women healers in our little school here. And five male doctors, all from amongst our Jewish brethren. More are on the way. They bring the healing knowledge of the ancients, going all the way back to the great doctors of the Greeks. We have Simon to thank for bringing them here, and he says there are many more who would love the chance to learn by being together."

"Ah, yes," said Simon. "But I would also say that the reason my Jewish brothers are so eager to come here or to whatever schools are established is gold! Money can buy a great deal of things they don't have and need in order to make advances, essential things, such as drugs, exotic herbs, operating tools, security."

"We have much of that already. Tell them, Magdala," said Milo, turning to his shy companion in the seat behind him.

"That is true," she said quietly. "We are constantly welcoming new local healers in the towns we visit. They bring such tools as they have. We help them organize gardens of herbs and healing plants, even enclosed gardens protected by trees and walls, where they can grow special herbs from Italy and beyond. Already we can barely keep up with the sick and injured who appear daily at our clinics. But we need everything! Especially teachers who have more knowledge of the human body. That's why the Jewish healers are so important. They have been able to open the human body and see inside it."

"Stop, Magdala! Say no more," Heimdal hissed. "You know the Church forbids such probes inside the body and they are severely punishable. You must not even imply that you do such things or even know about them. Your Jewish doctors must be restrained at all costs."

"I understand, m'lord," Magdala said, bowing her head.

"The clinics are a wonderful start," Sebastian said, rising from his chair and beginning to pace around the room. "But we are pledged to follow all of these courses. It's an enormous task. None of us may live to see any real fruition. But we have to start somewhere."

He paused, feeling the energy in the room. "We've already made a good beginning—clinics and schools up and down the Rhine. But we need to extend our energies to encompass the whole realm. We must divide the realm and send agents to each part of it. A system like the *missi dominici* is needed, a core of envoys who will enforce the king's will in every part of the realm. King Karl has already given his blessing to this plan and ordered all landed lords to support it with laborers and volunteers."

"That may be, my lord," Liudolf spoke skeptically from behind the others. "But I can only wish that those same landed lords were as interested in protecting our borders as they are in using the high king's gold. Seems to me this new plan may prove to be a distraction from tending to the realm's defense. We have enemies threatening all the border marches."

"You are right, my dear friend," said Adela, speaking for the first time. "But all that is no longer among the duties of this house and all of us. We have been given a new mission. And we must leave the rest to God and the king and concentrate on what we can do.

Who knows? Our tasks here, if they bear good fruit, could be more beneficial and long-lasting than anything we might contribute to the security concerns of our king."

Chapter 20

The Endless Road

Sebastian launched himself into the work of "civilizing the bloody land," as the king had put it: schools, literacy, elementary hospitals and small clinics, and pilgrim hostels leading all the way to Rome and the Saint James shrine in Santiago, beyond the Pyrenees.

Since they already had a solid start, Milo and Magdala continued developing the clinics, gradually expanding them into new territories. Though they spent considerable time at each new site, their main job was to organize and teach. When possible, they left a few qualified workers in each place and any available Jewish doctor in the larger facilities.

Sebastian was full of admiration for the pair. He sometimes found occasion to watch them move into a new village or town and create a small clinic in a barn or an outlying cave. Milo would build and supply, and Magdala would go unpretentiously into a town or village and sit with a begging bowl by the town church or village green, as she had done so often in Jerusalem along the Via Dolorosa. She would scrutinize the passersby and engage them if they showed sickness or infirmity. It did not take her long to establish a reputation as a healer and lead those in need to the new hospice.

Magdala never seemed to change. Despite the totally strange land she came from, and its very different people, she met everyone with equilibrium and gladness. Now that she and Milo were together, she was happy, and she smiled a lot, no matter how serious the work they did together. Finding remedies for illness and relieving plain folk's suffering was more than a passion for her; it was a sacrament.

And the work was constant, difficult - and dangerous. They often did healings that most people thought were impossible. Consequently, there was always a scent of superstition in the air among the common people who lived near the clinic.

At least she and Milo employed trusted friends and assistants to provide guards wherever they were engaged in healing. They quickly switched positions at the slightest hint of interlopers; Magdala stood in the background, holding cloths or jugs of water or building a fire for washing soiled clothing. Milo or one of the Jewish doctors would stand in her place.

But Sebastian was not satisfied. "Magdala!" he would scold, "you simply must stop acting like a doctor or even like a man. Your work is wonderful! We are making so much progress and helping so many people. But this is not Jerusalem! Most peasant folk here in Francia are far more narrow-minded and superstitious. And so are their lords. We must subtly do the good we can, with great caution, moving on frequently to avoid notoriety.

"We're a long way from changing the people's minds. They will not tolerate a woman handling the human body as you do. I hate to put a rein on your fine work, but when any outsider is present, except for an unconscious patient, you must confine yourself to teaching, gathering and growing herbs, and treating small wounds of the face and hands. You must not, under any circumstances, make it evident that you have touched someone's naked body—except to help a woman at birthing."

"And you and Milo most certainly must not allow your Jewish doctors to examine corpses! Ye gods! If you continue to disregard our customs openly, you will wind up being burned at the stake! And the Jews will find themselves castrated and skewered on a spike!"

Late that night, Milo tried to comfort Magdala as they lay together on a straw mattress at the end of the day. Magdala was distraught, weeping. "How can I give up doctoring and healing people? I just can't stand in the background when I know full well, better than most, exactly what to do?"

"I know, dear, but it's too dangerous. You won't be able to do anything if one of your patients decides to tell on you. It would take just one man who admitted you put your hands on his naked body, and you could be treated like a witch and burned!

"All right! But what, then? I was just beginning to be really good at healing, making a difference."

"Wait a minute! Milo said, sitting bolt upright in the bed. My father said we must "not make it evident" that you are healing. What if it wasn't evident? What if you just looked like a man and acted like one? We could dress you in men's clothes and put a mask on you and a turban or hat like the Jewish doctors wear. You could study men's gestures and ways of walking. It wouldn't be too hard since most people you care for are too concentrated on their pain or illness to look too hard at who's trying to heal them!"

And so they did it. Magdala was a woman only when they were on the road or in the privacy of their bed. They began to breathe more easily, and Magdala flourished.

**

Sebastian was very proud of their work. He fancied it was laying the foundation for great changes in medicine, even if those changes were far down the road. But he preached this warning every time he saw Milo and Magdala. And each time, they reassured him they were extra careful in everything they did concerning the new hospices.

Magdala was always the most knowledgeable of any healers, and she insisted on hands-on participation. Despite the disguises, Sebastian lived in fear that she would be caught. And she might have been in ordinary times, except now there was the daily distraction of war on the borders or riots in some towns and cities where they built their hospices. Everyone bustled about seeking security with one side or another and paid little attention to the work at the little out-of-the-way clinics. For the most part, people were glad enough to see at least something being done about disease and sickness.

And Simon! Sebastian came to feel over time that the trader had truly become a part of his family. He was almost like a brother. He had given up the riches of trade to engage in their nebulous pursuit of progress for the common folk. He had visions of planting towns, building potential trading centers and routes, and even finding a way to facilitate the return of actual money to replace the clumsy, uneven system of barter. Sebastian even sent Attalus with him on Simon's exploratory trips around the realm to build connections. He was convinced there was no better way for the young man to learn how to twist together the many strands of trade and build a fortune.

As for Sebastian's main group, there were tasks in profusion: overseeing the building and financing of hospices, recruiting agents, and convincing the churchmen to devote themselves to promoting literacy at all costs. Sebastian pleaded with bishops and abbots to expand their schools and admit anyone at all, regardless of class, as long as they were capable of learning.

The overwhelming challenge was the great lords. All of them had received or were due money from Charlemagne's treasury, but getting them to open their clenched fists for the common folk was like trying to pry open a bulldog's mouth. Much of his time was spent as an enforcer. He traveled from lord to lord and bishop to bishop, shaming them, reasoning with them, and even threatening to have the king confiscate their lands and properties.

There was far less trouble with the monasteries, where the monks were thrilled to get any support to pursue manuscript copying. That work surged in the ensuing months and years, including ancient Greek and Roman texts as well as religious writings.

Remarkably, Sebastian never minded the long days on the road and the constant effort and controversy they dealt with, simply because he could do it all with Adela. What might have been a grinding task from hell became a rewarding joint effort and a golden opportunity to be together continuously. It was hugely fulfilling, like no other time in their lives. Adela rode beside him every day. He marveled at how strong and durable she was, how straight she sat in the saddle, how consistently optimistic she was about the daily grinding task before them. Nothing seemed impossible as long as she was with him. People still called her "Adela the Fair," and her charms and beauty were considerable assets in garnering the cooperation of obstinate lords.

Sebastian was enormously proud of her but thought guiltily how little he deserved her, remembering their long separations and his many mistakes. He never imagined he would be rewarded with so much time with her.

The Lady Adela was indeed a welcome guest at every lord's manor or archbishop's cathedral. She could melt hearts. Still, they might have failed if Sebastian had not been a legendary paladin, a celebrated soldier, and a highly respected leader. As it was, both of them needed all their persuasive charm and likeability.

As the months of convincing and converting rolled by into a year and then another, a system like the old *missi dominici* did become established. A corps of agents kept track of the progress and reported even to the king.

Sebastian and Adela were always accompanied by Liudolf and a small troop of light cavalry. Even Bardulf and Drogo rode along, Bardulf to escape his harpy wife and Drogo because he had nothing better to do.

The group always seemed to be on the road. But the men had spent much of their lives on the backs of horses anyway, and Adela was a superb horsewoman, never seeming to falter or ask for relief. Eventually, little by little, from one circuit of the realm to another, they could see progress. For Sebastian and the entire tenacious band, that was enough.

***

Meanwhile, Adelaide flourished at the king's court. She had no trouble becoming its most prominent star. She had grown up as the daughter of a duke and the only privileged female in a house full of bounderish warriors. To protect herself and survive, she developed a wanton and aggressive personality. Most men, including her father, had given her a wide berth, preferring to avoid her sharp tongue and cynical wit. She learned to do what she liked and get what she liked.

Because she was improper and precocious, most women did not like her, but she didn't care. In her view, women mattered little. And the warrior thugs she observed around her were simply to be used or got round. Rarely did she relate to one or another because she liked him, but at an early age, perhaps because she was so uninhibited, she developed a healthy sexual appetite. She came to indulge it whenever she was inclined, provided her partner was attractive enough. Consequently, she also acquired the worst reputation of any woman in the Rhineland.

Adelaide never felt she was without recourse wherever she went, even in court. If stymied, she went down a different path toward the same goal. Defeat or denial only made her furious, and she plotted like a witch to brew her fortunes anew—or at least to exact revenge. Her assets were brains, nerves, and the focus of an adder. Had she been born a man, she would have likely become one of Charlemagne's generals.

But she did not stay long at Charlemagne's court. Only long enough to endear herself indelibly to the king. She wrapped him, Salome-like, around her little finger until he could not say nay to anything she desired. And then she left.

Chapter 21

A Camp Follower?

"Adelaide has taken up with our son Karl," Adela whispered to Sebastian as he came in with Liudolf from a morning hunt.

"What? What the devil are you saying? You can't be serious! How do you know this?" Sebastian said, throwing down his cloak and unbuckling his sword belt.

"Calm yourself, husband. Come," Adela murmured softly, leading Sebastian by the hand to a secluded bench in the garden. "A courier was here from the army with a message for you. He said that our Karl sends his greetings and that there has been a significant change in his life. Apparently, he's very anxious to speak with you about it but can't leave the army at the moment. The courier also said that a well-dressed woman with red hair was with our Karl when he was given the message."

"What! How can that be?" stormed Sebastian.

"Please contain yourself, my love. I'm almost at my wit's end, and I need you to be strong and clear-headed. One of our sons may be sleeping with your old lover."

"Adela! How could you bring that old story up? I thought we agreed never to speak of it again."

"I know, I know. But I can't stand to think of Karl being with her."

Oh, Lord, Sebastian moaned to himself. Adelaide was back in their lives – again, so much trouble! But he could see her taking advantage of a young man as naive and inexperienced as Attalus. But how did she snare their Karl, who was mature and perceptive enough to see through her wiles?

"I should have known she wouldn't want to stay at court for long," he admitted to Adela. Not enough freedom. Too many 'sweet doves.' But why, of all people, did she have to go to our son? Do you think she's doing it to get back at me for refusing her?"

"Adelaide must have gone to Karl straight-away, wherever the army was," Adela added, wringing her hands. "I knew there was a spark between them. She much preferred Karl to our poor Attalus. Apparently, the king's court has become too stale for her, and she needs some new stimulation."

"But I can't believe she's become a camp follower," Sebastian groaned.

"Yes, well, she had to go somewhere, and it was surely not going to be back to us. Besides, Karl is moving up now in the army. Everyone says so. He can probably afford to keep her in grand style, even in the field." Adela began to cry, and Sebastian hastened to put his arms around her.

"Listen, love, I don't believe it! Karl just wouldn't do this. He doesn't chase women; they chase him. After all, he's a captain in the heavy cavalry! His place in the army is far more important to him than any particular woman, especially one like Adelaide, who would demand far too much of him. I know it's hard to disregard the message, but let's hold judgment until we've looked into this."

"And we need to find out soon before any such connection goes too far," Adela continued, wiping her eyes. "If I know Adelaide, she won't be just languishing there. She's probably Karl's chief advisor. Do you think she could resist jumping into whatever is happening? She's not the kind of woman who will just sit around and wait for her lord to come home and give her a little attention. She would go insane."

"No," Sebastian added. "You're right, and she'll want to know everything. And she is so sharp Karl might listen to her. He's a good fighter, but he's no schemer. If he is with her, I'll wager any advice he gives to the king or Charles the Younger will have originated in the inventive mind of Adelaide. She's sure to plot for Karl's advancement, and that means she will want to encourage him to go wherever the fighting is."

Adela leaned into a kerchief and blew her nose angrily. "It's my fault; I went away to the convent and left him to the mercy of my bloody father!"

"Nonsense, my love! You're no more to blame than me. I was away for almost all the years of his growing up. Besides, every boy from a noble house goes away early to be trained as a warrior. Your father was just a better teacher than most. He did too good a job with Karl." Sebastian released her from his arms and began pacing back and forth.

"Listen, I may have a chance to see Karl soon. The army's not in the field at the moment, but I think there's a standing force at Mayence, a few hundred permanently active men from the cavalry. Karl is certain to be with them, and so is the king. The rumor is there's something big brewing there. I've heard the king called in several of his most important lords and advisors. I'll hear from him soon."

"What is it about? Do you know?"

"I think it must be about the succession. As the king gets older, he worries more about what will happen to Francia after he's gone. We've talked about it before. But now he must be in earnest. He's looking for some ideas, some wisdom.

"So far, the king's sons have been no problem. But you know Frankish history. The ancient practice has been to divide whatever kingdom there was among surviving sons. That almost always caused bitter battles—unless there was only one surviving son! Our beloved high king had a brother, but Carloman died before a succession fight could begin." Adela was sitting now with her head in her hands. Sebastian hastened to comfort her.

"Listen, my dear, we must always assume that war is possible. But it is not inevitable. If I am called, I will do my best to keep a conflict from happening. I may be able to do something. And at the same time, I can see to Karl."

"Yes! That's it!" she exclaimed, grasping his hands. "You must go there, Sebastian! Everyone knows and respects you. You must go to the king. I don't know anyone else who could stop a civil war."

"Perhaps, Adela. But it hasn't come to that yet. I'll leave for the court tomorrow, and I will make sure to find out what's going on, if anything, between Karl and Adelaide." He wanted to assure her that the message must be a mistake. Karl just wouldn't have gotten involved with her. But then again, it was never wise to underestimate Adelaide.

133

Steger

Chapter 22

The Divisio Regnorum

Thionville 806

For two whole years after Sebastian's near-fatal encounter with the Danes, Charlemagne kept his promise. Sebastian enjoyed the king's full support and blessing to pursue the countrywide welfare program. Eventually, however, Charlemagne broke his promise in the name of a greater need.

As Sebastian suspected, the issue was a succession and how to divide the empire. In the past, this had been a cause of bitter civil war. Charlemagne had escaped the risk due to the obscure death of his brother Carloman. But the king had three sons, and he called on his former paladin to help him find a way to avoid future conflict.

***

"But he promised!" Adela protested, stifling a cough. She lay abed long after the day began, and she felt a bit warm to Sebastian's touch when he woke her.

"What is this, Adela? Are you ill? I won't go!"

"Nonsense. You must go!" she said, struggling to sit up. "It's too important—for us as well as for the king."

"I know, my love, but I feel I ought to stay at least until I know you're all right. This isn't like you."

"It's just the change of seasons, dear. I always catch a little something this time of year. I'll be fine. Go! But come back as soon as you can!"

"All right, if you're sure. I shouldn't be gone long. It's not a military mission. The king only wants me to help him write his will and decide how the land must be divided when he dies. His sons are also coming to the conference at Thionville. I must go if I care about keeping the peace after the king dies. With any luck, I'll bring you back good news on both the king's account and ours."

He pressed her to him to embrace and kiss her. She seemed languid and untypically tired to Sebastian, but she hung onto him for a long minute. Then she gave him her most beautiful smile and shooed him away. "Come back soon," she called after him.

"I will, love."

Sebastian hid his apprehension as he rode away with Liudolf. But there was a heaviness in his chest. "She didn't look right," he confided to Liudolf. "She's almost never sick. Damn the king! I wouldn't go if it weren't so bloody important.

My God, that smile she gave me! It's burned into my soul! She is the greatest gift of my life. God's gift! You know, these last few years, since I left the king's service, have been the richest and happiest of our lives? Everything we do seems to prosper and flourish. She said we're God's agents, Adela and me! Fancy that, after all the mayhem I've been through and the ungodly things I've had to do! Now, for two years, we've been almost constantly together! I'll tell you, Liudolf, I'm afraid to leave her, afraid things will change.

Listen, old comrade, don't be such a worrier. It's just a cold. It's that time of year. And you better stop thinking about her and how good it's been and all that, lest you put a hex on it somehow.

Sebastian told himself Liudolf was right, but it took a long time for him to tear his thoughts away from Adela. Eventually, his anxiety grew in a different direction as he pondered the king's dilemma. King Karl needed to make an acceptable will. But if he could not produce one to the satisfaction of all three of his sons, conflict was almost a surety and could lead to the empire's disintegration. He pushed his horse into a gallop.

***

Sebastian went straight to Aachen to ride with the king to Thionville and discuss a plan on the way.

"You're doing good work, my old son!" the king exclaimed as they rode together, apart from the escort. "Everybody says so. It's a grand thing to try and change the soul of a people. But that's what you're doing, and I love it! As you say, it might even be the best part of my legacy!"

"But not as important as this meeting, High King. Right?" Sebastian said, only partially jesting.

"Now don't start, you knave! You know as well as I do what could happen if I die leaving three bloody heirs without an agreement. Why, they'd be trying to cut each other's throats before my bones were cold."

"Right, sire. I agree completely. But it won't be easy. No heir ever gets enough land if he's got a brother."

"Right!" the king mumbled. "Don't even know if I could have avoided a fight with my brother Carloman if he hadn't gone and died . . . mysteriously. Uh-hum."

Sebastian let that bleak mystery waft away. "Well, my king, I have some ideas that might help us avoid such a fight. Would you like to hear them?"

"Spit 'em out, lad! That's why I sent for you."

Sebastian had thought for weeks about a plan for the succession and talked with Heimdal, Milo, and anyone else with a crumb of an idea. He was thrilled by the consensus he'd managed to conjure up and could not wait to share it with the king. A long, uninterrupted ride together was the perfect way to present the bold idea.

"Here's the key thing, my king. Charles the Younger is your firstborn. He has the right to inherit the whole of Francia and the title of emperor. But he must give significant lands to his brothers and co-heirs which they may rule as sub-kings fairly and independently."

"That's how it is already," the king exclaimed. "So, shouldn't we just continue with the present arrangement?"

"I am inclined to say no, Your Highness. I think it's important for you to make one of your sons far stronger than the others. He must be so strong and have such support that his brothers will not dare to oppose him." Sebastian watched guardedly as the king furrowed his brow and stroked his mustaches. He went on.

"We already have a leading candidate in Charles the Younger. He commands the army in your absence, a very able general. And he has mettle, a good temperament, and a steady hand. Most of the great lords of the land like him. He already has their confidence."

"Right. That's exactly what I think."

"Yes, my king. But he must be clearly seen to be far more powerful than both of his brothers together, so they know without a doubt that they could not stand against him. You must give Charles the lion's share of the realm!"

Sebastian paused momentarily to let the king take in the idea and then went on quickly, "Charles the Younger's share must also contain the most dynamic parts of the realm. I'm talking about the Rhineland and the land between the Seine and the Maas rivers, including Paris, Reims, and Nijmegen in the ancient lowland home of the Franks."

"Why, that's almost half the empire and the richest parts of it," the king blurted out. "The others will never agree!"

"That's exactly the point, my liege. Charles the Younger must be twice as strong as both of his brothers together. They will not have the strength or the will to fight him."

***

Arriving early in Thionville, Sebastian and the king set to work immediately, welcoming each lord and high churchman. They were careful to spend time with each contingent, explaining in detail the provisions of the *Divisio, Regnorum* as it was designated. Most of the notables attending the meeting understood the need for a bold strategy. Eventually, they agreed that the realm should be divided as proposed—until the arrival of a substantial army of Aquitanian troops escorting Louis the Pious, his son Lothar and the venerable Benedict of Aniane with his entourage of black-robed monks.

Their arrival was unlike the other lords, even the king himself. The other contingents drifted in, taking time to greet old friends and allowing their escorts and attendants to set up camp in a leisurely fashion. Not so the Aquitanians. Theirs was almost like a movement-to-contact formation. There was a strong advance guard, followed by King Louis the Pious and his son Lothar. After them came the main body of soldiers, several hundred of them. Then the monks riding mules and the baggage carts, followed finally by a heavy rear guard. Every soldier wore armor and a helmet. An abounding number of flags and pennants sprang up just as the cohort entered the camp.

Sebastian could tell at once by Louis and Lothar's frowning coolness and hostile postures that they already had a good idea of what was being proposed, and the number of soldiers accompanying them indicated they meant to back up their objections.

Although the king greeted them warmly, the meeting quickly turned into a chilly confrontation. Aquitanian agents lost no time moving among the delegates, disputing the proposed division. By the second day, the camp had become a beehive of gossip, specious speculations, and denouncements. Benedict's influence undoubtedly carried much weight among the clergy from all regions. But the hottest resentment came from Lothar, Louis's youthful son and Charlemagne's grandson, who went about nakedly undermining the proposed *Divisio* and the "conspiracy" of the Rhenish lords who supported it. He fell just short of condemning the king himself.

"And you, Count Sebastian!" Lothar called out as he strode into a grouping of army leaders gathered around Sebastian at a makeshift field house. "Normally, I would greet you politely at a meeting like this. But we have heard disturbing news about the proposal before us. It's a scheme to redivide the empire and will not be in our favor. We also know it is your work. You're always whispering in the king's ear. You should know from the outset that it does not please us, not by any means! And we will oppose you— gravely, if necessary."

"Lord Lothar." Sebastian gestured to the youth. "Won't you come and sit with us? Let me explain to you the hidden importance of the division."

"Bah! There's nothing hidden about what you're doing. You just want to keep the realm's power in the hands of the eastern Franks! You want to keep the ability to tax us heavily and use our armies instead of your own to fight the battles of the empire."

Sebastian was taken aback by the young lord's fervor and obvious loathing of the eastern Franks and himself. He worried the lad might go far enough to convince his father to resort to violence if the proposal was sustained.

"And another thing, while I'm telling you what does not please us, great councilor Sebastian! We are sick of you telling us in Aquitaine how we should spend our money and our time. 'Benefits for the people,' schools, hospices! Drivel! That has never been our way! These are peasants you're going on about. Peasants must know their place. They are incapable of 'learning to read.' They make good soldiers, is all—if you don't bedevil their peasant minds with unfitting ideas."

Now Sebastian was getting angry. But he controlled his impulse to slap the youth across his haughty mouth. Instead, he said as evenly and kindly as possible, "Lord Lothar, let me invite you to Aachen and the school of Lord Alcuin, which boasts some of the best minds in the realm. There I would love to show you what great changes we hope to accomplish in this realm, changes which you might benefit from should you one day ascend to the Frankish throne."

"Humbug! I'd sooner cut my own throat. You're stealing our money and wasting our time. That's the real truth of it. And now you're trying to steal the throne. I warn you, we've had enough!" With that, the fiery youth turned on his heel and strode away without another word.

Later, in council with the king, Sebastian related the incident with Lothar. "Sire, they have come with an army. We don't have enough warriors here to oppose them should things get ugly."

"Ah, Sebastian, why do you think I've been king for so long? I sent for Charles the Younger and a goodly wedge of the army of the Rhine as soon as my scouts told me what forces Louis was bringing. Trust me, Charles will be here soon."

And indeed, Charles the Younger appeared the next day at the head of Charlemagne's beloved heavy cavalry of the Rhineland army, combat veterans of years of fighting in the Saxon wars and against the Vikings.

Chapter 23

The Roots of Decline

Within a week, what had begun as a peaceful council on the future of succession rapidly became an armed confrontation. There were so many troop contingents from all sides in the fields around Thionville that the king decided to hold the meeting in a nearby village green instead of in the stately royal palace built by Pepin the Short, Charlemagne's father. His son Charles the Younger sat with him, and on one side facing him sat Louis of Aquitaine and his son Lothar. On another side facing the king sat Pepin, king of Italy, Charlemagne's third son. No one knew as yet what Pepin would say or do about the proposal. But he also had brought troops, although far fewer than those of Louis and Lothar.

The day had run much of its course, with lord after lord offering an opinion on the *Divisio* proposal. Louis declined to speak, but neither did he consent to sit in council with the king in a private meeting. His son Lothar, however, had much to say, and he said it in the most belligerent and reckless way. Most of his ranting had to do with accusations that the king was violating Frankish traditions and openly robbing Aquitaine and Italy. Had this been a less precarious situation, the king would have had him arrested. As it was, Charlemagne could barely look at him and rolled his eyes in relief when Lothar arrogantly stepped away.

There followed several minutes of ominous silence while the participants processed Lothar's angry words and veiled threats.

Suddenly a rider appeared, galloping out of the ranks of the king's heavy cavalry precisely down the middle of the field. The big bay stallion labored over the newly wet ground but was powerful enough to hold his balance. The rider was in full armor, including a shield, but attached to his spear was a large white flag, which he waved continuously. Halfway through a second gallop in front of the astonished nobles, he wrenched off his helmet to reveal his face and long black hair streaked with white.

Stopping in the middle of the field in front of the king and his sons, the rider turned his face repeatedly to both sides so that there could be no doubt about who he was. Then he began to circle the horse, facing one side slowly and the other of the gathered nobles and churchmen. All could see clearly that it was Charlemagne's celebrated paladin.

Sebastian was close to madness. But he had already decided that if he died in this insane attempt to stop a looming battle single-handedly, he would cast away all doubts and force the sons to listen to reason or face terrible consequences.

"Comrades! I call for peace at this parley!" he shouted in a slow, booming voice, repeating the words several times as he rode back and forth before the gathered noblemen. No one spoke. Everyone knew him, and almost everyone respected him.

"Brothers," he began, his voice clear and calm but weighted with concern. "There are many of you here who are surprised and troubled about the largest share of the empire being given to the high king's oldest son. Why, you ask, can there be no equal sharing?" Sebastian paused to let numerous muted comments subside.

"Because, my friends," he declared, raising his voice, "There can be only *one* emperor! He is our unifier, the face of our people, and our very survival depends on unity under one ruler!"

Sebastian urged his horse closer to the gathering of clerics close to King Louis. "Our emperor rules alone by divine right, just as God rules his kingdom absolutely. God rules as the 'I Am Who Am!' Like our great God, the emperor and King of the Franks—all the Franks—embodies the law! Absolutely!" Louder comments from the assembly, some shouts of "Amen" and "Mightily!" and other belligerent cries of "Nay!" and "Not true!"

Sebastian rode back to the middle and continued addressing the whole assembly. Hot and sweaty under the heavy armor, he nevertheless spoke strongly and passionately. He could sense the tide turning somewhat, and he felt exhilarated.

"Finally, my brothers," Sebastian shouted, his face turning to Charlemagne and then to his son Louis, "the emperor cannot have rivals from within if he is to defeat our enemies from without... The emperor must make vital decisions quickly. It is imperative that he be strong enough to withstand all enemies, dissent from within, as well as threats from without.

"I ask you, therefore," Sebastian shouted as he turned Joyeuse one way and the other, "Why are so many of our warriors here today? Does anyone wish to murder kinsmen and friends, think you? If so, what has become of the Frankish people whom our great father Karl der Grosse, here present, raised into equal greatness? Do you not realize that there is no other race of people like us, like the Franks? Our empire spreads from the great ocean to the far steppes of the east. And there are no pagans left inside this entire empire! There is no power like ours. We are capable of becoming a second Rome, a Christian Rome, strengthened by our common faith!

"All this is thanks to your great king and emperor, present here and now!" He made a wide-armed gesture and a deep bow toward Charlemagne.

There were muffled cheers and only a few scattered obscenities. Sebastian was again encouraged. But he felt a tingling in his spine every time he turned his back to Lothar and the hotheads he had brought with him.

"So then, why? Why, I ask you, do we stand here before one another on the brink of destroying King Karl's great dream? You have seen how our magnanimous king has emptied his treasure chest to give the people the fruits of his glorious reign. Through you, he has given that treasure to *all* the people, highborn or low. Why did he do so? Because in his boundless wisdom, he knows that if all the people grow stronger, the realm will grow stronger—and safer—and more prosperous!

"But you, my friends—what are you doing here? There are some here with mayhem in their eyes. I say to them: Would you kill your brother? Would you ruin all the progress we Franks have made together?

He paused for a minute, continuing to circle and meet the eyes of foes and friends alike.

"If you want to fight, there are enough enemies. There are the Northmen and Danes who raid our towns on the shores of the northern sea. They even boldly threaten our coastal cities as far away as Aquitaine!" He looked pointedly at Louis and Archbishop Benedict.

"The Saracens, too, raid our southern borders. They threaten our marches in Spain and make forays over the Spanish mountains into Francia itself! How can you allow this?

"On our eastern flanks, we see more boldness from Slavic tribes who endlessly strive to make inroads into our lands.

"Oh, yes. There's plenty of fighting to be had, and we are few compared to the hosts who wish to march into our lands, take what is ours, and conquer us. And yet you stand here lusting to shed your brother's blood while the wolves are at our doors. It is madness!"

There was movement in the ranks now as warriors uneasily shook their heads and exchanged glances with each other.

"Aren't we all Franks? All brothers? Do not we all love our great land?" Moved by Sebastian's words, many lords, even those of Louis, began to look down at their feet and then up at their rivals. Even many of Louis' churchmen uttered a veiled "Amen."

"Fie on anyone who would say nay!" More affirming nods and louder affirmations.

"Yes, you know I am right! There is no need to fight. We can come to an agreement. We can have peace amongst ourselves. We *must* have peace amongst ourselves if we are to survive. Do you want to retain that Frankish greatness? Do you want to live in New Rome? Or not? Tell me! Shall we have peace together? Let me hear your voices, brothers! Shout it to me!"

A moment's hesitation. And then an explosion of raised voices. "We will have peace! We will have peace," echoed many of the nobility and a goodly number of the clerics. They shouted it repeatedly until. Finally, many crossed the small space between the groups and grasped each other by the forearms. And then there was a great roar from the masses of troops on both sides of the lines as Sebastian's words were relayed to them.

Sebastian breathed a great sigh, bowed to the king and each of the king's sons, and then galloped his horse off the green. The next day each of the sons approved the *Divisio Regnorum* of the sons, and the armies began to disperse.

As he watched them go, Sebastian mused out loud to Liudolf, "I thought I'd be a dead man by now. It's a mystery how it all worked out. Nay, it's a miracle!"

"Well," remarked Liudolf as the lines of troops marched by, "this is the first time I've seen a king's council that included so many warriors. And all of 'em heavily armed too!"

He paused for a minute as Sebastian's sunny expression turned into a frown.

"What do you mean, Liudolf? Didn't you see their faces and hear all that cheering?"

"I did, old brother. And don't get me wrong, you did an amazing job snuffing out the flames. To be sure, the soldiers on both sides were all Franks. But they usually follow their closest leaders. That's all they know. I suspect that they were just happy not to have to cut each other's throats this time.

"What's more, seems to me there weren't no smiles on the faces of Louis and Lothar, that blatherprating son of his. We're lucky he didn't start a war all by himself! I'm telling ye, we've not seen the last of him. Or his pious father!"

Sebastian momentarily dropped his eyes to the muddy ground and spat absently after the retreating troops. "You may be right, old comrade. If so, God help us."

As Sebastian watched, he was joined by both of his sons. Both were eager to speak but for different reasons.

***

"We didn't plan to be on opposite sides, Father," said Attalus as they settled into the common room of an alehouse on the way out of Thionville.

"No indeed, Father!" Karl chimed in. "How could I imagine I would be confronting my brother in a battle? I had no idea that Attalus was with Lothar."

"And I had no idea that Louis the Pious and Lothar were so at odds with our high king—enough to bring their quarrel to a fight," Attalus quickly added. "I'm with Lothar by his personal invitation. I knew and served with him when the army was still under King

Karl's command. It's entirely by accident that Karl and I find ourselves on opposite sides. Certainly not by choice."

Sebastian raised his hand to interrupt them. "Listen, Attalus, before we speak of other things, I need to talk to your brother. It's urgent. And as you are not involved, may I ask you to order our meal? We'll only be a short while." Puzzled, Attalus assented, even though he burned to know what the secret might be.

Outside, Sebastian quickly grasped Karl's shoulders and looked him square in the eye. "Now, son of mine, what are you up to? Don't lie to me. What has happened between you and Lady Adelaide?"

"What?" Karl said in bewilderment. "What are you talking about, Father?" Suddenly it dawned on the young man that Sebastian believed he was having an affair with Adelaide. He stepped back and shook off his father's hands. "Bloody hell! Who has been telling you of Adelaide and me? Father, how can you believe that I would . . . The devil, take it! There is nothing untoward between me and that lady, nothing!" he said hotly.

"She came to me not long ago because she'd left the king and had no idea what to do next. She needed to set herself up in Worms and see what she might find. I did nothing but help her get established. I escorted her around—to meet people, mostly. She paid for everything. We enjoyed each other's company, but that's it. There was absolutely no intimacy whatever! I don't need an older woman, Father. There's always plenty of pretty girls around the army."

Sebastian was limp with relief, and he embraced his son forthwith. "You can't know, Karl, how glad I am to hear this. Someone from the army who doesn't like you sent this villainous message. Someday I'll tell you how bad the situation would have been if the rumor had been true. But not tonight! Tonight, let's celebrate that we are no longer on a battlefield and the crisis is over. Let us enjoy each other! I am so glad to see you!"

Inside, the ale was already on the table, and a hot meal of fish and fried bread smeared with lard was served. They traded news as they drank, laughed, and joked at a few common memories. The conversation stayed light until after their dinner. Then Sebastian began to address the grave issues facing the realm and themselves.

"You know, my sons," Sebastian began quietly, "I hate to admit it, but what happened today may only have been the beginning of troubles between the high king and his sons. I doubt that what I did this day can ever again be repeated. Two of his sons and at least one grandson are totally dissatisfied with how the land is to be divided. We will see more of this as time goes by, and certainly whenever King Karl dies. You must be prepared for it."

"Well, from what I've seen today, I want no part of Louis - or Lothar," Attalus exclaimed. "Father, can you think of a way I might be relieved from their service?"

"I can, and I'm glad that's what you want. I'll speak to King Karl as soon as possible and ask him to assign you to work with me amongst the people. There's a good chance he'll approve it, and we could surely use you."

"Wonderful!" Attalus exclaimed. "That means all I need do now is tell my command the high king has released me to return home with you. We can provide the confirmation later. But I must leave you before the army moves to collect my things and tie up loose ends. I'll see you back at Andernach." He embraced both father and brother and quickly departed.

Good! Sebastian thought as his youngest son went out of the door. Adela would be enormously pleased, and Attalus will be saved from the clutches of that fool Lothar.

Once Attalus was gone, Karl anxiously sat Sebastian down before the fireplace and began to share some life-changing news. "Father! I have some very important news as well, and I desperately need your help. I didn't want to say anything in front of Attalus until important conditions were met and decisions were made. But here it is . . ."

In his excitement, Karl stuttered but then took a deep breath and straightened his back. "Believe it or not, the high king has offered me command of all Frankish forces from the estuary of the Rhine to the Danish border! It's the whole north! I'm to protect the ports and strengthen the fleet against the Vikings. I'm to take the fight to them if I can. It's a thousand men, Father! I don't think I can handle it. I believe he did it because he thinks I'll succeed like you always do. But I don't even know how to begin! I'm desperate to have your advice."

Sebastian rose to embrace his son. Though he wanted to shout and slap Karl on the back, he restrained himself in view of the seriousness of the situation. It was an assignment impossibly demanding and fraught with peril. Sebastian almost wished he could tell his son not to take the assignment. But he knew Karl would take it anyway.

"Well, young warrior," he began calmly, returning to his seat, "I knew something like this would happen to you someday. You deserve it. You're as brave and fit as any man I've ever seen. You even saved my life in a pitched battle. And you're a great leader. Everyone likes you, even the high king. As long as he's alive, you'll have plenty of support. And when the king does die, you'll still be all right if his successor, whoever it is, lets you alone and gives you what you need."

They sat for hours discussing the challenge Karl faced. In the end, desperately seeking something that might constitute useful advice, Sebastian summed up what his own experience had taught him about the challenge in the north.

"The Vikings are ferocious fighters, relentless, and they're not afraid of death. I'm sure you won't be able to beat them at sea. We've proven we can build ships like theirs, but we still don't have enough men who can fight as well as navigate at sea.

"However, you must try everything, and perhaps you'll be lucky enough to catch and outfight them occasionally—but only if you have a healthy advantage in numbers. My best advice is to strengthen our ports first. Fortification is the answer to everything. Everywhere! Behind strong walls, you can frustrate the Vikings with an impregnable defense. They will give up and eventually go away. You must also organize a call-up system so that you can quickly alert and bring up potential reinforcements. Every available free man must be committed to the system."

"But Father, don't you think our best Frankish troops, our heavy cavalry, can defeat them in open battle?"

"Normally, Vikings won't fight that way. They'll strike quickly, plunder, rape, and burn, and then take to their ships before you will ever be able to get there with a larger force.

"Listen, my son, I'm afraid the Vikings are just going to get stronger. If I were you, I would rely on fortress defense. And keep a reserve of cavalry in case you see an opportunity to catch them strung out and unawares. Make every lord and count in the entire north fortify his towns and villages and store enough food and water to withstand sieges."

"God help me," Karl moaned. "That will be so costly! The lords in the coastal areas are bound to resist."

"You must make them do it, Karl! Punish them if they don't. Threaten to get the king to deprive them of their lands. He will do it if he has to. All he will need to see is one more of his significant ports and towns raped and destroyed by the Viking raids."

"I hear you, Father. And thanks. I'll be sure to keep you informed. But I must leave tomorrow. If what you've told me to expect proves as bad as you think, it may be quite a while before I see you again. I want you to know that I . . . I will miss you enormously. I'm grateful for everything." They embraced again.

"Go with God, son. And don't ever let your doubts get the best of you. Press on! Above all, stay alert. At least you may be lucky enough to avoid the quarrels I know will happen between the brothers and their father if Louis is the one who becomes king. That, even more than the Vikings and Saracens, could bring down our proud land."

They were finally preparing to retire when an exhausted Liudolf barged clumsily through the inn door.

"Ach, God! Sebastian! Some of the king's troops said you might be here. Thank God I found you! You must go home at once. Adela is ill—very ill. She has been taken to Fernshanz!"

Chapter 24

All Things Come to an End

Fernshanz

"I know he will be sorry," she said to Father Pippin as he hovered over her bedside, smoothing a pillow or squeezing Adela's pale hand. "He will tear himself to pieces thinking about what he feels he should have done and didn't. He will be sick remembering how long he stayed away from me."

Adela had been attacked by some mysterious infectious disease she had picked up at one of the hospices. She lay sweating and coughing night after night until she realized the worst: she might be dying. She had immediately insisted on being transported back to Fernshanz. Milo and Father Pippin had set out with her from Andernach the next day. But by the time the boat reached Fernshanz, pneumonia had set in, and Adela could barely remain conscious. Father Pippin had been with her constantly, and now he sat at her bedside.

"Father, he will blame himself terribly, thinking he had not loved me enough. He will spend the rest of his life believing he failed me."

"My dear lady, you can be sure he loved you above all others, including the king." Father Pippin hesitated a moment and then grasped Adela's hand.

"Listen, my lady, I never told you before. I didn't think it was necessary. But Sebastian made a confession to me on that last campaign when I went with him to Saxony."

Adela tried to sit up but fell back, coughing. At length, she repeated the word. "Confession? I never knew him to go to confession. He never seemed to trust the Church enough."

"Well, he did. One night around a campfire on the trail, he spoke to me for a long time about his whole life. Perhaps it was

150

because he didn't have much hope that the mission would succeed. And he was distressed about having to leave you again so soon. I think he feared that he might die on that last campaign and never see you again."

"Father, I know you aren't supposed to reveal what someone tells you at confession. But I can't help but wish I knew what he said."

"It's all right, my dear. It wasn't a formal confession. He didn't hold me to silence or ask me for penance and absolution. But it was as sincere and complete as any I had ever heard. He bared his soul that night, and we talked for hours about everything, especially you."

"Ah, then please do share it with me, dear Father."

Pippin took a long breath and looked into Adela's eyes.

"Much of it was about regret, my dear. He rued the time lost from you more than anything else. And he regretted all the work and the fighting. He felt it had blackened his soul. All those men he killed because he was a champion, the culture in the army of wanton violence that he had to endure for so long, the hatred in his heart for evil men like Konrad.

"But most of all, he regretted the pain he caused you. The long absences, the loss of faith when he thought he would never be able to be close to you again, the affair with Lady Adelaide."

"Ha!" Adela exclaimed weakly. "I should still be angry with him about that. But I've managed to understand it. He thought he'd lost me forever, and he needed somehow to fill his loss. Besides, she and I have become good friends since then," she said with a low laugh that sounded like a tiny bell.

She turned her head aside as tears filled her eyes. "But he will be sorry for the rest of his life. I know he'll believe he should have been strong enough to love me only—and totally."

"But, my lady, don't forget the one powerful allurement that forced his absence—the awful, overpowering influence of the king and his enormous empire! Add to that Sebastian's uncommon sense of duty, and you will find the major source of his imagined neglect."

"Ah, indeed, dear Father. My lord! You would think King Karl wanted to own the world! The real guilty party is the king. He's the one who kept us apart."

"Yes, it did seem your husband could never say no to King Karl. But did he love the king more than you? Never! Of course not! There were things about the king he abhorred. And he almost left his service several times.

"But a man like Sebastian cannot live his life for duty alone. Such men must go beyond it. They must have a cause to throw their minds and bodies into without being daunted by the sacrifice. Such men are rare and different. In my experience, almost everyone needs to have a sense of belonging. They need to identify with something to feel safe and secure. You can be proud, my lady, that Lord Sebastian has dared to pursue his convictions in spite of the dangers."

"I know that, Father. You have him exactly. But there were other demons. Oddly, he always suffered from his fear of failure. He never let it show, but he eventually confided his fears to me in our most intimate moments. He had to struggle all his life to overcome some deep feelings of insecurity, which he kept hidden from all except me. I believe it may have had something to do with his being an illegitimate child."

"Ah, I did not know that. But, in spite of that, I do know that he is a man of deep faith. That night as we sat together by the fire, he told me that at the end of his life, he trusts that he will be able to feel that God will forgive him for his sins, in spite of everything, and that he has used the talents God gave him to good purpose."

"That's true, Father. In spite of the fact that he hardly ever agreed with the Church, he always believed God was there for him, ever since he was a small boy."

"My lady, your husband's strong allegiance to the king was mostly because he saw in the king a way to make incredible change. Sebastian believed in his bones that if he could just get the king to stop going to war every year, King Karl would turn his hands to doing something about the awful condition of most of the people in the land and make lasting laws on their behalf."

Adela nodded and closed her eyes.

"And, praise God," Pippin continued, "that's what seems to have happened in these late years of the king's life. I am so proud of Sebastian for his part in that profound change."

"Yes, and so am I," Adela said softly, struggling to stay conscious. "I know that Sebastian loved me more than any other human. But he also believed in the king's dreams. Now I fear he'll think that he has not only lost me but that he may live to see those dreams frustrated."

"You may be right, my dear. There are too many threats to this Francia that we love. Even if your husband has been able to avert the present crisis, the danger is high that the king's sons and grandsons will always seek power and challenge how the empire is divided during the time of succession."

"I know," Adela said, stifling a cough. "My greatest fear is that he will come to feel that the purpose God gave him to pursue, the purpose of his life, has been thwarted."

"Nay, my dear, never. His faith is strong, believe me. He'll continue to try with all his heart to change whatever he can for the better."

"But how wretched he must feel! I'm sure he's been told I'm dying. Oh, Father, he won't come in time."

She reached once again for Father Pippin's hand.

"Tell him I love him... all my heart... now... always. Not afraid. New life now, new life. Together . . . always."

Chapter 25
Letting Go

Andernach

Why do we mourn the passing of grace and beauty more than the deaths of men and women less handsome, less charming? Sebastian pondered as he rumbled along, weary and sleepless, on the sweaty backs of one galloping beast after another.

Every person is a creature of God. Beloved, no doubt equally, by God. Shouldn't they all be equally mourned? He asked himself. No, absolutely not! It's what one does with the life one is given, he reasoned. Adela is beautiful and good and has made the world far richer with that beauty and virtue.

Ah, but what about Adelaide? he considered. What about her dazzling beauty? She has thrilled hundreds of men's souls. Does that not also make the world richer—something like the beauty of an exquisitely carved stone? Or a wonderfully made quilt? Or a finely bred stallion? Wouldn't a man grieve the same for the passing of Adelaide simply because her beauty, which so many have enjoyed, also enriched the earth?

"Humbug!" Sebastian shouted aloud. "There is no one, nothing like Adela."

But he was too late no matter how hard Sebastian pushed Joyeuse and his small remuda of extra horses. Adela died the night before he arrived.

***

So far, her body had not been removed to the church, and Sebastian was able to lay his head on the bed by her shoulder and hold her cold hand. Eventually, he fell into an exhausted sleep.

When he awoke, he was stunned to see Adelaide sitting quietly in the corner of the room.

She held up a hand as if to ward off an unpleasant reaction. Then she said gently, "Sebastian, I was here before she died. I came as soon as the troops were called up. A messenger from Andernach came looking for Karl or Attalus to tell them their mother was ill. I traveled night and day, and I've been here a day or two already. Since then, I cared for her and nursed her, together with Father Pippin.

"Listen to me before you say anything. I know it will be hard for you to believe, but Adela and I were able to reconcile, even to love each other in those last hours." She paused a moment to let her words sink in.

"But why . . . why did you come?"

"My dear, dear man, don't you know that Adela has always been one of the most important people in my life, even when I hated her? She's the only other woman who has shared your love. And you are the only man I ever really loved." Sebastian lowered his head and waved a hand as if to dismiss the thought.

"Sitting here in the dark after she died, I realized that death has a way of banishing conflict. I only felt love for her."

Sebastian looked up in surprise. It was a sight he had seldom seen. Adelaide was crying.

"She changed me, Sebastian. She told me at the end that I was her sister. She even said I should look after you! What generosity! What kindness! She was not only thinking of you, she was thinking of me—her rival, her enigma."

She moved closer and sat on the other side of the bed, with Adela in between them. She took Adela's other hand. "I once hated her because she stood between you and me. But I came to see that you and I were not meant to be. I know that she will always be the only woman in your heart. But now I feel I can share your love for her. I'm a far better person because of her. I know you'll find that hard to believe. But perhaps one day I'll be able to show you."

"But what now, Adelaide? What will you do?"

"I have no idea. For once in my life, I don't have a plan. The only thing I've been able to think about is Adela. But now . . . I can't go back to the king. I think he's a bit insulted that I left without his permission. But I just needed something else. And the army is in the field.

"I was so mad at you when you rejected me that I was ready to take up with one of your sons. But neither of them would have me—not that I tried very hard. Besides, now that I really know what kind of woman she was, I wouldn't do anything she wouldn't like. I assured her there was nothing between me and either of the boys."

Sebastian peered into her eyes to see if this was another of Adelaide's clever deceptions. What he saw was a dejected woman staring down at the body of a friend, still weeping, spiritless, at the end of her rope.

He hesitated, suddenly aware that what he was about to say would seem entirely incongruous, shocking to many, even the king. But, he thought, what would Adela do? He knew right away.

"Listen, Adelaide. The world is going to fall apart out there soon. No one will be safe. In spite of our little victory at Thionville, chaos is beginning already. Neither the emperor nor Louis and Lothar give a damn for one another, and I'm sure we're in for some very hard times over the next years. You are going to need a port in the coming storm.

"Besides, I owe you. You saved my bloody neck in Constantinople! You can stay here—or at any of my manor houses—as long as you like. Adela would want it."

Adelaide uttered a low, mournful wail and buried her face in Adela's outspread hair. She cried for several minutes. Her shoulders shook, and she clutched the pillow as if to hold onto it for life.

Sebastian was astonished to see how undone she was. It was a side of Adelaide he had never thought to see. He put his hand on her shoulder and murmured, "It's all right, it's all right. We both must grieve." He helped her sit upright and gave her a cloth to wipe her glistening face.

"I mean it, Adelaide. You can stay—at least until you find a new path for your life—however long it takes. This is what Adela would say. And I say it too! You will be welcome as long as you have need."

He paused momentarily to give her a chance to recover her composure. "The steward will find you some rooms. Do you still have attendants?"

"Just Ajax," she intoned wearily. "My attendant ladies found some soldiers who would marry them. Ajax only lives to protect me."

"Wonderful," Sebastian groaned. "Try to keep him from murdering somebody."

"He will be no problem."

"And Adelaide, you mustn't hope that there can ever be anything between us again, right?"

"Oh, Sebastian, don't be silly. I'm tired of all that. I've had enough men to last me forever. Besides, you're too old and battered up. Have you looked at yourself lately?" she said with a wry half-smile.

"But I will love you still," she added sincerely. "Just in a different way."

***

As she had wished, Adela was buried next to the Fernshanz chapel beside Hugo, her little son by Konrad, and Sebastian's parents, Ermengard and Attalus. For once, the whole family managed to assemble there. And the whole village and all the people of the surrounding area crowded as far as they could into the small churchyard to pay their respects to a woman they had all learned to love.

Father Pippin said the Mass and gave the eulogy. None of the family spoke. All felt that Adela was simply beyond words. Sebastian did see that there was a feast for everyone. He opened all the storehouses to do so, and many of the people stayed for three days after the funeral.

After the first day, Sebastian disappeared and was gone for a week. No one knew where.

Chapter 26

Requiem

Sebastian stole away in the middle of the night with only Joyeuse and a few provisions. He reached his destination just as the rising sun bathed the old cabin in a golden beam. The sudden light seemed to offer a welcome.

He dismounted and tied up the horse in slow motion, still staring at the cabin door, expecting she might fling it open at any moment and run to him. It was all he could do to open the door and go in slowly.

Memories of the last time they were together in that place flooded into his head as he took in its warm simplicity. He closed his eyes, the better to see her. He even imagined he could smell her perfume. When he opened his eyes again to the empty room, he felt a stab of pain. Her loss was like a crucifixion. He lay down on the rough blankets where they had slept together and wept.

He mourned for several days, hardly eating or drinking anything. He walked tens of aimless miles in the forest. Once, he took a long ride to a small brook where he and Adela had enjoyed a picnic with the boys. He smiled at the memory of roughhousing with them and everyone singing together.

He fell into the habit of speaking to Joyeuse as they rode through the silent forest. "It was Adela who taught those boys how to be good men," he asserted for the thousandth time, "thoughtful, open-hearted, honorable. She taught them how to enjoy life and be grateful for it. She gifted them with a piece of her soul."

The horse pricked up his ears the better to listen.

"She gave me life, as well!" he said aloud as if he had suddenly become aware of it. "She taught me how to laugh and enjoy pleasure and even how to weep without shame and be sorry. And what she taught me about love was like knowing what was in the heart of God.

"To be sure, we were apart for too long. But when we were together, it was the best of times! Wasn't it, old friend? We filled each other up. We ate from the same bread of life."

Joyeuse issued a low rumble in his throat as if to agree.

Gradually as the days passed, he began to feel less sorrow and even a sense of peace. He forced himself to remember the good of his life with Adela and not wallow in the sorrow of her death. He tried to remember everything they had ever done together, even what she had said and how she had said it. He remembered her kindness, her unselfish daily life, her luminous beauty.

Ah, yes, her beauty! He felt again the ecstasy of seeing her after a long separation. How lovely she was! But he knew she treated her beauty as if it didn't matter. She never even acknowledged—or refused to know—that she was so beautiful. But everyone was aware that she was—in every bone, and especially in her heart and soul.

Eventually, by filling his mind with all the good that Adela had been and how grateful he was for their life together, he came to a sense of peace, of gratitude. Father Pippin admitted to him that Adela was in pain in those last days, but she remained unafraid of death. She only considered it a door to go through, beyond which lay another time, another place. And she was certain that was where she would find him again.

Finally, Bardulf and Drogo tracked him down. He returned with them reluctantly when they insisted that the new "poor people plan," as Bardulf described it, desperately needed his leadership. He vowed to visit the cabin whenever he came back to Fernshanz. Then he immersed himself in work.

Months and even a few years would pass before he needed to go to the king again.

Chapter 27

A Bizarre Proposal

Andernach

Meanwhile, Adelaide had moved herself to Andernach. Life on the Rhine was apt to be livelier by far than the remote woods and fields of Fernshanz. Despite her hard life and many adventures, she changed only slightly from year to year. She had always been physically active and still enjoyed robust health. Her brain never stopped working. With Milo's help, she learned to read and read avidly whenever she could get a book or a new parchment. It became her chief defense against boredom. She worked hard to retain her opulent figure with long walks and diet and, for the most part, succeeded. Her ability to charm people with her fabled stories and incisive wit remained undiminished.

The problem was her reputation. Despite the fundamental changes in her life, they followed her no matter where she went in Francia. She was known all over the realm as a predator of young men and a woman who thought and acted like a lord but had nothing of her own. Her brother was still alive and had children, so there was no chance of her having her estate. She was simply Count Sebastian's "ward." Almost everyone thought she was his secret mistress.

By default, Adelaide came to be in charge of Andernach. Everyone else in the family was ordinarily away doing the business of Charlemagne's bequest. Sebastian was glad to give her something to do, and she ran the place grandly. Gradually she gained more and more visitors, at least those of the male kind.

Adelaide was irresistibly entertaining. She was fun. Lords and notables of the army and even of the Church often stopped for a night or two at Andernach or even a week while making their way up or down the Rhine. There were opportunities for festivities and receptions. Gradually, Adelaide overcame her clouded reputation. In spite of that, she was not happy.

When Sebastian returned to Andernach one day after almost a year on the road, she confronted him. "Well, finally! I thought I'd never see you again. If it weren't for the occasional visits of Milo and Attalus, I'd never even know if you were still alive!"

Though she scolded him, Adelaide was always thrilled to see him. Her stomach never failed to cramp whenever he appeared. Of course, she hid her feelings well and jousted wittily with him. But looking at him for the first time in a while, she would have to turn her head away lest he notices her face and neck turning bright pink. For her, he was still 'a beautiful man', even with all his scars and the white streaks in his hair. "I still love him, dammit!" she would say. "When will this ancient passion ever fade?"

"Well, madam, from what I've heard, you don't need me. You are the toast of the Rhineland. Everybody I've run into seems to have been here once or twice, and they all say the hospitality was superb and the entertainment and food amazing. And that's fine with me; the more the lords have a good time at my expense, the more they will be willing to open their tight fists for our work."

"Yes, well, I had to do something. This place is certainly not Constantinople, mind you, but at least it keeps me busy—some of the time."

Later that night, they sat together around the fireplace in the middle of the great room. Adelaide seemed anxious and kept getting up to pour wine or stoke the fire. Initially, the conversation was all about the details of daily life at Andernach or about Sebastian's work on the road.

Finally, after copious cups of wine, Adelaide got up and stood in front of Sebastian, arms akimbo, frowning, her face distorted with pain.

"Sebastian! I'm going insane! What I do here doesn't amount to a pig's fart—naught! The estate runs itself; the stewards take care of it. The occasional parties are all right, but most of them are boring. The men are Franks, not Byzantines. Most of the men who come here cannot even read. All they know about is the bloody land and the eternal fighting.

"Lately, I've been having to keep some of them from devouring each other, depending on whether they are for the king or one of his sons. I tell you, Sebastian, this land is heading toward serious troubles. There is so much division! I'm sure there's a big storm brewing! On top of all that worry, almost every man who comes here thinks he can get me to sleep with him, as old as I have become! I hate that old game. I'm sick of it!"

She buried her face in her hands and turned away toward the fire. Sebastian was astonished. It was very rare to see any tears in Adelaide's eyes.

He rose and put an arm around her shoulders. "Here now, sit down, dear girl. It's all right. Let me help you. Tell me what I can do."

"There's nothing you can do! I'm just going to turn into a pile of hardened bones. I have nothing of importance to do. I don't even have any friends. The only person who loves me is bloody Ajax." Her shoulders shook, and she turned away again to subdue a sob.

Sebastian rose with a look of alarm. "Oh, I didn't have any idea you felt this way." He took her in his arms and rocked her like a child, murmuring, "It's all right. You will be all right. Everything is all right! You're strong, and you're healthy. People do like you. All of my family likes you."

She settled a bit, and finally, Sebastian said quietly, "And I still love you, my dear. Granted, it's become a different kind of love now. But you and I were once very close. We left indelible marks on each other. Those can't be removed in spite of all the time and circumstances that have passed. After all this time, we're part of one another, in a way. A good way."

She turned to look into his eyes and saw that he was really sincere, not just pitying her. She squeezed his neck and told herself, "It's not the love I want and likely never will be. Still, it's him. It's Sebastian, and I will take what I can get of him!"

After a moment, she let him go and turned away, saying candidly, "Well, yes, I admit that must be true after all this time. But I'm not your wife. I know I can never take Adela's place. And I know you feel guilty for ever having loved me. That's why you stay away so much. In your heart, you wish me gone."

"Not so, dear Adelaide!" he erupted emphatically. "Listen to me! I've gotten used to your being here. I'm glad about it. You add to my life as you do to my whole family. We can't do without you now." He released her and gazed, elbows on knees, into the fireplace. "But you are right—I do mourn my wife still. The grief never goes away. And I keep wishing I'd been different for her. I wish I'd been what she wanted and deserved to have."

"You were, Sebastian," she said, putting an arm around his shoulders. "Trust me," she said, deciding suddenly to allay his pain by making light of her passion. "I loved you for about an hour," she lied, "as passionately as I could. But then we both moved on. Adela was not just Adela, she was you! I realize that now. She was your other half. Be glad! Most people search all their lives for their other half without finding it. How could I compete with that?"

"Thanks for saying that, Adelaide. It's exactly how we came to feel about each other. And that's why I still feel so strongly that I must do penance for neglecting the gift she was to me. That's why I work so hard and am gone so much. It's not you." He paused for a long while before taking her by the shoulders to look into her eyes.

"And there's something else. Because we are so close and because of what you've told me tonight, it's become something of the highest importance for me."

"Uh-oh, Adelaide said, shifting uneasily. "This is going to be something to do with me, isn't it? Something hard, I'd wager."

"No, it's not bad. It's something that could be very good indeed for you – just as it was for me."

"What in the world...."

"Shh, let me tell you. After that business in Constantinople, the murder I committed, and what I thought was your betrayal, I fell into a profound depression. By the time I got to Jerusalem, I was ready to kill myself. I almost did. But Milo saw what was happening to me and made me go with him to meet a seer, a medicine woman. It was Magdala."

"You mean our Magdala, Milo's wife?"

"Hmm, I guess they are married by now, though we don't seem to have had a ceremony. Magdala is very different. She's quite spiritual but doesn't care much about anyone else's customs. No matter.

"I finally agreed to meet with her out of love for Milo. He wanted me to go earnestly, and I couldn't refuse him. At first, I thought Magdala was a charlatan, a kind of witch-woman who knew a few healing tricks so that the simple folks she treated thought she could do miracles." He got up and began to pace back and forth around the fireplace.

"But as I got to know her, I discovered that the miracles she performed were mainly due to her profound understanding of life and death. For several days, I watched her healing people. I saw how much of her healing was about comforting people with her intense compassion, renewing their faith, and, on occasion, helping them enter into death.

"I had several sessions with her, and then she gave me a mission: I was to go out by myself and spend several days and nights alone pondering some questions she gave me."

Adelaide was fully engaged at this point and anxiously awaiting the story's outcome. She stood up and stopped Sebastian in mid-pace, grasping both his hands. "What questions, Sebastian! What mission?"

He took her by the arm and began to walk with her around the room. "She sent me out into the desert to be alone, to examine my life and try to find my true self. She warned me that if a man can discover who he really is at his core, it will either be the most painful experience of his life or the best. She told me I must fast for three days and drink very little water. Finally, she told me to contemplate the meaning of love and the meaning of death." He paused and turned away from her to warm his hands at the fire.

"Well, what? Speak up! Did you find the answers?" Adelaide demanded eagerly. "Did you change because of that? What? You can't just leave it like that!"

"My dear Adelaide. I think it's better if I don't tell you everything right now."

"Why, for Christ's sake?" she cried out, digging her sharp fingernails into his arms. "This may be what I've been looking for all my life—some real purpose."

"Because I want you to see Magdala yourself. I think she might have the same kind of effect on you that she had on me. I was able to change completely because of her. If I could do that, at least you should give it a try. What do you have to lose?" He was startled to see her shoulders shake as she turned away, trying not to shed more tears.

She straightened her back and turned again to him. "It's odd," she said, wiping at her eyes, "I've had the strangest feeling— something like awe, ever since I met Magdala, and she helped me recover from my illness. I keep asking myself, could this mysterious young woman actually change my life? It puts a chill running down my backbone just to think of it. And then I think - if she could change a strong warrior like you, why not me? I'm ready, Sebastian! Go ahead! Tell her to come and help me. I will do the best I can to believe and make it so."

Chapter 28

Becoming Rich

It took Sebastian a few weeks to arrange a meeting. He brought Magdala back to Andernach for a welcome rest and closed the place to visitors. On the second day, he brought her to Adelaide. Fully aware of what Sebastian was asking of her, Magdala wasted no time taking Adelaide for a brisk walk to a brook deep in the nearby woods where there would be no interruptions.

As they sat facing each other on a blanket by the water, Magdala took Adelaide's hands in her own.

"I'm not exactly sure, dear Adelaide, why we are here or what it is that you're actually seeking. Lord Sebastian tells me you are unhappy. Well, if I am to help you, I must know who you are, my sister. Let me ask you first, what is your opinion of yourself?"

Adelaide was taken aback. She began to wonder if her willingness to see Magdala had been misplaced. "Ach, good Lord! What is this? I don't want to talk about myself. I'm not ready to confess all my sins to you like a priest and repent for being such a wicked woman!" She barely stopped herself from expressing her irritation at such an invasive question. But, thinking twice about the question, she replied after a minute's silence.

"I'm sorry," she said with a sigh. "I'm just never asked provocative questions like that!"

"I don't want to know about your sins, dear one. I want to know about you, how you see yourself, why you are unhappy with yourself."

"Well, that's all right, I suppose. But now that I think of it, I don't know, Magdala. I've never spent much time thinking about who I am. You might think I'm afraid I will find some appalling answer lurking in my soul's shadows, but I've never even thought about it."

Magdala kept a good grip on Adelaide's hands and nodded knowingly. "Go on, try to think about it now. We might discover why you feel so dissatisfied," she said softly.

Adelaide paused again for a long moment. "Well, I suppose my story begins with the circumstances I grew up in. I have always wanted a larger life than what was set up for me. I had no mother. My father didn't know what to do with me, and he never really bothered to talk to me in any depth. He was gone a great deal, soldiering with the king. And when he was home, the house would be full of men. I learned at an early age that they were mostly predatory and rapacious. So I strove to manage them by sharpening my tongue and making them feel ridiculous or small."

"Did you not have any grandmothers or aunts or any women friends?" Magdala prompted with a gentle smile.

"I did not. My female relatives were all dead, and most women avoided coming to my father's manse."

"Why did you not choose an acceptable mate among your father's associates?"

"I never considered the loutish soldiers Father brought home to be acceptable. I just studied how to control them so that they would do my bidding or leave me alone." She withdrew her hands from Magdala's and rose to stand and stare into the crystal-clear stream and listen to its faint bubbling noise. The sound was calming.

"I struggled to have people admire me, or at least be wary of me," she said, almost whispering as if just discovering a fault. "I've always been considered quite beautiful. My best assets were a sensual face and a voluptuous body. I wanted to be free, as my father and brother were, to do whatever I wanted. So I used those assets to good advantage wherever I was."

"Looking back, do you regret how you spent your life?"

"There never seemed to be any other course, Magdala," she said, turning around. "I refused to live the dull life of a Frankish wife. And I could not go off to war every year as the men did. So I played around, using this man or that to get what I wanted. I even used Sebastian to help me find a way out of my circumstances." She flumped down again on the blanket.

"I'm ashamed to say it, but I beguiled a good man like Sebastian into promising to marry me. He was an easy mark since he was full of suffering after the king gave Adela to Konrad. Then, God forgive me, I abandoned him for Simon, Sebastian's friend, who was able to take me far away from Francia. Eventually, I found myself in Constantinople, where I became a famous dancer and courtesan."

"Ah! The place where you learned to dance." Magdala added in appreciation.

"I was quite happy there—until Sebastian stepped back into my life. His sudden appearance made me realize that he was the best man I ever met and that I loved him and wanted him as my husband. But he refused to stay with me in Constantinople. At that point, everything fell apart, and I had to flee for my life."

"Yes, I know that story," Magdala replied. She paused for a minute and began again carefully. "I think you have told me enough that I may be able to see why you are so unhappy. Do you wish to have my answer?"

Adelaide was surprised and uncomfortable at having revealed so much of what she thought of herself. Nevertheless, she was eager to know what Magdala thought. "Oh, yes, please," she said with a faint note of uncertainty. "For heaven's sake!"

Magdala stood up and then fell on her knees, hands clasped together in front of her. "Come, kneel with me here. She took Adelaide's hands, closed her eyes, and took a deep breath. Then she looked directly into Adelaide's eyes, "To begin with, my dear Adelaide, what happened in your life to create the woman you became was not your fault. You had no guidance, mother, or kin to give you a sense of security and moral support." Adelaide gave a slight nod.

"But I also think you are exceptionally gifted, my lady. You have a remarkable mind and an imaginative personality. You are creative and inventive. These are precious assets. You could have used them in a much different way, however."

Adelaide raised her eyebrows.

"Instead, as you have said, you always wanted people to admire you. So you dressed splendidly and expensively. You absorbed yourself in caring about what others thought of you. You chose to use your physical allure and talents for an adventurous life of pleasure and power. What I see is a woman who has been mostly self-centered all her life."

Adelaide winced but managed to hold her peace.

"On another level of great significance, you seem to have abandoned any kind of moral standards or principles of conduct . . . or spirituality. I know that is hard for you to hear, and I'm sorry if my words offend you."

Adelaide sighed deeply, covered her eyes uncharacteristically, and bent her head. "No! No, Magdala," she said quietly. "That's the right picture." After a moment, she raised a face contorted with pain. "You're the only one who has dared to tell me that about myself. You are right. But it's the only life I knew. I see it with different eyes now that I've grown older, and things have changed for me. There are people I admire, people who are genuine and without deceit. I . . . I want to be like that. But . . . but I don't know how."

"Wait. Give me a few moments."

Magdala needed more than a few moments. There was a long silence while she closed her eyes and became quite still. At last, she took a deep breath and returned to an anxious Adelaide.

"Listen, my poor dear. What I am going to propose to you may be the answer you desperately need. It is a way for you to become rich." Adelaide drew back in surprise.

"Not with money," Magdala said quickly. "This way will be extremely difficult. You say you want a completely different way of life. To have it, you will have to change yourself fundamentally— completely." Adelaide drew back a bit and raised a hand to her mouth as if she were about to receive a prison sentence.

"It may require fearful sacrifice—as bad as cutting off an arm, perhaps. It will require more courage and discipline than you have ever had to summon. And you must be prepared for a long battle. That may be the hardest thing."

Adelaide turned away suddenly and began to weep and hang her head. Eventually, she turned back and replied, "I believe . . . No! I know you are right. But what is it? What can I do?"

169

Magdala reached across to hold Adelaide's hands again. She said gently, "What I think you need most is humility."

"But what is that?" Adelaide cried. "Must I humiliate myself? Must I become like a serf or a slave?"

"Not at all, my dear. Humility is not at all the same as humiliation. What you must do to be humble is to accept that you must be yourself—no better, no worse than anyone else. Don't ever say you are something you are not or say you can do something you cannot. But also, don't deny the good things you are as a person and your abilities and virtues. Look down on no one. Look up to those who can teach you something of value. Humility is simply a reverence for truth. If you add compassion to that, you will change your life."

Adelaide remained with her head bent, eyes closed, biting the edges of her lips. Finally, she said, "I can see you are right, Magdala. But it would be like cutting away a huge part of myself. It's such a different way to look at things. I don't even know how to begin. As for a moral code or spirituality, I don't know that I have any of that."

"I will tell you, my dear. In spite of your fears, I am offering you a way to become truly rich. But it means you must abandon yourself and give what's left of your life to others. If you are truly sincere about wanting to change your life, join us in our work!"

"What?" Another moment passed as Adelaide dealt with the surprise. "I don't know anything about your work except that you work among the common people, the poor, even the serfs. I know it's a demanding, ugly, dirty job, and I'm afraid of such people! They're full of disease, aren't they? And they're filthy! I have absolutely nothing in common with them. Besides, I don't know a thing about healing—even if I could stand to be around them."

"You don't have to. But you are right, and there is risk. You must reconcile yourself to that. As for work, there will be plenty of work that you could do right away without any training. You could provide supplies, mop the floors, clean up the tables after patients, hold the hands of people who are dying."

"Mercy! I can't do that! I would abhor it! I probably would faint away at the first sight of blood."

"Come now, you're a strong woman. You're smart, and you learn quickly. I believe you've seen plenty of blood during the course of your audacious life. From what I've heard about your survival through the years, you can do anything you make up your mind to do.

"Yes. You will hate the work at first. But that is exactly what will make you humble. You said you wanted to change, didn't you? Then you must absorb yourself in something entirely different—try helping others instead of yourself! That's how you will become rich!

"Of course, it will be painfully hard at first. But, perhaps, the more you do it—if you do it—the stronger you will grow and the more content you will find yourself to be. It's a mystery, but that is what happens."

Chapter 29

Metamorphosis

Adelaide did become stronger. She began like a gambler preparing for an all-or-nothing venture. She threw away all her fine gowns and shoes, gave her jewelry away, and disappeared from the friends and social life she knew. She left strict orders for the servants at Andernach to say that she had simply gone away and specified no particular destination.

Then she went to join Milo and Magdala in their work. She did exactly what they asked of her—any menial task, any dirty detail. Ajax loomed over her, clearly befuddled and anxious about the woman he cared for more than his life. But he pitched into the work beside her, doing any of the heavy lifting and most of the really dirty work. He even disposed of the frequent corpses that too often coincided with the work of healing.

She moved from hospice to hospice in the cities, towns, and villages of Francia, wherever there seemed to be the most need. When Sebastian saw her for the first time, he didn't recognize her, dismissing her as some sweaty, stringy-haired, sunburned village wench hired to do a bit of cleanup. That is until he spotted Ajax. His jaw dropped as if he had seen a demon, and then he whipped around to take in the room again.

Adelaide didn't stop mopping the gritty floor of the makeshift clinic. She simply said, "Don't!" when Sebastian reached out to her. Then she said, "Go outside and wait for me until I finish this floor."

He paused to look askance at Milo and Magdala, who simply shrugged their shoulders, and then walked meekly out of the clinic to wait.

She finally appeared, sweat staining the armpits of her simple dress and dirt between the toes of her sandaled feet. She sat beside him on the bench and looked him in the eye. Suddenly, she broke out laughing, and it was the old hearty laugh he had heard so often when she was having high fun in grand and elegant places.

"Sebastian, my darling boy! What's the matter with you? Don't you recognize your old lover?" She laughed again at his open-mouthed discomfort.

"Oh, Sebastian, stop gawking! I'm fine. Never been better, as a matter of fact. What did you expect to find—me bending over a stricken peasant dressed in a ball gown?"

Sebastian pulled himself together and managed a smile while he reached over to take her calloused hand.

"Jesus, Mary, and Joseph, Adelaide! I knew you were doing good work with Milo and Magdala. They sent me an occasional note, which always included good words about you and what an asset you and Ajax have become."

"Yes, well, it's true. Ajax does much of the work I am charged with doing. But I often get a chance to look over the real healers' shoulders and witness the miracles they're performing. They are amazing! Everywhere they go, they bring goodness and hope." She laughed again and squeezed his hand.

"I am learning, Sebastian, and I love it!"

"But . . . but you look so different. I didn't even recognize you at first."

"I don't care," she said nonchalantly. "That's hardly what matters to me anymore. Guess what? I want to become a healer, even a doctor, like those high-minded, precise Jewish doctors who know how to cut into and cure a human body."

"Shh, my dear, you mustn't say that out loud. They are forbidden by our laws to do such things."

"Well, that is nonsense! I've seen them save the lives of people who were otherwise doomed to die. Anyway, I don't go around telling anybody about the wonderful work they do. I'm just telling you that I want to do it. It's my new ambition!" Sebastian couldn't help but be captured by her enthusiasm and energy. He smiled broadly and then laughed with her.

"Meanwhile, I just do what is needed—Ajax and me, we're a good team. And I couldn't give a tinker's damn for what anyone thinks!"

Later, when there was a good moment, Sebastian took Magdala aside. "You did it, Magdala! You cured her. You made her happy, or at least content. She has something to live for now. Just as you did with me. I'm so beholden to you, so grateful!"

"Well, my dear father-in-law," she said, taking both his hands and placing them on her belly, "you will have more than that to thank me for—and your son Milo, of course. We are married. Father Pippin said the mass and presided over the ceremony the last time we were at Andernach. And now we are joyously expecting our first child, your grandchild, perhaps the first of many. Milo says we must call this first one Sebastian!"

"Ach, don't lay such a curse on him! But I am enormously pleased. I can't think of anything better than this new babe for all of us. But now you will have to come off the road and return to Andernach for the birth."

"Nonsense, Father-in-Law. In the bleak lands where I grew up, a mother-to-be might work all morning in the fields or garden, lay down her tools at noon, have the baby, often cutting the cord herself, and then go back to work for the afternoon, with the baby in a sack tied around her neck! I certainly will not stop until I have to. Whatever for?"

Chapter 30

Rex Mortuus Est!

Aachen, January 28, 814

The wild ride to Aachen took several days through punishing storms and heavy snow. Sebastian had to thaw out frequently and rest Joyeuse, the fifth stallion of that famous name, until they reached the Rhine crossing on the road to Aachen. Once across the river by barge, he was met by troops with fresh horses stationed there by the king to escort him to the palace. His arrival was none too soon.

The king's bed in his inner chambers looked like a big, rough-sided crib with a high back and a primitive wooden toilet chair aligned beside it. Serfs hourly removed the chamber pot beneath it. The bed was large enough for a wife or a mistress and several children, and it took up a sizeable portion of the room where he worked and slept. It was obvious that Charlemagne did not like sleeping alone, as several other straw-filled mattresses lay on the floor around a large fireplace, blazing at the moment at full capacity in an effort to hold back the piercing cold.

Sebastian found the king propped up on a bolster with several pillows under and around his body. For a minute, he didn't think he was the king. The man in the bed wore a peasant's long tunic and a coarse wool cap. The only thing that implied it was the king was the familiar old blue cloak he always wrapped around himself when on campaigns. He wore no crown or diadem, and his long, tousled hair and untrimmed beard made him look like a madman.

Sebastian observed him for a moment from the door in profound sadness. In spite of the thick canvas mattress filled with soft wool and moss, the king was obviously in considerable pain. He thrashed about, shifting one leg after the other from one side of the bed to the other and slapping weakly at the pillows as if to drive away the ache. But he straightened at once when Sebastian was announced.

"Well, ye certainly took your bloody time getting here," the king croaked. "Suppose I'd died before you came?"

"I humbly beg your pardon, my liege. I came as fast as a good horse could bring me."

"Yes, yes, of course ye did. But I wanted ye here weeks ago. I wanted to visit with you again about the old times. But you waited too long, damn ye. And now I'm dying, Sebastian! Imagine that!"

Sebastian bowed low as he approached the bed. He had been thinking of nothing else but the dying king since he'd left Fernshanz. And he could not "imagine" a single hopeful outcome.

"Come here, you devil, and give me a hug." Sebastian gladly complied but was stifled by the foul odor coming from the king's unwashed body. Ach! What has happened to the man who gloried in the feel and cleanliness of water? Not long ago, he swam every day.

"Well, dammit, sit here on the bed with me. There's no time to talk leisurely about our gallant past. We must spend what time is left to talk about the bloody future and what I need you to do from now on."

Oh no. He's going to give me a new mission—even on his deathbed! Sebastian thought dismally.

"I already know you won't agree with everything I have to ask," the king said as if he had read Sebastian's mind. "But, by God, I'm the king, and you must heed my words—even if I'm dying. You hear me?"

"Yes, my king. I've always heard and heeded. You know that."

"Well, this time, there are many things. What I've got to say won't be easy to hear. In fact, these last tasks may be the hardest things I've ever asked you to do." As he spoke, the king heaved with an effort to take a deep breath.

Sebastian almost groaned. He cringed inwardly, his belly churning and his heart already beginning to pound. It was doubly alarming because, this time, the king had said it would be hard! In the past, he had always claimed, "It will be easy for you. It won't take much of your time." What could be harder than all the years he had spent as the king's paladin in the Saxon wars, in Brittany, Pannonia, Denmark, and the three years in the East where the king's business had put him and his companions at risk daily? All those missions, pernicious to himself, he had endured, all that time away from home because the king assured him it was absolutely necessary and would be easy!

Charlemagne paused and gazed out of the window at the approaching gloomy night. His head drooped, and his whole body slumped into the pillows. His once powerful arms trembled as he reached for Sebastian's hand, and his voice quavered as he thought of his death.

"God's blood, man," he said finally, "I wasn't through with this life, don't ye know? Not by a long measure! Let me tell you something, old lad, I don't want to die! Life on this earth is good! If it weren't for the blasted pain, I scarcely would want to go to heaven!"

He looked up beseechingly, and Sebastian was shocked to see something like fear in the old king's eyes. "I'm not sure our blessed Lord is going to have me anyway," he said. Sebastian waved a hand as if dismissing the thought.

"Oh yes, but he will, by thunder!" The king rallied and raised himself enough to utter a weak shout. "I'm his bloody David, ain't I? I made half the world Christian for him, din't I?" He fell back again into the pillows.

"Uh . . . well, yes, you did, my king."

Sebastian's back was to the fire, and the king bent forward to see him better. "You never really approved of me, did you, you righteous scoundrel," the king jibed in mock anger.

"Not so, my liege," Sebastian replied indignantly. "You know I always loved you and followed your will."

"Yes, but you always had your precious 'reservations,' and you always tried to get me to do it all differently. Well, I didn't have the bloody time—nor the inclination!" He paused and gazed again into the fireplace as if he could conjure words from the flames.

"But now I'm thinking you might have been right—at least some of the time. Don't smirk, you bugger! Well, you can bloody well watch me die. You'll be sorry enough when I'm gone, and things begin to fall apart. That simpering priest son of mine, Louis, the so-called Pious, will never be able to hold it all together. And God help the Franks if Louis dies and that crazed upstart Lothar comes to the throne!"

Sebastian was determined not to be drawn again into discussing the brutal politics of succession. It would only make the king angry and rob him of his remaining strength.

"I'm dying. Sebastian, Charles the Younger, and Pepin are gone. Dead they are, just when I need 'em. Why did God take them, the good sons, and leave me with the runt of the litter? Louis! And he doesn't have a clue about what to do—except go to Mass for half a day and pray it'll all go away!"

For a long minute, he was silent, but then he began to speak softly, almost apologizing to Sebastian.

"I know what I'd do if I were young and sound of body. I'd bloody well go to the source of our problems and invade Denmark! Denmark's the problem now. If I could, I'd wipe 'em out, burn their towns, chop the head off every buggering leader I could find."

The spontaneous tirade made the king cough violently again. As Sebastian came over to thump him on the back, he could see red specks on the pillows around the old autocrat's head.

But the king rallied once more and suddenly took a different tack as he looked at his long-time favorite. "I made you do so many dangerous things, old lad. I'm sorry for that now. But you have to understand why I did it. I'm the king, b'God! And 'twas God Almighty who made me the king and not my brother Carloman."

"Aye, my liege, assuredly," Sebastian hastened to say, listening with rising astonishment as the king revealed more of his deepest convictions, the Holy Grail of his life. "And it was God himself," the king declared passionately, "who told me to save this land for the Christians against the pagan savages. And I did it, by Jesus! That's been a heavy burden, Sebastian, my son. But, by thunder, a king rules by divine right and the rood of Christ, don't he? And what he has to do is in the name of God! Like David, I had to do God's will and by whatever means at hand!

"That's why I used you so hard. You were the Sword of God in my right hand, so to speak."

Sebastian's jaw dropped as he heard this rare unbosoming. But what the king said next made his dumbstruck paladin sit up and listen with awe.

"But God gave you a command as well! He said to you, 'Make the king seek peace. Teach him to seek a different way to do my will.' And I did change, din't I? Several times and more as I drew toward the end. It wasn't what I liked to do. My heavy cavalry was always a quicker way to solve problems. But you made me know I needed to begin doing things differently—set a better example, so to speak, for them that come after me."

Taking a deeper breath, he lowered his voice and whispered, "And because I had a great deal of killing to atone for."

Sebastian reached over to take the king's hand. He could see by the firelight that the great monarch was weeping.

The king's grip tightened momentarily, and he blurted out: "You must help him, Sebastian. You must be Louis's advisor as you have been mine." Sebastian's mouth fell open, and he closed his eyes. This is what he feared most, almost feeling sick. I've got to tell him no this time, he resolved. Once and for all! It's too much! How could he think that one man could do all that he asked? And even to attempt to do it, he would have to abandon their great work with the people.

"And, listen, to do that," the king went on, speaking intensely, "you'll need the Church. You must go to the Church right away after I'm dead. Oh, I know you've had your grievances with it. But I have made it very powerful and influential. It's become a bulwark of sorts to civil conflict, and they—the bishops and such—agree with me wholeheartedly that there should be more good done for the people. That's excellent! That's very good! We're together, at least on that. And that must continue, above all!

"Go to the pope, go to the archbishops! Make 'em aware of the dangers that Louis will face. Make 'em swear to help him. But continue to protect the pope as I have always done.

"We mustn't make a mistake and think that the Church doesn't matter. The Church legitimizes the king! If it says, '*Deus lo*

179

volt,' the people believe that I am king by the will of God and that no mere man may even attempt to change that! Even more so now, the people must believe that Louis will also be king by divine right!"

"I understand, my liege, though I fear that one day the growing power of the Church may become difficult to control."

"Not if the king—the emperor—remains strong! The king must always have veto power. He must never allow the pope or any other churchman to tell him what he must do. The business of the Church is souls, not power, damn it!

"Now, the second thing: We must ward off any dissension, anything that distracts us from being on the same focus."

"Aye, my king," Sebastian agreed, wondering where this tack was going. He feared the worst.

"I feel we're not focused! Hell's fire, there's so much division between the eastern and western parts of the empire. We don't even speak the same language anymore. You have to become one of Louis's main advisors. You must show him how to keep everything together."

Sebastian bent forward slightly to ease the painful tightening in his stomach. Here it is again, "you must do this, you must do that," he lamented to himself. But now he's dumping everything on me. It's as if he wants me to become himself! I've got to get out of this somehow. God help me! He took a deep breath, thought for a minute, and decided to be bold.

"Sire, all this is an enormous task you set before me. To do as you ask, I would have to live at Louis's court. I would have to abandon the wonderful work you have allowed Adela, my children, and me to do so far.

"Listen, my king, and I feel what we're doing for the people all over the realm may be as important as defending the realm. As I've said to you so often if the people are stronger, the king will be stronger. In fact, the work you've given us to do may be remembered as the best part of your legacy to your people—the very best you could ever do for them."

The king paused momentarily and then blew his nose loudly into a rag. "My legacy, eh? Schools and learning stuff, is it? Learning to read, eh? B'God!"

"Yes, my liege, and medicine and doctors, roads and bridges . . . all that. Yes! All that! If we succeed, that is what you will be remembered for . . . mostly all that!"

"Humff! All right, all right. I know you're right. Ye can't do both. I don't mean that you must live at Louis's court. You couldn't stand it anyway. But you must be there whenever serious decisions are to be made, *right*? He's got to be convinced of the need to build ships and train the local militia to counter the threat of the Vikings up north and the Saracens on the Roman Sea. They raid now with increasing boldness. They must be stopped! Louis must be convinced to fight them! Or at least make peace with them," he added, looking away and clearing his throat.

"I will do what I can, my king."

"I know you will, old friend. I suppose you can't spend the rest of your life leading armies. There are younger men for that now. So, er, ahem—I will release you to the work you are doing now."

Trying not to look elated, Sebastian turned away to clear his throat and take a deep breath. He turned back to the king with a straight face and uttered simply, "I am most grateful, my liege."

The king snorted and scratched his groin. "Actually, I always wanted to do something permanent for the people when we'd done with the fighting—simple stuff, like you and Milo and the Church, are doing."

Sebastian coughed again to hide his chagrin. "Sire, our work is far from simple or easy. You cannot believe how reluctant some of your counts and bishops are to spend money on what we want to do."

"By God! Who are they? I'll have their hearts ripped out!"

"It's all right, my king. We're making good progress. The Church does ease the way for us, and many nobles are coming around."

"Ah then, it's a grand vision!" The king sighed deeply. "If I just wouldn't bloody die, we could make this whole land the equal of Rome or Greece! Is it not so?"

The king leaned forward awkwardly and grasped Sebastian's hands again. "That's why I've left you alone these past years, Sebastian. And it's paid off!"

"Yes, my king."

"I wouldn't be surprised," Charlemagne whispered, "if what you and your people are doing will indeed be my legacy."

The king suddenly turned his face away and coughed violently into his pillows until he was gasping for breath. Sebastian rushed to his side but could think of nothing to do but pound his back. Finally, the fit subsided, and the king could be coaxed to drink water and lie back. But there was bright red blood all over the pillow.

***

He slept finally. Sebastian continued to hold his hand as a deep quiet filled the room, broken occasionally by the crackling of the fire. Sebastian reflected on his long life with the king. He could hear Charlemagne's voice in his reflections.

"'But, but, but,'" the king would complain. "That's what you always say! It's enough that you've avoided being here at Aix as much as you could. I had thought to do a little hunting with you once more."

That was what Sebastian loved so much about the king—his enthusiasm for almost everything he did, his love of life, his genuine affection for his family, his friends, his mighty army, and, most of all, for the Frankish folk.

One story was a favorite of the king. Sebastian could hear his voice in his brain. "Remember that time we slew the big boar? You were just a skinny shaveling. What a thrill it was, too! Kneeling on the ground, just you and me, and letting the black devil run himself up on our spears. We barely held him off! You didn't budge an inch, though, and that was your first boar hunt!

"That's when I first began to like you. I swear by Jesus's mother, that beast was bigger'n you!

"And remember all the times when we could swim together with the other men at court? We had such wonderful times in those warm waters, such glorious baths after a long campaign. And we sang, din't we? Loud and strong so even God could hear us! Oh! We had some lovely moments together."

We did indeed, High King, Sebastian said to himself, his eyes filling with tears.

"And best of all," the king's voice continued in Sebastian's head, "were the times we were able to get our heads together. You and Alcuin helped me see the future—a future where every soul could read and be free from hunger and disease. You gave voice to my hope for the days when I could cease having to fight and when I could think about things other than war. Actually, it was you. You came to represent the ultimate peace!"

That's why I fought for him. That's it! Sebastian realized as he gazed into the fireplace. Those words, "the ultimate peace"— that's why I sacrificed so much for him and came to love him, as wrong as he so often was. I loved him for his vision, the goal behind all that fighting every year, and the main purpose he had in mind and strove so hard to create. I knew that in my heart, but my brain kept telling me otherwise. Yet, it was the ultimate peace he sought.

***

Sebastian sat on the bedside with the king for at least an hour after his last breath. He was grateful the king had forbidden anyone to disturb them until called. There were no tears after his father Attalus had died, only a sense of great loss and fleeting, panicky visions of a waiting abyss.

Finally, the chamber door squeaked open a crack. A few more hesitant seconds and Count Arno filled the doorway and marched boldly into the room, his ponderous body making the floorboards complain.

"Is he . . . ?"

"As you see, Count. The king is gone."

Arno started, stepped back, and covered his mouth. A weird sound came from his throat, something between a cough and a small shriek. But he was a proud man and not second-in-command at the palace for nothing. He quickly recovered. In crisis situations, Arno was a master at affecting a lofty composure and an officious bearing. Sebastian was sure there was little sorrow for the king in Arno's cynical heart. Instead, as Mayor of the Palace, he would already be plotting how to use the king's death and remain in power.

"Well then, Count Sebastian," he pronounced imperiously, "you must get out! There is much I have to do. I must ask you to leave at once."

"Careful, fat man," Sebastian growled. "Remember what happened to you the last time you tried to run roughshod over me."

Arno took several steps back, the blood draining from his face. But he summoned his courage and the sure knowledge that he did indeed have the power of the king at the moment.

"My dear count, you must know that as Mayor of the Palace, I am to act in the place of the king if he is unable to rule. Obviously, there is no king at the moment, and I must act in his place, at least until his heir arrives. I must send for his son immediately. I hope you will not force me to use my power to arrest you."

"Arrest me! You pompous talking pig! You couldn't get a single soul in this whole palace to arrest me. Who, indeed, is going to arrest one of the king's paladins?"

Sebastian sighed, realizing further talk was a waste of time. After all, the king was dead. Let Arno see if he could handle the uncertain and frightening future.

"I will go…for now. There's no need to stay. But I'll return! Don't fail to inform me about the king's funeral and when King Louis arrives."

With that, Sebastian took one last look at what was left of the once almighty monarch and brushed past the ever-indignant Arno and out of the palace.

Chapter 31

The Spider's Fate

Arno had gone too far. During Charlemagne's illness, he had met secretly with Lothar to devise a plan to redraw territorial boundaries and clarify that Lothar was to be publicly proclaimed emperor and overlord when Louis died. Perhaps Arno thought to surprise the king by completing a treaty that would adhere to the arrangement Sebastian had negotiated, making the oldest son always the most powerful. More likely, he was currying favor for the day the son might succeed the father. His position as Mayor of the Palace in Aachen was also undecided.

The dukes and landed lords who lived at the king's court in Aachen knew of Arno's meetings with Lothar. They considered it bald-faced plotting. None of them had ever liked Arno in any case. He lorded it over them and often frustrated their efforts to speak with or influence the king. He never missed a chance to insult them subtly and hold his position as Mayor of the Palace over their heads. They had endured more than enough, and the king's death, together with this latest scandal, emboldened them to take their revenge.

They convinced the palace guards that Count Arno was plotting against the dying king on Lothar's behalf. The nobles then had the hapless high steward arrested and confined. He was manhandled, sputtering and cursing, into a locked room until they could organize his trial. It did not take long. He was summarily tried for treason by peers of the castle and region, none of whom had any love for the unfortunate count.

Arno was doomed even before the faux trial began. He was permitted only a brief moment to defend himself before them but was never allowed to present whatever defense he might have made fully. He began to speak rather eloquently at first, building a plausible defense. But the peer nobles laughed at him and imitated his waddling way of walking. They pooched out their bellies and puffed up their cheeks. No one listened to him. The louder they laughed, the more befuddled he became until he was terrified and could do little more than stutter and beg for their understanding and mercy. In the end, they acted quickly and condemned him unanimously.

Guards put him in irons immediately and took him to a wall by the palace's front gate. On instructions from the peers, they stripped him of all clothing except his long black gown. This they pulled up to cover only his head and shoulders and tied his hands together. Then they hung him by his hands from a rope, where he dangled blind and helpless against the palace wall. There he sagged and swayed for most of an entire day.

Every visitor, man or woman, every townsman or trader coming to the palace, could observe the alabaster body with its beefy legs and grotesque belly in horror.

By happenstance, Sebastian returned with his usual escorts to the front gate just before sunset. He had promised to come back and participate in plans for the king's funeral. They had to push through a small crowd gathered at the gate to gawk at the spectacle. "God on earth! What have they done?" Sebastian exclaimed, his gorge rising in his throat.

Without hesitation, the guards immediately opened the gate for the famous paladin and his entourage.

Though he knew already, Sebastian hissed to the sergeant in charge, "Who is that?"

"Why, it's Count Arno, m'lord. Seems he did betray the king."

"Cut him down at once!" Sebastian barked angrily, his eyes flashing acrimoniously. "I will take full responsibility. On my oath, you will not be punished. Dead or alive, take him and my men to a private room. If the count is still alive, provide whatever my men may need. I'll be there myself shortly."

With that, Sebastian charged off to confront the noble peers of the palace. He found them drinking and celebrating the "fall of the spider," as they put it.

Sebastian approached them and stood in the middle of the room in silence. They also became quiet as they observed the hostile visage of the king's famous paladin.

"Speak, Count," someone said. "We have been anxious to see you. Now that the infamous charlatan has been deposed, we have much to discuss. And we need you to lead us."

Sebastian fired a glance at the man and almost spat out the words. "How could you do this? It is a heinous act. Incredibly unworthy of all of you! You're peers of the realm. How dishonorable! Shameful!"

"What, what?" said one of the ranking army generals. "How dare you speak to us this way? You know the man was little more than a sorcerer. He beguiled the king. He hated all of us and treated us with disdain. It's high time he was removed."

"He must die! He must be hanged!" cried several voices at once.

"No!" Sebastian shouted, turning in a circle to face down each man. "Do you even know what you're doing? He is a count of the realm! Where is your respect for the king? He was chosen by our king! Who knows why King Karl chose Count Arno? But I would wager it was because that spider gave our king vital information on his enemies. I know of several conspiracies against the king which Count Arno's army of spies thwarted."

Sebastian continued pacing around the floor, staring gravely into each nobleman's eyes. "We are less secure now, gentlemen. We have lost our great king, and you wish to murder one of his most effective servants. Shame! What are the people to think if they see one of the highest lords of the land dangling like a butchered hog by the front gate? If that can happen to one lord, is any lord safe? Besides, it was a barbaric act, most unworthy of this assembly."

Several lords moved restlessly away from the middle of the room, and none wanted to meet Sebastian's eyes.

Finally, striving mightily to control his anger, Sebastian said, "I had him cut down, lords. If he's alive, he's being treated now by my men. I will look into this business with Lothar. If Arno really meant to harm us, which I can scarcely believe, you must execute him only after a fair trial. If not, you cannot be seen to have made such a mistake."

Sebastian noted with satisfaction the numerous mumbled voices of agreement.

"Reconciliation is impossible," he continued. "If Arno is innocent and survives, I will send him to Andernach, and you can say he is in permanent exile. I will see that you never hear from him again."

One of the dukes in residence, a senior royal advisor, stepped up and said in a loud voice, "My good count, as always, your advice is invaluable! You are right in this case. We acted hastily. Once again, we're greatly in your debt. How can we reward you?"

Sebastian moved toward the door. As he opened it to make his exit, he turned to reply. "Sir, as it was with our illustrious father, the High King Karl, I am bound by oath to offer my advice and service to whomever the next king and emperor will be. I need no reward for that. As for the unfortunate count, I hope we need never speak of this again." He exited quickly in a moment of nervous silence.

***

In the end, Liudolf and a few guards bundled the once proud second-in-command of an empire into a simple cart in the early morning half-light and whisked him away to Andernach. It took several weeks, but he did survive with the ministrations of Magdala and the household staff. His health, however, was permanently impaired, and he never recovered the sharpness of his mind. He became little more than a simpleton, living like one of the peasants in a small hut near the manor house. He spent his days working at this or that menial chore, happy with his freedom and lack of responsibility. Adelaide never failed to visit him when she was at the manor. She was known to be his special friend and caregiver. He worshipped her.

Chapter 32

Prelude to the Fall

Francia 814 – 833

To say that the years after the death of Charlemagne were a time of chaos and uncertainty would be to liken it to an apocalypse—long, hard winters beset by storms and deadly cold. Floods and constant rain, followed by drought, famine, and pestilence, besieged the land for years on end. Louis wrestled with such problems as best he could, but the profound natural disasters beat him down. When he failed to help them, the people lost faith in him. They returned to old ways of coping. Superstition was rife throughout the land.

Nevertheless, Louis the Pious managed to keep the empire together for roughly half of his twenty-seven-year reign. However, he was forced to lead frequent campaigns to put down revolts in all the provinces along his borders and even Rome. Still, if he had sired only one son to succeed him, he might have had a tolerable reign. But he had three, and that was his downfall.

***

Emperor Louis had always harbored doubts about his father, Karl's favorite paladin. When Sebastian was present, it was like having Charlemagne in the room. Sebastian felt this tension too. He dreaded going to court because he almost always disapproved of the emperor, whom he felt was weak and indecisive. Unlike Charlemagne, he did not seek out "wise men" from all parts of the realm. He surrounded himself instead with churchmen and old cronies from the nobility of Aquitaine, who were quite different from Frankish lords in the rest of the realm. Louis felt this disapproval and refrained for many years from calling Sebastian back to court. For his part, Sebastian was profoundly grateful as the years passed.

Then one day, a messenger appeared from the court, bidding him ride post-haste to meet the emperor at Aachen. The days when Sebastian's aging bones could make a nonstop ride without rest were over. But he and Liudolf managed to cover the long miles in two days.

"Welcome, Count Sebastian, welcome!" the emperor began effusively. "It's been too long. I trust you are managing to cope with these parlous times," the emperor began nervously, motioning for Sebastian to sit.

"We manage to survive, for the most part, my liege." Sebastian chewed the side of his mouth as he waited anxiously for the emperor to get to the point of the visit. Thankfully, Louis obliged.

"We have no time to waste, dear count," the emperor blurted out as he began to pace back and forth in front of the central fireplace. "I need your help most urgently. Suddenly all three of my sons are threatening revolt over my plan to apportion the empire after I am gone. It seems none of them is satisfied, least of all my impetuous tartar son Lothar."

Bloody hell, Sebastian thought as his pulse began to quicken. This really is serious. I dread what he's going to say next.

"Sebastian, I remember how you single-handedly prevented a battle between my father, King Karl, and me some years ago. I have always been profoundly grateful for your clever handling of the situation so that no harm was done that day.

"But now I am faced with the discontent of all three of my sons. And Lothar, as usual, is the ringleader. Somehow, they have convinced the confounded pope to join them in their complaints. In short, I would ask you now to advocate in this dispute, as you did for my father for so many years. I want you to go to all of the complaining parties—if you can find them—and see if we can discover a way to bring them together with me so we might come to a resolution. I need you, Sebastian. And I would be most grateful."

Good God! Sebastian groaned to himself. He's just like his father. What in the world makes him think I can do what he asks?

I've only briefly met the pope once, and I haven't seen Louis's sons in years. He looked down at the floor and cleared his throat, desperately seeking words to convince the emperor that he was not the man for such a wildly complicated task.

Seeing right away that Sebastian was preparing to decline his proposal, Louis played his trump card. "Ahem . . . I see you are hesitating, good count." He stepped closer to hover over Sebastian. "What if I were to promise to renew my support for your cultural efforts," he said with a shrewd smile.

Sebastian's head came up abruptly, and he stared into the emperor's eyes to see if he was serious.

"Your clinics and hostels, your schools that you care so much for?" the emperor went on, relishing the look on Sebastian's concerned face. "I can announce to the lords and bishops that I give my full support to your efforts, just as my father, the High King Karl, did, and I expect them to do the same."

In the end, that was the price Sebastian accepted for his services. He and Liudolf set off the next day to see the pope, who, by great good fortune, was already in Bavaria, ostensibly on papal business with church leaders in that province. Since the pope traveled openly with a large entourage and heavily armed escort, Sebastian had no trouble finding him after several days' ride.

***

Pope Gregory IV never wanted to be the pope. He was a mild-mannered man and somewhat timid. But once he was forced by the nobles of Rome to accept his election, he vigorously pursued some pet obsessions. One was his conviction that the papacy must be recognized as superior to the emperor.

Emperor Louis the Pious disagreed emphatically, taking his lead from Charlemagne himself. He publicly reprimanded the pope for accepting his position as pontiff before formal approval of the choice came from himself, the emperor.

This fundamental dispute between Church and State played a crucial part in the sundering of family relations between Louis and his sons. Both sides would use it to define their positions and attract allies. It opened the first crack in the unity of the empire.

***

"Most Holy Father," Sebastian began, kneeling on one knee in Pope Gregory's temporary council room. "I am delighted to see you again. You may not remember me, but I met you once before when you were a bishop, and I was in Rome on the business of King Karl the Great. I was much impressed by the good things you were doing then to resurrect the great buildings of that illustrious city. Thank you for giving me an audience so quickly."

The pope smiled abstrusely and indicated a small bench before his slightly raised dais. Sebastian was not encouraged by the pope's cool demeanor. So far, it was not a promising start.

"Thank you, Holy Father. I will return to the urgent reason Emperor Louis sent me to you. It concerns the ancient Frankish custom of dividing the realm among the surviving heirs on the demise of a ruling monarch."

"Yes indeed, Count," Gregory said, breaking his chilly silence. "That division was settled upon some years ago. It's an unfortunate practice that has been the cause of many wars and even murders."

"That's exactly why I'm here, Your Holiness. You know, of course, that our emperor lost his wife some months ago. He has since married another, a Bavarian princess named Judith, very beautiful and quite intelligent."

"So I've heard, my dear count. They say Louis has quite lost his head over her."

Sebastian coughed. "Ahum . . . yes, he is quite fond of her and wishes to please her in every way. And that's the problem, Holy Father. You see, Queen Judith has had a child, a boy named Charles." He paused briefly to let the news sink in and began again.

"Apparently, Queen Judith is demanding that Emperor Louis provide an inheritance for her son as well. When I left his company at Aachen, he was in the process of carving a rather large territory out of the land promised to Lothar, his eldest son and the heir apparent to the empire's throne."

"Ah," the pope said, looking away and stroking his beard. "Well then, what is it the emperor wants from me? I am not exactly a counselor on marriage rights."

"No, Your Holiness. But you have great influence. The king wants you to come to him at the court and mediate this grave issue between himself and Lothar. He knows you have a good relationship with Lothar in Italy, where he rules as king. He hopes that you will be able to prevent a possible rebellion.

"Will you do this, Your Holiness—as soon as may be? The emperor is very anxious to have you."

The pope hesitated a moment before giving a surprisingly cheery answer with a beaming smile. "Why, yes indeed, most worthy count. I shall come as soon as it can be arranged. Only name me the place."

Sebastian left the pope's presence, eyes wide open in astonishment. Perhaps there was hope for success after all! Still, a voice in Sebastian's head whispered to him that it had been all too easy.

***

The next mission was to Lothar, who, at the time, was also in Bavaria conferring with his brother Louis, later known as "The German." He found them both in an impregnable fortress high in the Alps.

"Ah," Sebastian began, bowing to both men. "Princes of the realm! How good to find you both together. I have come bearing gifts and an invitation from your eminent father. May God give him peace and good fortune."

"Yes, well enough," Lothar interjected roughly. "But before you get on about my illustrious father, what about these gifts you speak of? You're famous for your surprises, O great paladin of the king!"

Sebastian ignored the sarcastic jibe. "Of course, gladly! Gentlemen, will you please come to this window facing the courtyard below." He parted the curtain and opened the window despite the cold mountain air. There, fidgeting restively in the hands of Liudolf and several attendants, were two magnificent blood bay stallions, each deep-chested, stocky and strong, spirited and adroit— perfect warhorses.

"My lords, these are my gifts to you. They are the sons of my own horse Joyeuse, who is the grandson of my first Joyeuse on whose back I fought many wars against the Saxons with your grandfather, Karl the Great. That superb stallion gained quite a reputation then. You may have heard of him."

"Joyeuse!" both brothers exclaimed enthusiastically.

"Who has not heard of that one?" Lothar said fervently. "They say he was the champion of all horses! I know men who would pay a fortune to have a foal in that line."

"You are right, my king. Joyeuse and his offspring are probably the reason I have stayed alive for so long. So I am very glad to present one of these fine stallions to each of you, hoping they will always bring you similar good fortune."

"All right, all right, good count," Louis said. "What is it you want from us in return—half of Bavaria and both of our wives?"

"No, no, my kings, I want nothing at all from you—no land, no gold, nothing . . ." He paused. "Except . . ."

"Except what?" they called out together.

"I suspect you already, Sebastian," Lothar pronounced with a new edge in his voice. "You're a clever bugger when it comes to something serious at stake. What is it this time?"

Sebastian ignored the rudeness of the young king. "Your goodwill, my king, is what I want . . . and a promise to meet with your father and me somewhere very soon in the interest of peace and justice."

"Peace and justice!" Lothar snorted. "I suppose you think it would be 'just' to give the bastard of that whore Judith half my kingdom!"

"I'm sorry, my king. I was told the boy is your godson," Sebastian said in low, measured tones.

"Damn you, Sebastian, for reminding me of that! I was duped into agreeing to call him my godson. But I'll have nothing to do with him now. The whole baptism was just a plot to steal what is mine."

"I apologize, King Lothar. I knew nothing of how you felt. In any case, your discontent is precisely why I'm here." He paused, took a deep breath, and decided to cast the die. Boldness was the best way to challenge the tempestuous prince. "I came to convince you not to go rampaging into the Rhineland against your father, especially on faulty evidence and rumor."

"You cheeky devil! Are you calling me a liar? I know what I know!"

"Not at all, good king. I merely suggest that you might not have all the facts. In any case, we can agree on such facts if you consent to meet with your father as soon as possible. We can bring everyone's point of view out in the open and come to a fair division concerning the land. You will have the largest say in those negotiations, of course. After all, you are the king's primary heir. The king has always acknowledged that firmly.

"But," Sebastian drove on quickly before Lothar could think of a response, "Queen Judith's young Charles is also your father's son. According to Frankish custom, he must have an inheritance too, is it not so?"

"That may be, but my father is trying to give away half of my lands!"

"Lothar, dear king," Sebastian said quietly, seeking to flatter and reassure the impetuous prince, "I will be there when you meet with your father, the emperor. It was I who helped him establish the current division of the empire. That was more than twenty-five years ago. And it has held up very well since then. We can do it again . . . if you will just meet with your father in peaceful, unthreatening circumstances. I guarantee that we can work out a division suitable to all concerned . . . as we did before."

The brothers said nothing, but it seemed that they had at least listened carefully. Sebastian broke the weighted silence by proposing gaily, "Gentlemen, we are far too serious. Let us go and meet the stallions! I wonder which one of you might have the courage to mount one? And after that, a good supper, nay?"

Ultimately, the brothers agreed to meet with their father within a fortnight. They asked nothing else, no conditions, no demands. Again, as with Pope Gregory, Sebastian felt a shred of doubt creeping up his spine as they prepared to return to the emperor.

Chapter 33

The Field of Lies

Rothfeld, June 833

The emperor was at Worms, and Sebastian raced with Liudolf to bring the news quickly, but the alpine roads through Bavaria were few and often treacherous. He was uneasy. There was something awry about his meeting with the pope and the brothers. All had easily agreed to negotiations with the emperor—too easily, too much smiling, not enough questions.

When they finally arrived at the palace in Worms, Sebastian drove his sweaty horse through the palace gates and right into the main reception hall of the palace. No one dared stop him. He dismounted and knelt before the shocked emperor.

"Sire," Sebastian exclaimed at once, "they have all agreed! But . . ."

"Please rise, good count, and come with me to my chambers. Will someone come and take care of this man's horse!"

When they reached the emperor's chambers, he indicated a place where both could speak privately.

"Now, Sebastian, tell me. You said all had agreed. That scoundrel Gregory as well as my two reckless cubs?"

"They did, my emperor. It was almost too easy. It was as if they already knew what they would do, even the pope."

"But you heard no anger, no counterdemands or threats?"

"None, sire. There was just this feeling I had that pervaded our conversations . . . a sort of hidden sneer behind a fist, a furtive look the boys gave each other. But what they actually said is what you wanted to hear. They will come to meet with you."

"Well, good enough, then! Let us make arrangements to go at once. I will meet them halfway, say, somewhere near Colmar in the Alsace. That's fair to all.

"I will take a small force with me for security, some of the standing army around Worms, and my personal guards since you're nervous about it. But not enough to frighten anyone. And I am bringing Judith and the boy with us. Lothar does not know Judith well. If he did, I'm sure he would love her, as I do."

"Sire, is that wise?" Sebastian exclaimed in alarm.

"Of course! I wish to show that I mean to have a peaceful and fair council amongst family, with the blessing of our pope. After all, Lothar is the boy's godfather from a promise made when she was first with child.

"I don't believe that Lothar will bring a sizeable force from Italy across the Alps just for a meeting's sake. And Louis the German, as he's called now, hasn't been invited, but I don't care if he does come. The more of my sons, the better. I hear the pope, bless his disobedient soul, has troops now too, but I'm sure he hasn't a clue how to lead them. Besides, he'd better learn soon how to get back in my good graces. I swear I'll bring him to heel if he doesn't. I've dealt with popes before." He calmed himself for a moment and went on, almost gaily.

"As for my dense eldest son, he's quite a careless thinker, you know. It will be easy to confuse and convince him that he will still have the lion's share of the realm, even after the reapportionment on behalf of Judith's Charles."

"Is that true, sire?"

"No, but Lothar is not very knowledgeable about geography. He will be content with what I do if I keep calling him 'co-emperor.'"

"Begging your pardon, sire, but if you deceive Lothar about the division and he discovers it, there will be war."

"Nonsense, Count. You overestimate him. All I have to do is flatter him before everybody, and he will be content enough."

"Uh . . . Your Highness, may I suggest that you might delay the council and gather a larger force than you have mentioned . . . just in case?"

***

Every league of the long march down to Colmar increased Sebastian's fears. The emperor had almost completely ignored his warnings, confident that Lothar and the pope would not be prepared to fight against their emperor. He discounted his second son, Louis the German, as not having the same serious resentments as his brother Lothar.

Early on, Sebastian sent Liudolf and several other scouts ahead. From every crossroads, they came racing back to report the movement of large numbers of troops from different directions, converging on the plains of Rothfeld, near Colmar.

"Your Majesty, we must turn back or find a good defensive position and wait," Sebastian urged.

"Nonsense, my good count. Of course, they would not travel without forces to protect themselves, but Lothar and the pope would not dare attack their emperor! Press on."

Sebastian cursed himself for not protesting strongly enough before the king to make him think twice about the rendezvous. Now it was too late.

As the armies faced each other through the day, Louis's forces seemed to get thinner and thinner. Every hour, queries from his troop commanders came asking what to do about monks and priests from the pope's contingent moving among his troops.

Finally, the emperor came to his senses and realized he and his small army were in grave danger. "What can I do, Sebastian?" he blurted out fearfully. "Can you get me out of this?"

Sebastian breathed in deeply and finally looked the emperor in the eye. "Sire, it's too late. We've had no messages from anyone. I don't believe they mean to negotiate. We are already surrounded and outnumbered badly. I think the next thing we will see is a courier with a white flag coming to demand your surrender."

"Oh, no! This cannot be happening," the emperor moaned.

"My king, I fear you have only two choices: you must either fight or surrender. I cannot make this choice for you."

"But what would you do, Sebastian? You have always been successful in war."

Sebastian hesitated as violent memories and old battlefield images flashed through his mind.

I would fight, he thought to himself. That is just who I am . . . if I were a younger man . . . and if I were in command. In the past, we were often successful simply by boldness—smashing into the foe's center with the heavy cavalry, aiming for the flags where their leaders stood. But I am not in command, and Louis is not Karl der Grosse.

A voice intruded on his reverie. You say you would fight. Ha! But what about that oath you gave God that you would never kill again? What do you think you would have to do here?

Yes, he answered himself. In the past I would have fought, even if I might die. But now, a bloody battle is the last thing I want to see. It's true—I've sworn to God twice that I would never kill again.

"Sire," he said hoarsely, "you must surrender. You haven't a chance. We would be wiped out. Why let so many of your faithful men die in vain?"

***

They took King Louis to a church in Soissons several leagues away. Judith and the child Charles were separated and spirited away under heavy guard to different secret locations.

A few weeks later, Louis the Pious, emperor of all Francia, son of the peerless Charlemagne, was put on trial in the Cathedral of Notre Dame de Compiegne in front of many great lords of church and state gathered from all parts of the empire. He was made to confess publicly to all sorts of wrongdoing: oath-breaking, violating the public peace, inability to control his adulterous wife, and even murder. He was blamed for all the unrest and confusion across the realm, neglect of the state, and poor leadership.

Louis at least had the courage to face the accusations bravely. He was forced to read out a statement confessing to all charges. Before the penance was pronounced, he stepped forward, threw his sword belt down at the base of the cathedral's altar, and said, "Do with me what you will; I place my soul in the hands of God."

He then stood straight with his eyes on the narrow window at the back of the altar as bishops and other high churchmen imposed their hands upon his body in absolution while he repeated his confession as it was read out, line by line. It was a scene of utter humiliation.

Finally, Louis was made to swear as part of his penance that he would never seek power of any kind for the rest of his life.

***

Sebastian and Liudolf were escorted to Soissons shortly after the emperor was taken. They were treated well and with respect, but they were clearly under confinement. After two days, Sebastian was brought before Lothar in one of the church buildings.

"Well, Sebastian, what shall we do with you? It seems you chose the wrong side this time," Lothar said with a sideways grin.

"I came here from my home to choose no side, my king, but to act as a minister for peace, to bring together you and your father for negotiations. Not to fight. You know that, King Lothar. That's what I conveyed to you and your brother in Bavaria, is it not?"

"Yes, that's true. But my father lied to us. He never intended to negotiate. He brought a strong force to meet us. And you showed up with him—in your chain mail and helmet!"

"King Lothar, what prince travels anywhere without a strong force to keep him safe? Your grandfather never moved without a force twice the size your father brought to Rothfeld. And I am in the habit of wearing my armor whenever I travel.

"I will not speak for your father's intentions," he continued. "But my intentions from the beginning were clearly to facilitate negotiations. Ask him! He will tell you that I urged negotiations even to the last moment.

"I will also say this, my king: I fear that I was the only party in this whole occurrence who did not stray from the truth. Even our good pope never revealed to me his true intentions."

Lothar laughed heartily. "Ha! You are right! Turns out that 'our good pope,' as you so kindly put it, ain't so saintly after all. God bless him! He has been with me all along because he doesn't like our father and wants to be able to claim the supremacy of the papacy.

"That's fine with me; I'll say that it is so if it makes Gregory happy. But I'll do whatever I please once I'm formally declared emperor."

Sebastian bowed his head and stared at the floor. Lothar mused at him for a minute and said, "You are right, Sebastian. I suppose we should rename Rothfeld 'Lugenfeld', the 'Field of Lies.' But that is what statecraft is about, is it not? Putting one's governance and one's self ahead by whatever means? It's all about who gets what in the end, right?"

Sebastian stood up, bowed slightly, and said, "I should go now, Your Majesty, by your leave. I can add nothing more—except that, if it is your will, I shall leave tomorrow for my home and the work I have been doing for our people."

"Ah yes, the poor bloody people! Go see what you can do for 'em. They won't thank you. They'll just ask for more. By all means! I never intended to punish you anyway. I know that you meant no harm. And besides, one of your sons is in my army, isn't he?"

"He was, Your Majesty. He was on the field with you the time you and your father Louis confronted your grandfather, King Karl, and I came between you to negotiate peace. Remember? After that, you gave my son Attalus leave to come home to help me in the work I've been doing."

"Ah yes, dear count, I certainly do remember. You did us all a favor then. I was less ready and ultimately glad of your intervention. But, as I remember, your son was a good captain amongst my troops. It's been quite a while, but tell him it's time for him to return."

Sebastian felt his gut wrench at the thought of returning his son to this conniving ruler. Thinking fast, he said, "My king, would that I could. But I had to send Attalus to Spain to buy horses for me and for the work that we do. There are never enough horses. His grandfather, also named Attalus, was an excellent horse master, and I believe my son has the same talent."

"Yes, I remember that story. Interesting. Hmm . . . there's always been some mystery about who your father was. Ah, don't bristle so. I'm not going to ask you," Lothar said with a laugh.

"No matter. You're a pretty good breeder yourself. That stallion you gave me is the finest I've ever had. I should let you go just because of him. Great horse!

"Well, go along then, with my blessing! I know I can trust you, Sebastian. I hope I can count on you in the future."

"I shall always be at the service of the ruler of the realm, Your Eminence. I wish you good health and peace."

***

Sebastian and Liudolf rode home under a cloud of dismay and regret. How could the son of the great Charlemagne have fallen so low? All that had been accomplished in Karl's long and glorious reign seemed shattered asunder like pieces from a broken mirror.

No matter what happened, Sebastian was determined to stay out of any coalition whatever. He would work furiously to reinforce all three of his estates, forcing any enemy to pay a prohibitive price to overcome any one of them. He would announce to everyone that he would take no part in any fighting unless attacked and until a clear plan for the fate of the empire had been agreed upon.

For the most part, Sebastian's plan worked. His lands on the upper Rhine were threatened but never attacked. They proved too thorny to be worth the effort. After Louis the Pious was dethroned, the brothers could not agree on the division of the empire or who should be the overlord. Ten years of bitter civil war ensued. Louis the Pious was even restored to the throne for a while in an attempt to restore peace, but then he died. Again, more war.

Finally, in 843, ten years after the infamous "Field of Lies," the empire was permanently divided in a treaty in the Burgundian village of Verdun. All unity was broken. What emerged from the treaty was Louis the German as king of East Francia, Lothar as king of Middle Francia and Italy, and their half-brother Charles as king of West Francia. Pippin of Italy had died in the meantime.

The civil war ended. But the empire, Charlemagne's great symbol of Frankish unity, was dead.

Epilogue

Light in the Darkness

Fernshanz, August 843

I'm old! Sebastian said to himself. I have to face it finally. I can't keep riding all over the realm endlessly trying to beg and persuade all those stubborn old counts and those bloody-minded new warlords to support what I'm doing. They don't understand. And they refuse to hear about it. To make things worse, war is happening all over this land and on all of our borders. That's all they want to talk about.

Besides, no one's been calling on me lately to arbitrate their incessant quarrels. They'd prefer to cut each other's throats! It's happening from one end of the realm to the other. God help us! It's what I feared most when the great king died. I said then that divisions within would destroy the empire.

The news had just reached him that Louis the Pious's three sons had signed a momentous treaty dividing the empire at a place called Verdun on the River Meuse in Burgundy. It called for the division of the entire empire into three parts: West Francia, Middle Francia, and East Francia.

In the west, there was Aquitania and Gascony. Humff! They speak a flowery, almost completely different language than the old Frankish tongue. I can't even speak it myself. At least here along the Rhine and in the east, the old Frankish tongue survives, though it's changing too. In the middle, who knows? There's everything from lyrical Italian to the coarse, sea-born speech of the lowland peoples. No wonder we can no longer communicate with one another!

Nevertheless, Sebastian considered himself lucky that no one came to call him to service again. He counted it a blessing that he could finally rest. Bloody well rid of those benumbed and heavy-handed meetings with stubborn kings and arrogant lords! Besides, he thought angrily, it's no longer safe to travel anywhere without a huge escort.

After Emperor Louis the Pious died, his sons competed violently with one another to take his place as the sole ruler of Francia. While Vikings and Saracens ravaged the empire's borders, each royal son tried to deceive and gain an advantage over the other. False alliances were formed, two against one, changing periodically to new coalitions until no one knew whose side to join or avoid.

Sebastian mourned daily his son Karl, who was killed in a battle against the Vikings in Dorestad. The wars of royal brother against royal brother had sucked up all the available manpower. No reserves were to be had to reinforce Frankish troops in the north, desperately trying to hold off heavy Viking raids.

He had heard that Karl was among the last to fall as the Vikings sacked and burned Dorestad again. Ironically, Bjorn Thorbjorn, the renowned Bloodaxe, died in the same Viking attack. Who knew if Karl and the famous Dane happened to cross swords with each other? Sebastian wept bitterly to think that Karl might have died on the same church steps where he had once saved his father's life in the fight against Konrad's raiders so long ago.

Sebastian had wisely sent his other son to Spain to study the horses raised there in the Frankish march facing the Umayyad Emirate. He advised Attalus to stay there until he was no longer likely to be called back into Lothar's army. This turned out to be a matter of years.

Eventually, Attalus, like his grandfather, the first horse master, created a good life for himself in al-Andalus. He married a comely, sun-kissed girl from a Gothic family he worked with in Barcelona. Her father owned land in the region of Pamplona and was glad to have Attalus as a son-in-law. His reputation as a horse master grew considerably. He was accepted as an important connecting link between the Franks in the north and the Christian communities south of the Pyrenees.

Sebastian was now the grandfather of six, three by Milo and Magdala and three by Attalus and his colorful Spanish bride.

Milo and Magdala continued to attend to the chain of clinics they had established, training new healers and midwives every year up and down the realm.

Milo became quite famous as a learned man, thanks to his long years of study with Alcuin, the great mind of Charlemagne's famous school for scholars in Aachen.

Milo could speak on almost any subject, but particularly on philosophical ones, such as the nature of man, virtue and the good life, and the responsibilities of every human being toward God and neighbor. He was formally promised high positions, even an eventual bishopric if he would just join the Church openly. He eschewed the invitation and the honor in favor of his preferred life among the poor and sick. And, of course, there was Magdala, whom he would never have abandoned.

To no one's surprise, Adelaide eventually became one of those successful doctors in the makeshift clinics up and down the Rhine. Little by little, she had looked over the shoulders of the healers until she had learned everything they knew. Then she took up with one of the Jewish doctors and became a partner in exploring the secrets of the human body. So far, she had gotten away with it, and she was deservedly famous in many quarters for her diagnostic abilities and talent for relieving pain and saving lives. Of course, all of her works were done in secret.

She visited Sebastian now and then at Fernshanz or Andernach, enjoying a rest from her labors with the afflicted. They maintained a warm relationship, each grateful for the other's long friendship and fondness. She considered these retreats her rightful home, and she intended to die and be buried at Fernshanz when the time came beside the graves of Adela and Sebastian.

As with many men of massive proportions, Ajax developed uncurable joint problems and could no longer travel with his beloved mistress. But he became a fixture at the main gate of the Fernshanz fortress, where he awaited her every day, rain or shine, heat or snow.

Simon, Sebastian's longtime Jewish trader friend, surprisingly came to live, at Sebastian's invitation, on one or the other of his three estates. He switched at his leisure between Andernach, Adalgray, and Fernshanz, depending on who was home or visiting. His wealth of knowledge about exotic, faraway places and great adventures made many travelers stop by for an evening or a week of good wine and conversation with him.

Sebastian often thought of his old blind mentor Heimdal, whose ghost roamed the woods and fields of Fernshanz. His wisdom and inexhaustible knowledge had served him and his father, Attalus, so well for many years. One day, it was said, Heimdal had limped into the deep forest around Fernshanz and simply disappeared. Apparently, no one had ever seen him since or even found his bones. Sebastian dreamed that one day Heimdal, old as he was, would just walk right out of the woods carrying a bunch of wild onions or perhaps disembark from a riverboat at the wharf carrying a bag stuffed with exotic herbs.

Sebastian's great companion and inseparable friend, Liudolf, finally married, more for the pleasure of eating tasty meals prepared regularly and for comfort in his declining years. But he still spent most of his time with a flagon of ale before a good fireplace at Fernshanz manor, reliving escapades with Sebastian and Simon.

Of the other members of Sebastian's long-time entourage, only Bardulf survived, still alive and relatively healthy because his wife Liesel, who had finally come to appreciate him, kept him relatively clean and well-fed, though she nagged at him endlessly. He spent most of his time anyway, telling tall tales at a small pub in Fernshanz village, where anyone might drop in and hear how famous Sebastian's little band had been and how Charlemagne himself owed his long and successful rule to the legion of exploits Sebastian and his peerless comrades had rendered on his behalf. He was a spellbinding spinner of fables.

Sebastian enjoyed his freedom late in life. It was astonishing just to get up in the morning and have the whole day ahead to do nothing at all but what one wanted. He could mount the latest version of Joyeuse and spend days just riding around the fields and forests of Fernshanz, inspecting his people's fortifications and condition.

Once in a while, he traveled to Andernach and Adalgray to look into the preparedness of his other estates, each of which was a bristling fortress. And every day, he thanked God the Vikings never bothered to raid upriver on the Rhine, probably because there were much richer targets along the coast. He'd heard they had even dared to sail up the Seine to attack the city of Paris itself.

He rued bitterly the impending dismantling of the empire. Frankish lands once had spread from the endless sea in the west to the steppes of the Rus. There was no longer unity from one part of the realm to another. He did his best to ward off the conscription of any of the men from his three manses, claiming they were essential to defending against the danger of marauding Vikings.

Some days Sebastian just sat in a chair beside Adela's grave, mourning her absence and that of his cherished son Karl, as well as the many golden friends, as he called them, who now were passed away—including among the first the incomparable Charlemagne.

On many days, Sebastian was left to reminisce alone over his long life. He still grappled with the question: What was it all for? All the conquests and perilous adventures? All those dead warriors! And now that the empire has been sundered . . . what did we achieve?

One gray winter evening before the fireplace, when Milo and Magdala were visiting, he asked them the same burdensome question. They provided a surprising answer.

"Father, you can't blame yourself or even Karl the Great," Milo began. "Let me tell you what my studies have taught me. For one thing, you helped the king bring Christianity to this barbaric land. That's obvious. But you helped him do much more. You and Alcuin encouraged him to create unity and law!

"I've learned that men crave security because they live in fear so much of their lives. They long for a common identity to cling to and a place where they are known and belong. They want to think that what they've chosen to believe in is right and good. And they want unity and law so they can feel safe. King Karl wrested both great virtues out of the poverty and ignorance that was once our Francia. In the future, those precious concepts of unity and law will continue to grow and become ideals, which will long survive him."

Sebastian marveled at his son's discernment and insight. Hmm, my son, the philosopher, he thought with pride. "Those are noble ideas, Milo, but need I remind you, sadly, that King Karl accomplished much of all that by force?"

"Granted, Father. He indeed had a hard time employing 'Sebastian's Way,' as you so often lament. But in the end, he was using it, wasn't he? Remember the Saxons you convinced him to spare twice? And he backed away from a potentially disastrous war with Denmark. All in all, by the end of his life, peace and unity did exist—at least within the core of the realm, if not within its borders."

Sebastian listened intently, for he was grateful to hear these words, though his heart had many doubts.

"Best of all, in my opinion," Magdala chimed in, "from one end of the realm to another, there is growing literacy and medicine. Slowly, to be sure. But once, only the clerics could read. Now this budding literacy will one day create invention and great change."

Sebastian marveled at her enthusiasm. She was no longer the shy, deferential maid she had been when she came to Francia. Now, she was a person of significant consequence.

"Once, illness and death were matters of evil spirits and inevitable," Magdala asserted earnestly. "We are far, far better off in terms of healing. There is knowledge now that we never had, even small schools of medicine where the worst pain and illness can be confronted."

"Yes," Sebastian said, "but now chaos is looming in the land, threatening everything we do."

"Don't despair, Father," Milo added. "New ideas lie dormant under the turmoil of these civil wars and assaults on our borders. There is still an infrastructure for a new civilization. Perhaps not a Roman one, but a much better one than we Franks have ever known. Those ideas will live beyond tomorrow, and someday, what the great king tried so hard to achieve will emerge—a land of justice and prosperity, a higher civilization where all things might be possible."

"You see, Father," Magdala added, "you were an agent of a unique and unbelievable king. There may never be another like him. Who knows what else his legacy may spawn? Yes! Despite the erosion of his great achievements and the disruption of wars and hardship, we can be certain that King Karl's legacy will last.

"And," she added softly as Sebastian's eyes began to close, "as was famously said of another inestimable man, Charlemagne was a light shining in the darkness.

"And the darkness cannot prevail against it."

Author's Note

Writing historical novels is not like writing murder mysteries or fantasy. Such authors can invent almost anything they like, time and reality be damned. Writers of historical fiction have rules. They have to obey history and weave their stories around it. It's possible to get away with a little poetic license, but one who strays too far from the facts risks the scorn of true history buffs. In this tale of the time of Charlemagne, I labored hard to match story time to real-time as closely as possible. I apologize if I'm off a bit here and there in this volume. Blame it, if you will, on the paucity of information in the scribblings of the monks who gave us what facts we have! Bless 'em anyway for at least giving us something to go on.

I especially thank Helen Wallace, Joyce De Ville Marzullo, Dave Rose, Chris and Rita Jensen, who read the drafts and provided invaluable feedback. Thanks also to Aaron Redfern, my editor, whose corrections and suggestions made the whole prickly briar patch fall together. Thanks as well to Jennifer Quinlan of The Historical Novel Society, whose vision and advice inspired all three novels of the Sebastian's Way trilogy.

Not least, thanks to my close friends Karen Fernengel, Joe Kerr, Jo Ann Stovall, and Frances Porteous MacDonnell, my lovely daughters, Angela and Kate, and stalwart sons, Steve, Tim, and Ben, all of whom cheered me on and kept me from going beyond the red line.

Made in the USA
Monee, IL
11 September 2023

42533150R00118